Special Deliveries: Life Changing Moments

D. J. Kirkby

This book is for my mother, the first sage-femme in my life.

Published by Sunnyside Press

Cover design by DesignforWriters.com

Story Copyright © D.J. Kirkby 2012

First Edition

British Library Cataloguing in Publication Data. A
catalogue record for this book is available from the
British Library.

Introduction

The birth of my desire to become a midwife

Special Deliveries is a compilation of stories based on my experiences as a midwife whilst I cared for women during pregnancy, labour, birth and afterwards. Although a work of fiction, each story in *Special Deliveries* is derived from my midwifery experience and modern practice, and is intended to reflect the experiences of the people I have had the privilege to care for. The stories have been deliberately kept short to mirror the short periods of time in which midwife and parents have to build an effective trusting relationship.

~~

The term midwife means 'with woman' in old English which is why both male and female registered practitioners are referred to as a midwife. The French word for midwife is *sage-femme* – which directly translates into 'wise woman'. I have spent many years vacillating over which term I think describes the role most accurately and have come to the conclusion that both are correct. Our role is to be both 'with women' at times when they need physical and emotional support and to ensure that we are very wise about everything that is normal in relation to being pregnant, giving birth and the first few weeks afterwards. If we aren't well versed in what is normal then we wouldn't be able to recognise when things become abnormal, which is when we refer to our obstetric colleagues. This is a symbiotic relationship that works very well as long as each professional resolutely believes in the skill of the other.

I grew up in a country where the term midwife was relatively unknown to the general population and there was no possibility of being given care from one in pregnancy, during labour or in the postnatal period. When I was nine, my family moved from a city on the East Coast of Canada to the relative wilds of the West Coast. We lived on almost an acre of land which was large enough to raise rabbits, chickens, ducks and goats, and I soon learned about pregnancy and birth. I can distinctly remember the first birth I was a witness to, not just because being present at a birth is a significant experience, but also because it involved our goat whom I was particularly fond of. Normally she followed me around most of the time I was occupied with chores outside the house so when she didn't appear one day despite me calling her, I began to worry and decided to go looking for her by following the usual trail of droppings she left behind.

Soon I was completely absorbed in the task I had set myself; head down but not watching where I was going, I stumbled often. Luckily I managed not to fall head first into the very substance I was following. The goat droppings were increasing in frequency and in quantity. *What is going on?* I wondered. Still following the clues left by our goat, I became aware that I could hear her bleating in what can only be described as an undertone and as I neared the shade under the tree from which my tyre swing was suspended I could see her lying on her side, panting.

She grunted, in greeting I thought and then from her bottom appeared a face framed by a pair of tiny hooves! Not sure what to do, I crept to her head and smoothed her face along the side of her nose where she most liked a caress. She relaxed and rested her head in my lap for a few moments until the urge to push came upon her once again. As she strained she lifted her head from my lap and bleated, her tongue flickering in and out. I knelt up and watched in fascination as her baby inched forward while she pushed, the progress slowing as our goat tired.

Hearing the front door of our house open, I looked in that direction and saw my mum. Reluctant to shout I picked up a stone and threw it towards the house, waving my arms frantically when the noise made her look in my direction and then beckoning her towards me. Mum moved fast, her face set in trepidation; fleetingly I realised she was scared because I was on the ground, seemingly non-verbal and not mobile. When she was near enough I pointed to the baby goat hanging halfway out if its mum and as if my finger was the missing instruction, the very wet baby slithered out onto the ground. I had been with our goat for no more than 20 minutes but it felt as if days had passed. Mum held me as I cried.

When I had regained my composure, Mum turned me towards our goat and to my amazement the little baby goat was already on its feet with its fur bristling out in many directions just like her mother's, except for the spot that her mum was still licking. The baby started to stand and turn around but collapsed in a jumbled heap of its legs. I giggled and then made my way carefully around the baby so that I could stroke her mum. My mum busied herself picking some comfrey to feed our goat. She was a qualified herbalist and put many of the plants growing on our property to good use.

'What you doing, Mum?'

'This is to help bring on the afterbirth and speed healing. We gave it to the rabbits after they birthed, remember?'

I nodded, though I hadn't seen the rabbits give birth, just knew they had because Mum said so. It wasn't until the baby bunnies were several days old that I got to catch a glimpse of them for the first time. I took the comfrey that Mum handed me and offered it to our goat who ate it with utter absorption, momentarily seeming to forget about her new baby. Then she grunted in that tone that was now familiar to me, the one that meant she was pushing again. Mum and I looked in time to see something bulge at the opening of her vagina. It was wet fur instead of the placenta Mum had expected and she rushed over to our goat and encouraged her to stand.

'I need gravity to help get this baby out before the comfrey goes to work!' Mum panted, holding our goat's head.

'Why?' I kept my eye on the progress at the opposite end from where my mum was.

'It makes the womb contract and then the opening to the womb will close which means the baby will get stuck.'

Oh, please push your baby out, I thought, concentrating all my hope on what I feared would be her soon-to-be-stuck baby.

Meadow Lark pushed without making much progress.

'Here, take her head.' Mum said and went to pull on the baby in time with her contractions until at last the second baby was on the ground. Our goat collapsed on the ground as soon as I let go of her head. I sat down so she could rest her head on my legs again but my mum said, 'Nudge her head round to the baby, she has to lick it clean so she can get to know it.'

I nudged her, she licked, the baby bleated and then staggered to its feet. Soon both babies began to bang her udder with their heads until their mum stood to allow them to feed. I refused to leave them to eat my own supper so Mum left me to my vigil until I was driven into the house by the night's chill. That night I floated to sleep cradled on the memories of the day. Sometimes I still do...

It was at that point that my desire to be a midwife was born, though I didn't know it. It wasn't until many years later, when I was in my mid-twenties, that I would be given the opportunity to move to England and train as a midwife. Four years after I moved to England to begin my midwifery training the first midwifery training course was offered in a university based in central Canada. Life can be funny like that.

I have had the privilege of working in a variety of maternity units and have seen first-hand how different units function and how the services they offered varied depending on where they were located, their resident population numbers and needs. I now teach midwifery and find that students enjoy anecdotal stories as part of their taught sessions. *Special Deliveries* is a compilation of stories based on my experiences from within the clinical conditions of the delivery suite to the more relaxed atmosphere of homebirths. The stories have been chosen to show that not only is the modern midwife's role complex, demanding and frustrating, but above all one that is a privilege to perform. These stories are snapshots of each event as succinct as most episodes of care in modern midwifery. Despite this I have tried to capture the jubilation and heartbreak of pregnancy, birth and the early days of parenthood within hospital and community settings that are all very much part of the experience of pregnancy, childbirth and beyond.

Within this book you will find stories about a singing vicar, baby whisperer, the multi-functionality of the humble cabbage, flat babies and many other tales intended to be entertaining, emotive, educational and a demonstration of the dedication of the frontline maternity staff. The stories are grouped into seven sections, which cover the axioms of most midwifery shifts: love, grief, wisdom, unexpected events, conundrums, mirth and an interlude or two (if we're lucky). I have used literary licence to alter identifying factors and events so that all the stories within this book, although based on elements of actual midwifery practice, have been fictionalised in order to maintain the anonymity of those I have cared for and worked with throughout the years. Therefore any resemblance to persons living or dead is entirely coincidental. Finally, all opinions in this book are entirely my own, and in no way attempt to reflect the thoughts of the midwifery profession as a whole.

Love

Chapter 1 - In it together

'Christ almighty, this thing makes my back ache!'
Mr Smythe said to the general amusement of the
rest of the parent craft attendees. His weathered
face crinkled around the eyes as he laughed.
Nature had been kind to him as he aged and his
hair was silver at the temples and nowhere else
which made him look younger than his 42 years.
He was wearing the Pregnadad tabard with
month nine weights fitted into their pouches front
and back. His wife Violet had pulled the side
straps tight so that the weights pressed firmly
against his back and bladder in a manner all too
familiar to her at this stage of pregnancy.

'Welcome to my body,' she said softly and
smiled at his antics. 'I'm glad we got this time
together.' She said to me, 'He tells me he
understands but I don't believe him. Now he can
feel what I mean. Time to rescue him, I think.'
Her voice was still soft but filled with love. She
went to help her husband undo the long straps
so he could get out of the uncomfortable
contraption. He passed it to the next man waiting
for a turn at experiencing what it felt like to be
pregnant, who pretended to stagger under the
weight of the Pregnadad tabard. They all
seemed to be in a silly mood tonight. I liked it
when parent craft groups gelled together like
this.

'Guess I should be glad you can't show me
what giving birth feels like,' Charlie said as he
walked over to where I stood, his arm wrapped

around Violet, rubbing her shoulder with his big hand.

Violet looked up at him fondly. It was a long way for her to look up and her jet black hair fell away from the creamy smooth skin of her face as she did so. 'I don't think that will be required,' she said in her perfectly enunciated English; proof that it wasn't her first language, especially not in this city where the pronounced dialect acted as a neon sign to indicate those born and raised here.

Violet had met Charlie in Singapore when he had gone there on a backpacking holiday after his marriage to his first wife ended. When I booked Violet early in her pregnancy they had delighted in regaling me with their love story. According to Charlie he had first noticed her violet-coloured eyes peering at him from behind the counter in the library.

'He fell in love with my coloured contacts,' Violet teased. 'That's how I got my nickname.' Violet's real name was Siti.

'No, I fell in love with you and your happy smile that makes everyone around you glow.'

It was true, I thought, Violet did project an aura of happiness that was very endearing.

'And I fell in love with you; a giant of a man with a gentle voice, sunburnt face and dusty clothes.' She had slipped her hand under his large one where it rested on his knee.

After two years of living a long-distance romance they had decided to get married. Violet moved to England and was in the process of going through the channels to be granted indefinite leave to stay. She had been here for two years now and was entitled to function as a resident, which included being able to work and access health care on the NHS instead of paying for it privately as she had had to do when she first moved here. As well as being present during the initial booking visit Charlie attended several of the antenatal visits during Violet's pregnancy which had given me a chance to get to know both of them. They were more overtly in love than any couple I had ever met in my career but not sickeningly so, and from what they said, had been this way since the moment they had first met four years ago, despite their 18-year age gap.

I met Violet's mum during the last antenatal check that I did before Violet went into labour. She was as diminutive as her daughter and also had a smile that filled the room.

'Mother has come to visit and is going to stay with Charlie and me for the first month after our baby has been birthed.'

Violet's mother nodded, smiled and gave Violet's hand a squeeze. 'First I am going to visit relatives in London before my grandchild is here.'

They left with arms linked together, their closeness and joy in each other's company reminded me of the relationship Violet had with her husband.

When Violet came in complaining of contraction-type pains two days before she was due she only brought Charlie with her.

'Your mum still in London?' I asked as I walked Violet and Charlie to one of the birthing rooms with a pool.

Violet nodded. 'She will come here again after our baby has been birthed. Too many people at time of birth is bad for harmony of the baby.'

I did the usual admission observations plus ones for labour and found Violet was contracting regularly and strongly enough to be in established labour. After a while she asked for pain relief. After discussing her options she decided that she wanted to get in the pool for some hydrotherapy and that she would try some gas and air later if she wanted extra pain relief.

I filled the pool and then said, 'I'll just pop out while you get changed. Press the buzzer when you want me back.'

'Where do I get changed?' Charlie asked.

I laughed, thinking he was joking then saw that he was holding a pair of men's swim trunks. 'Charlie, are you sure? I mean, it gets quite...messy...in the pool sometimes.'

'Is that ok?' Charlie asked at the same time as Violet said, 'I would like for Charlie to be in water with me, please.'

'Yes, it is fine as long as you are prepared for it to get a bit mucky in there and if you get out immediately if I ask you to do so. I have heard of other men getting in the water, just never been present when one has actually done so. You may need to scoop items out of the water with a sieve,' I warned.

'I remember!' Charlie said rummaging around in their bag and bringing out a white plastic sieve.

I was only with them for another hour before my shift ended and I handed them over to Gina's care. By this point Violet was well advanced in her labour and had her back pressed against Charlie's chest as he alternated between smoothing the hair off her forehead and passing her the gas and air as required. Sometimes a change of shift at this point in a labour can be difficult for the woman and her birth partner but as I said my goodbyes, I knew they wouldn't mind me leaving them. They had each other so all was right in their world.

A sucker for a happy ending, I silently wished them forever together.

Chapter 2 - Daddy delivery

The introduction of fathers to the labour and birthing process is a wonderful thing, at least most women will tell you it is, though not all dads would agree. I think it's a great thing if the father of the baby wants to be there and nothing but akin to a punishment if he doesn't. Furthermore it can be a downright hindrance if the reluctant squeamish father faints when his baby is half-way out. This has happened during several labour or births I have attended and is quite the distraction for a woman mid-contraction or, even worse, mid-push. Not to mention the fact that it means an unexpected additional person has to enter the room to attend the unconscious birth partner while the labour mum has to get on with it without the support she had hoped for.

However, some fathers are almost completely relaxed in the birth environment. They are able to assist their wife or partner as if they had been trained specially for that purpose. More importantly they are able to stop trying to help her, without acting offended, when she decides that she just wants to be left alone as all women do at some point during their labour. These are the dads that would be able to lend a willing hand with just about any aspect of their baby's birth. I know of several midwives, including myself, who are more than happy to involve fathers with these relaxed personalities further in the birth process.

I can remember a midwife I worked with as a student saying, 'You put your baby there in the first place so there's no reason why you can't finish the job now.'

Crude I can remember thinking but accurate, at least in relation to that particular father. I watched as she held his hands on his baby and helped him guide it out as his wife pushed. Now that's teamwork I marvelled to myself. I filed the experience away in a 'try it when the opportunity presents itself' space in my mind.

Many years later, fully qualified and experienced enough to be fully relaxed with the women I was assigned the care of, I began to pay particular attention to the occasional man who was also relaxed and able to deal with his wife's labour angst in a measured and confident way. One man was full of questions, and would ask them in quiet tones, listening intently to my responses as he gently rubbed his wife's back or supported her as she hung from his arms in a standing position. What was I writing in the notes? I let him read what I had written. What did that machine tell me? It measured his wife's temperature from a reading off the tympanic membrane in her ear. What did it mean when his wife stepped from one foot to the other? She either had tired legs or was trying to instinctively adjust the baby's position in her pelvis. He asked her which it was and she said she just felt fidgety. Why did his baby's heart beat change all the time? That is a sign of a healthy baby because it meant that the heart rate was reacting to changing oxygen levels as it moved around or reacted to the contractions, in much the same way our heart beat would change as we exercised or relaxed. Why did I listen to their baby's heart beat more often as the labour progressed? To make sure his baby kept on coping as well as it had been so far. Why did I need to wash my hands after taking my gloves off when I had washed them before putting them on? To remove the powder left on my hands from the inside of the gloves and to ensure that no debris had managed to pass through an unnoticed or microscopic hole in the gloves onto my hands. Would a shower or bath be of any use in helping to get rid of the back pain his wife was complaining of? Perhaps, or she might benefit more from an ice pack, she was welcome to try both or either; whichever she preferred. His wife opted for the ice pack which the ward health care support workers made up in batches by freezing water inside gloves. The sight of those frozen gloves never failed to amuse me for some reason. He helped his wife once again by holding it where she indicated for a few minutes at a time and then removing it for a few minutes.

The questions continued until Tracey snapped, 'Gary, enough!' and to me, 'I'm sorry, he's always like this, he was exactly the same when I was in labour with our son.'

'Nothing to apologise for,' I assured her. 'Gary's asked some good questions and it's nice to have a father so interested in everything that is going on. Is it too distracting for you?' I asked, wondering if this was her real reason for telling her husband to stop.

'Me? No, I'm used to Gary's inquisitive...' Her voice trailed off as she began sucking on the tube attached to the cylinder of entonox. A new contraction was building, and Gary slipped into the routine they had established between them, rubbing her back in long sweeps from her shoulders down to her hips. They had learned through trial and error which movements of his hands on her back she preferred and which made her irritable.

Gary looked over his shoulder at me. 'I've always been like this,' he said in a quiet voice. 'I can remember following my granddad around all day while he went about working on his allotment or spending the day with him at work as a landscaper and asking endless questions.' He was silent for a few moments, concentrating on Tracey's needs as she recovered from the contraction. 'I've got those times to thank for owning my own successful landscape business now.' He smiled.

'That, and your thirst for knowledge, I expect.' I smiled back. Tracey and Gary were a lovely couple and it had been a pleasure to be involved in their labour care.

They both laughed.

I took a deep breath and while Tracey was contraction free and therefore able to concentrate, I broached the topic I had been considering for them. 'Very occasionally there is an opportunity for fathers to get more involved in the birthing process...' I began.

'How?' Gary asked as Tracey turned her full attention on me.

'If Tracey is coping well with pushing and you are also coping well when she is pushing then I would be happy for you to get some gloves on and help me support your baby as Tracey gives birth, as long as this is acceptable to you both.'

'Woot! I'd love to!' Gary looked like a child who had just discovered that Santa really does exist.

'You both need to keep in mind though that if I ask Gary to stop helping and move aside then he needs to do it straight away and without question.'

I looked at Tracey and she smiled, opening her mouth to respond before changing her mind and shoving the entonox mouthpiece in instead. Once she had recovered from that contraction she sipped some water before saying, 'I think that would be amazing if Gary got to help me deliver our baby.'

'Awwww, babe.' He put his arms around her. 'I love you.' Tracey cradled her face into his shoulder and murmured a response.

I'm a real sucker for emotionally charged scenes like this and felt tears prickle my eyes. I composed myself by spending time getting the notes up to date and documenting this new decision that they had made.

Not long after Tracey began to push. She had been close to fully dilated when I had last performed an internal examination on her so we had known that she would reach this stage before too long.

'Better get your gloves on, Gary,' she gasped at him.

He looked at me. 'Wash your hands first. Make sure you dry them very well or you'll never get the gloves on,' I advised.

He went into the ensuite toilet and I used the sink in the room to wash my own hands. By the time Gary had got his gloves on, which involved a considerable amount of faffing about as he tried to get his fingers in the right spaces, I could see a small section of their baby's head. I had handled equipment while doing a set of observations on Tracey and her baby so I washed my hands again before taking the delivery pack out of its wrapper and getting my own gloves on. I left the delivery pack closed so as to keep the contents inside sterile until the last possible moment before the head began to crown.

Once the head had crowned I showed Gary where to stand so that I could place my hands over his and help him to support his baby as Tracey pushed. She was very in control of pushing her baby out and it wasn't long before there was a baby girl entirely out of her mother's body and in the hands of her father. I showed him how to lift their daughter onto Tracey's abdomen and spent a few moments enjoying the sight of this new family getting to know each other before getting back to my job of observing what was going on with the rest of Tracey's labour as she still had the placenta inside and no labour is complete until the placenta is delivered. I didn't think that would be a part of the delivery that Gary would be so keen to be a part of though, so I got on with the job myself trying to interfere as little as possible in their family time.

Chapter 3 - A prayerful birth

I began the shift with my own personal black cloud of grumpiness following me around. It was mid-August and I was thoroughly fed up with the rain and heavy cloud we had been experiencing off and on for a few weeks. My mood lifted slightly when I found out that there was a woman in labour on her way in; time always passed quickly when I was occupied with caring for a woman in labour. Much preferable to the alternative of finding equipment to clean or slogging through online training, though these times of no patients to care for during parts of the shift were becoming scarcer the longer I was qualified.

The woman I was to care for and her husband arrived. I greeted them at the door noting how calm she seemed and I instantly doubted that her labour was advanced enough for admission. She was requesting a water birth, the room was unoccupied and so I escorted them to the room with a birthing pool. We chatted of inconsequential things as we walked: introductions, our names, and the weather.

'God is watering the soil so that the crops have all the ingredients necessary in order to ensure a good harvest,' Mark, the husband, commented.

Nonplussed I replied, 'Is that a fact?' not at all surprised when his reply was a simple, assured, 'Yes.'

Once we were settled in the room and I had a chance to look at Sue's maternity notes I would find out that he was a lay preacher. At that moment I simply wondered if I had a weirdo on my hands.

Your God is flattening and ruining the hay with all his heavy downpours and it needs harvesting now, I thought, but aloud I said, 'That's an interesting way of looking at this awful weather.' I opened the door and ushered them into the room with a smile which mirrored theirs.

The room opened to a view of the bed at the far end close to the large window which was covered only with nets, the heavier curtains pulled open. I left the lights in the room off so as not to put the room on display to anyone walking past outside as we were on the ground floor of the building. The room was in the shadow thrown by the trees outside but there was enough light to work by for the time being without closing the curtains and turning on the lights. A dimly lit labour room was often more soothing than a brightly lit clinical environment. Birthing pool in situ or not, this room was part of a large maternity hospital and dim lights helped to disguise the emergency buzzer, oxygen and other medical gas outlets on the wall at the head of the bed, the Now Please Wash Your Hands sign over the sink and the bright yellow biohazard bin liners.

I did some basic observations on Sue: temperature, pulse, blood pressure, frequency of contractions and listened to her baby's heart rate, all of which were within normal limits. I talked to Sue about how long she thought she had been having regular contractions for and learned that they had become regular about four hours ago though she had been having irregular ones since the early hours of the morning. This meant she was likely to be in established labour and I spent some time monitoring the frequency and duration of the contractions by keeping a hand on her abdomen to determine the intensity of the contractions. I noted that Sue's only reaction to the contractions was a sudden silence that lasted for the duration of the height of the pain. She was contracting regularly enough to convince me that she was in established labour though you wouldn't know it from her relaxed demeanour. I explained my findings to them both and pointed out the birthing pool in the far corner of the room. It offered good pain relief to a lot of women and was often used once they were established in labour though discouraged prior to this as some research had shown that the relaxation from the water could cause contractions to diminish before this.

'Let me know when you feel that you need some pain relief and I'll start filling the pool for you then; it takes about 15 minutes to get deep enough.'

'I don't need it right now, thanks,' Sue said, then fell silent, her faraway look and deep rhythmic breathing making it obvious that she was concentrating on a contraction. Mark held her hand, rubbing his thumb over her knuckles.

When she smiled with relief at her husband and made eye contact with me again we knew another one had passed.

'I'm going to pop out to get you a jug of water; would either of you like tea or toast?' They both wanted some, so after showing them where the buzzer was in case they wanted me before I returned, I took Sue's maternity notes and left to get them admitted to the ward.

'They want anything?' said Carol the auxiliary nurse as she came out of the nearby nursery.

'Ice water, tea and toast for two, please.'

'Got'cha. You want a cuppa while I'm making?'

'That would be lovely, thanks!'

The ward clerk had finished at 2 p.m. so I settled in her office to use her computer in order to admit Sue. The ward sister popped her head in. 'Is Mrs Travers in established labour?'

'I haven't done a VE so I don't know dilatation yet but she's contracting 2:10 moderate. I'll admit her and see how she gets on over the next hour.'

The sister went to her office to make the necessary alterations to the patient detail board while I finished filling in the numerous pages necessary to admit Sue on the computer. Date of admission, observations, recent blood results and so on. I read Sue's notes over carefully, as this was the first time I had met her and I needed to ensure I was up to date with all the pertinent issues from her pregnancy. Carol came into the ward clerk's office and shut the door.

'Erm,' she began with a strange look on her face.

'What's up?'

'I was going to take Mr and Mrs Travers' drinks and toast in then bring your cuppa to you but I think you should go in there with your tea because they're acting really odd.'

I stood up, holding the notes. 'Odd? In what way?'

'Well they're singing...hymns!'

I laughed. 'Both of them?'

'Yup!'

'He did say an odd comment to me about the weather this morning and I noticed on the notes that he is a lay preacher so I'm guessing that might be why they're singing hymns.'

'Okaaaay, whatever...'

'Could be worse! I've been out of there about 15 minutes now so it's time I got myself back in there.'

'True...but better you than me anyway. I wouldn't want to be in there listening to them hymns for the rest of her labour! I'll bring your tea in though, 'cos I'm good like that.' She gave me a cheeky grin and headed towards the kitchen.

As I approached the birthing pool room door I could hear them singing Amazing Grace, perfectly in tune with each other. I waited until they had finished then knocked and entered. Sue was kneeling on the bean bag and leaning over the bed, Mark was sitting on the bed holding her hand smoothing his thumb over her knuckles as before. I walked round the other side of the bed and crouched down to Sue's eye level.

'How are you coping?'

'They're stronger now.'

'Do you want any pain relief?'

'No, I'm ok, thanks.' Sue smiled then closed her eyes before lowering her head onto the pillow waiting on the bed before her.

'I think we gave the tea lady a fright when we started to sing a hymn while she was in here sorting our tea and toast,' Mark said.

'Singing hymns calms me, reminds me that I don't spend my days in pain usually,' Sue explained.

'I sing along to help Sue keep pace and because it calms me, too.' Mark smiled serenely.

'If it helps keep you both calm and feeling in control then that's fine with me. You both have lovely singing voices,' I said gratefully.

With Sue's permission I did another set of observations of her contractions and her baby's heart beat. They sang as frequently as I checked on her and their baby's well being and monitored the progress of her labour. The next few hours of Sue's labour passed in a pleasant haze of gentle noise interspersed with talk about what they would like to experience as part of their birthing plan, if possible. Eventually Sue asked to be moved into the birthing pool. When she began using gas and air as additional pain relief, breathing that in, instead of joyously singing hymns, I knew it wouldn't be long until she began pushing. Less than 30 minutes later Sue gave birth to her baby.

'Sue, here, reach down and bring your baby to the surface of the water.' I placed my hands on her arms to guide them to the baby quickly. Sue grasped her baby and pulled it up onto her chest, looked at it, kissed it, gently lifted it further until she could see they had a daughter, and then tipped her head back to look at Mark as she burst into tears. Mark did the same and sobbed out a prayer of thanks for this blessing of a perfect baby as he cupped her delicate head in his hand while she stared with wide open eyes at her parents. Feeling privileged yet again to be able to experience moments such as these, I sat quietly in the dimly lit far corner of the birthing pool area and watched them for several precious moments before it was time to get on with the rest of the work involved in the birthing process. Moments like these never failed to make me happy, whatever the weather.

Chapter 4 - Allah

If I was asked to declare one absolute about the labour and birthing process, I would say that it is that each woman will cope with her labour very differently from the last woman who went through the same process in that room. Some are silent, some sing, some chatter away with a note of hysteria audible in every sentence, some behave as if they are on a social outing in between contractions, some swear, some get physically aggressive and others repeat one word endlessly throughout the course of their labour and delivery.

I was on the labour ward with no one assigned to care for when the call came through that Mrs Bashir was now in established labour and on her way in. I assumed that her husband had made the call because I had met them earlier and knew from that experience that Mrs Bashir did not speak much English. Her husband was first-generation British so there was no problem with his grasp of the English language but having to have my words translated left much to be desired in terms of feeling I was giving Mrs Bashir the best care I could offer. Lack of connection equals lack of confidence. Although Mrs Bashir had been quite responsive when her husband had translated earlier, asking several questions in response to my attempts to explain the difference between latent and established labour and when they should return, I felt that there was a distinct lack of connection between myself and Mrs Bashir and could only assume it was due to this language barrier. Having sentences translated slowed down the communication process to the point where it felt laboured, no pun intended.

As I had cared for them when they were here earlier and I now had no one else occupying my time, I volunteered to take over their care when Mrs Bashir was admitted this time. I had a couple of options so far as communicating with Mrs Bashir went. I could resort to a picture book we had on the ward for just this sort of thing though I felt it best used when the woman came in unescorted so as not to insult her or her translator's intelligence by appearing to treat them like children. I could make use of the phone-based translations service which again might insult her husband by introducing a stranger (albeit down the phone line) into the proceedings when he could do exactly the same job, or I could continue to use her husband as the translator and ignore the fact that it felt like there was a barrier up between me and Mrs Bashir. By the time they arrived I had decided on the latter.

I groaned inwardly when they introduced me to the older woman who had accompanied them as Mr Bashir's mother. I assumed that Mrs Bashir must have her mother-in-law with her under duress, as I couldn't imagine anything I would have liked less than to have to labour in the presence of people I was related to through marriage. Projecting my feelings onto the situation was not only incredibly unprofessional but also very inaccurate. The atmosphere was completely different this time around. Mrs Bashir made it clear that she felt I was there to support her, she was all about smiles and eye contact and grasping of my hand when the waves of contractions washed over her. Her mother-in-law sat quietly on a rocking chair in the corner of the room taking it all in as she moved the chair back and forth in a soothing rhythm. When the time came for an internal examination Mr Bashir translated, told me his wife had given her permission though this was obvious from her vigorous nodding. His mother barked out a few sentences and he told me that she had said for him to leave the room during the procedure. He said he would be waiting outside and to send his mother if I needed him, that her understanding of English was excellent, then he gave her a very mischievous look and left the room. Men! I thought. They could grow up, have responsible jobs, get married and start families of their own but they were always cheeky rascals where their mothers were concerned.

The membranes ruptured as I was doing the internal examination, straw-coloured fluid flowing out of Mrs Bashir's vagina and cascading around my gloved hand onto the absorbent pad underneath. She was six centimetres dilated so this was a perfectly acceptable stage for this to happen naturally. The baby coped well with this change; its heart beat a healthy gallop within the normal range. Mrs Bashir who had up until now been mostly silent with the contractions let out a long moan with the next one.

'Allah!' her mother-in-law barked.

Mrs Bashir went silent and when the contraction ended the elder Mrs Bashir walked to the door to call her husband back in.

I explained my findings to him, his wife was well established in labour, things were unlikely to stop now until their baby was born and tried to explain that although we could guestimate how long a labour might be we couldn't say for sure, even when pressed.

When Mrs Bashir stood, instinctively rocking her hips in preparation for her next contraction, her mother-in-law immediately said 'Allah' again but this time in a softer tone.

'Allah,' Mrs Bashir repeated. She then used this word during her contractions for the rest of her labour. She used the same soft tone her mother-in-law had, almost breathing the word out instead of speaking it aloud.

'She is calling on Allah to give her the strength to cope with the rest of the labour and delivery,' her husband explained in response to my quizzical look at one point.

It certainly seemed to work for Mrs Bashir who made steady progress in labour from that point on until she gave birth to a baby boy who came into this world appearing as relaxed as his whole birthing process had been.

Chapter 5 - Polygamy

Caring for Trish Campbell-Turner-Morgan widened my horizons to such an extent that in retrospect it seemed as if I had gone through life previously believing the world was flat. The day I booked Trish was the first peek into a world that I had only the vaguest awareness of through trashy documentaries which prominently featured the kind of people whose outwardly hostile appearances would make me cross the street rather than brush past them for fear of inadvertently provoking them.

'You have an unusual surname, Trish. I don't think I have ever seen a triple barrelled one before!'

'Ah, well, I like to think I am an unusual person,' she replied enigmatically, grinning at Mandy and Brian sitting beside her. They laughed and nodded. Trish had introduced them by forename only, giving no explanation for their presence but explained that she wanted them to participate in her pregnancy and birth when I asked.

Okaaaaaaay, I thought, this booking may be hard work. 'Oh, in that case I look forward to finding out more. Can you give the name of your spouse, please?'

'Mandy Morgan.' Trish indicated the woman beside her. 'We also...'

'No, it's not a porn name,' Mandy interjected defensively, as if that was the next question I would ask. She jutted out her chest and said,

'Lots of people seem to think these combined with my name equal porn star.' Brian's eye's strayed to her chest, lingering there as if he were no more capable of appropriate social etiquette than a lust-struck teenager.

'I can assure you that thought never entered my mind.' I sketched a vague smile in her direction, made a note of Mandy's name and returned my focus to Trish and the next question on the booking form.

'And Brian Turner,' she said before I could ask my next question, indicating the man next to Mandy.

I stopped, pen poised and eyebrows raised.

'We're polyamorous,' Trish continued. 'In a polygamous relationship.' She looked at me. I could feel the mood in the room change to one of cautious expectancy. I knew I had this moment to gain their trust or to lose it completely.

'Well that answers my next question then. I'll put both Mandy and Brian down as your next of kin, shall I?' Their smiles lit up the room.

As I got to know them all I grew very fond of them. Their relationship was unlike anything I had known but it seemed to work well for them. During the pregnancy the story of how they met emerged bit by bit.

After a few years of domestic bliss Mandy and Trish had decided that having a child would be just the thing to cement their joy. They had known that conceiving a child, for them, was going to be slightly more complicated and a lot less spontaneous than it was for heterosexual couples. They said that what they hadn't been prepared for was the sheer, unadulterated back-alley type of seediness of it all. Finding a suitable donor who resembled both Trish and Mandy, who would agree to sign away parental rights, and who was willing to go to a sexual health clinic to prove he was free of any sexually transmissible nasties (on a regular basis during the time they were trying to conceive) was going to be enough of a challenge. Furthermore this Mr Perfect Father would have to be willing to put hand to flesh on a daily basis every month during the days in which Trish was fertile, in order to produce a donation of sperm which Mandy would then insert into Trish with a syringe. Romantic it wasn't they assured me, but said they felt that the effort had been worth it.

They explained that they had tried to find a donor through word of mouth at Martha's, their favourite gay and lesbian nightclub, but it had all ended up too complicated and verging on more intimacy than they said they wished to have with random men who partied there. Trish and Mandy joined Baby 4 U - a sperm donor website that a friend told them about. They regaled me with stories about the challenge to find anyone who lived close enough to them to make the sperm collection and insertion a workable reality and the lewd suggestions they received. They had printed off some of the emails they had been sent and showed me during one visit.

'Look at this one!' Mandy thrust the paper at me. The email declared that the potential donor preferred the **natural insemination** method.

'We replied telling him that he'd best find himself someone who wants to be in a relationship with him then,' Trish said before handing me another email. This candidate got himself removed from their list of potential donors because he insisted that he be allowed weekly contact with **his** child.

'We were looking to create our child, not his,' Mandy said.

Another man wanted to **spend quality time getting to know each other** before **sharing** his sperm. 'I don't want to get to know him as a person and since when does paying him for his sperm equate to him sharing it with us,' Trish muttered.

'We sent him an email back saying all we wanted to know about him was his vital statistics and sexual health profile,' Mandy chimed in. 'We never did hear back from him.'

'What we hadn't counted on was falling in love with Mr Perfect Father when we finally found him at a picnic hosted by the local LGBT social network.'

'What's not to love?' Brian preened as Mandy and Trish smiled at him.

Peculiar as I may have thought their relationship, one thing I was sure of was that they genuinely loved each other.

During the booking process Trish had declared her religion to be Pagan. When it came time to go over her birth plan I became aware that she wanted her labour and birth to be as alternative as her lifestyle. The way people behave during this time is as varied as can be imagined, from the silent women to the singing women. Pagans, as I would learn, were all about exuberance and full-on enjoyment of every moment of their labour and birth. The fact that she wanted a homebirth came as no surprise at all and as her pregnancy processed without a hitch, I was able to fulfil her wish. Trish, Mandy and Brian's birth experience has filled my memory with visions of near darkened rooms illuminated only by flickering candles. I used a torch to fully light only the necessary area of Trish's body and no more during her labour and birth. The perfume of incense drifts through these memories like scented thread weaving into the fabric of the new-age style music that played while Trish laboured with almost joyful abandon. There was no intensely quiet arrival for their son. Instead he was taken along the laborious path accompanied by his mother's vocalisations and various mobilisation techniques including pelvis rocking and immersion in water until he was virtually chanted out into the welcoming world. Emotionally exhausted but with a head full of positive thoughts about the cleverness of the female body, I left the four of them curled up together on their king-sized bed. Their son would certainly experience an alternative version of the traditional family composition but I was confident that he would also have a chance to grow up surrounded by family who enjoyed each other's company and who had overcome great challenges to find each other. Several of my nights after Trish's birth experience were filled with dreams of rooms of women who rubbed vast pregnant bellies whist chanting 'You are a Goddess' in a never-ending loop while men danced in a protective circle around them. Those dreams were a bit psychedelic and totally different from the ones I usually had but like the polyamorous Trish, Mandy and Brian, once I got used to the uniqueness, I realised that I liked them really rather a lot.

Chapter 6 - Head lice and seed pearls

I breathed out with relief as I managed to squeeze my car into the only parking space in the area. The hostel was located close to one of the main shopping precincts, which meant available parking was a rarity. Annie Pinhale and Daz Furlang had been added to my caseload through notification from social services and this was the second time I had been out to the hostel to see them; the first was to book them in and this time was to discuss the results of Annie's screening tests. Social services were involved because Annie and Daz, at just 16 and 17 years of age, were still minors and they had been living rough on the streets since early spring. I crunched through the autumn leaves scattered on the path, which led me to the hostel like brightly coloured beacons. After buzzing me in through the main door the house warden escorted me to the waiting room and then went to fetch Annie. I chatted to some of the other residents who were in various states of recline in the common room and sorted through the results to refresh my memory.

'Hiya.' A soft voice penetrated my concentration. I looked up and around until I located Annie draped against the door frame. Once again I was astonished by the disproportion of her dreadlocked hair compared to her tiny build; pregnancy bump invisible under her hoodie unless one knew to look for it. No wonder she needed to lean against solid objects whenever she walked. I wondered why Daz hadn't come down to get me this time.

'Hello again, Annie!' I gathered my equipment and followed Annie as she led the way to the lift resisting the urge to hold the ends of her hair as we walked, much as one would do with a heavy dress train at a wedding. In the lift she predictably leaned against the wall and as I followed her off the lift I noticed a smudge on the metal surface where her hair had been.

'…and so I said to her, yeah, right? Like you can't be doing that, it just ain't right!' Annie looked at me as she finished her complicated story about an altercation she had got into with another girl over seating arrangements in the soft lounge downstairs. I nodded uncertainly, which seemed to be the correct response because Annie flashed me a smile as she opened the door.

I made myself comfortable in the only chair and asked, 'Where's Daz?' Hoping the answer wouldn't involve them separating. They had seemed to utterly adore each other and I was certain that they both were the best thing that had ever happened to each other in the past few years.

'Gone to the shops.'

'Ok we'll make a start without him, shall we?'

Annie nodded her head as she scratched at her scalp using the blunt end of a pen to reach through her dreadlocks. I took that as a yes rather than just a movement in rhythm with the pen.

I began Annie's antenatal check by going over her blood and chlamydia screening results. 'Everything has come back fine except for your iron levels which are a bit low so you'll need to take iron tablets once a day and also your chlamydia results have come back positive so you'll need to take antibiotics for a week and Daz will need to get tested, too.'

'What's that mean, the clapidia one?'

'Do you remember when I talked to you about infection you can get from having sex and how you can pass it on to Daz if he doesn't have it? The infection that you can't always tell if you have it?'

Annie nodded and scrabbled through her information leaflets in her booking pack until she found the black-and-orange chlamydia fact sheet. She waved it at me questioningly.

I nodded. 'Well that's the one that the results have come back positive for. If you take the antibiotics and use protection while having sex until you, and Daz if he tests positive, are clear then the infection will be gone.' Back then, as now, chlamydia testing was targeted at the 15–24 years old pregnant cohort in particular, though available to anyone older who needed it. Nowadays the chlamydia factsheets are a less harsh green and yellow and have a whole team who specialise in testing, giving results and treating patients. It means less work for the busy midwife but also one less opportunity to connect with some of the women on her caseload.

As Annie scratched her head again I noticed dots of white embedded in her light brown hair. I stared. Annie noticed. 'Wot?' she challenged.

'Those white dots...' I began.

Annie preened. 'You like 'em? They're little beads that look like pearls. Daz sewed them in special for me for a mate's wedding we went to last week.'

I made appreciative noises even though I couldn't decide if they were pretty or pointless. 'That must have taken Daz a while to do,' I said as I noticed that there were hundreds nestled amongst her dreadlocks.

'It took him all day! Loves me he does.' Annie's voice was filled with happiness. I could only agree. Daz had mild attention deficit hyperactivity disorder and it would have been immensely challenging for him to remain focused on this one task of sewing all those tiny beads into his girlfriend's hair.

'Gonna get it all cut off today...' she said as Daz entered, ducking his head as he came through the doorway, seeming to fill the room with his lanky frame.

'Got it, babe.' He was carrying a prescription labelled bag from the local chemist. 'Hiya, miss,' he said to me.

'Hey, babe!' Annie stretched her arms up and pulled him down for a kiss.

'Hello, Daz!' I said as he plonked himself on the edge of the bed.

'Get your hair cut off?' I continued my conversation with Annie.

'Yeah, I got nits, didn't 'cha see me scratchin'?'

'I saw 'em this mornin' when I was lookin' to see how many pearls had come off. Went to doc to see if he'd give me 'n' Annie a script for lice killer stuff 'cos we don't have the dosh to buy it,' Daz explained.

'You get the scissors?' Annie asked.

'No, but Helen said she'll let us borrow hers.'

I did the full antenatal check and left with my scalp crawling with imaginary head lice. Much to my dismay I discovered that the imaginary ones are much more difficult to get rid of than real head lice.

The next time I saw Annie I wouldn't have recognised her if it hadn't been for Daz's familiar face grinning beside her. Her dreadlocks had gone and in their place she had a choppy elfin hairstyle that was much more suited to her delicate features. I was impressed that she had gone through with getting rid of her dreadlocks but even more impressed when I found out that Daz had managed to get Annie's hair to look like that without any help from a trained hairdresser.

They had told me of many horrid things they had experienced in their short lives and their relationship was one that had set them on the right path again and had given them strength to believe in their own self worth. They were thrilled to have a baby on the way and I was quietly confident that with the right support they could learn to be good parents. I was pleased to be able to help them on this part of their journey and determined to try and talk Daz into signing up to train as a hairdresser. That young man had natural talent which would be wasted if he didn't go to college.

Interlude

Sister Morgan

Sister Morgan, whose giant personality seemed to crackle around the ward with a life of its own that belied her diminutive stature, was nearing retirement and 'used to a different breed of doctor' as she never tired of reminding us. She was clearly used to a different breed of midwife too and made this clear by insisting we refer to her by her senior midwife title of Sister, instead of by her first name as we did with all the other senior nurses. Usually the ward was run like a smoothly oiled machine under the not-so-tender ministrations of Sister Morgan. She never seemed to tire and was always about making sure the team was on active duty unless officially on a break. She was very fond of teaching the students and, whenever the pace on the ward slowed enough to provide an opportunity, would drag them into the sluice for an impromptu 'how to' session on anything from checking the placenta to preparing cleaning solution. Although the duties of being a senior midwife included administrative duties such as the duty roster, timesheets and the like, Sister Morgan seemed to like nothing better than the physical tasks associated with being a midwife. And by this I mean all of the tasks. Depending on the ward she was currently working on Sister Morgan could be seen with her cardigan off busily occupied at myriad tasks from checking stock, delivering a baby, carting linen bags to the drop area, making tea for patients, serving meals, showing mums how to bath their baby, to wiping down equipment. I can clearly remember a dressing down she gave a student midwife once who had dared to suggest her learning experience might be better if she was set the task of doing something other than making beds.

'You do not feel it is your place to make beds?' Sister Morgan's voice was dangerously soft, a mixture of confusion and enquiry.

'Not really.' The student midwife fidgeted under Sister Morgan's scrutiny.

'What do you think you should be doing instead?'

'Well I could do the baby baths instead.'

Sister Morgan stared, her silence an ominous chasm between them.

'And Elaine could make the beds.' The student rushed to fill the silence, not watching her step, and fell into the waiting abyss with Sister Morgan's anger weighting her as she fell.

'So as a student midwife you think it is more appropriate for you to bath babies and for Elaine as a health care support worker to make the beds?' The question wasn't really a question as the student was about to find out.

The student nodded and smiled. 'It gives me time to teach the mum how to care for her baby, to check how the mum is feeling emotionally without making it obvious that's what I'm doing. We have had a lot in class sessions about it, we've been strongly encouraged to keep up the learning in our clinical placements and I feel ready to put what I've learned in class into practice. My personal tutor said...'

I made a scared face at Wendy, one of the other midwives on duty. Sister Morgan's views on the midwife's role were clear and she did not feel that there was much in-depth information to be gained from the mum while teaching her to bath her baby, seeing as she would be distracted by her baby's cries and by trying to learn the new techniques.

'Pish!' Sister Morgan interrupted the student. 'I couldn't care less what your tutor said in the classroom. Unless she is regularly setting foot on this ward wearing her uniform and ready to work then she doesn't have the wherewithal to talk about what you should be doing and where you should be doing it. This is my ward and I'll thank you to take instruction from me whilst you are here!'

Safely out of Sister Morgan's line of vision, I raised my eyebrows at Wendy. Sister Morgan didn't think much of midwives who left clinical practice to go into teaching full time. Particularly those teaching on these 'new fangled' direct entry courses as she called them. In recent years midwifery training had switched from being an add-on to a nursing qualification during an 18-month mostly clinical placement to a three-year degree course, where the clinical and theory time was shared equally during the course. This meant that student midwives could enrol on the course without a nursing qualification and they were unable to do even the most basic of clinical observations such as temperature, pulse and blood pressure monitoring without supervision. Sister Morgan thought this, and the fact that they came to the ward with ideas placed in their heads about how they should behave on the ward which didn't match her ideals, was outrageous. No one likes change but Sister Morgan did have some very good ideas about what best practice meant and in this case I agreed with her. A midwife's place was at the woman's side as much as possible and things like making beds allowed us to delve into women's emotional well being without appearing officious, often drawing them into revealing more than they had intended and much more than they would have if we had rushed in and out of their room on official midwifery business like daily checks.

The student's face fell and her cheeks flushed as she looked around frantically as if seeking an escape route.

Sister's Morgan's eyes softened. 'Come with me.' She beckoned imperiously.

The student swallowed noisily and followed. 'I'm sorry, Sister...' she began.

'We are going to write some prescriptions!' Sister Morgan said.

'I haven't studied drugs yet,' the student said nervously.

'Prescriptions for cups of tea! Anyone can write them and give the doses out as long as they have the necessary ingredients. What do you think they might be?'

'Erm, tea? Milk? Sugar? A cup and saucer?' The student floundered, obviously suspecting the correct answer wouldn't be as simple as it seemed.

'Yes indeed, all those but most importantly time to listen to the patient!'

Truer words had never been spoken on that ward and the student learned a valuable lesson that day. Time was one of the most valuable tools we could use as part of the care we gave our women. Time to listen while they told us far more than they ever would have if they could see that we were preoccupied with trying to complete all the other tasks that needed doing during the course of a shift.

Grief

Chapter 7 - Butterfly baby

Writing about Sister Morgan reminded me of an unforgettable learning experience that I had as a student. Grief is an unfortunate part of some births, and it is vital that every midwife, preferably during her training, learns how to support parents through times such as these. I was fortunate to be able to work with a senior midwife on such an occasion and the lessons she taught me were so important that I have passed them on to all of my students over the years. The key thing I learned from Peggy was the significance of open windows.

'The window!' whispered Peggy urgently. I looked up in confusion. I was sure I had heard her correctly because my ears were fine tuned to catch even the faintest undertone that came from her. As a student midwife I had to act quickly on every instruction my mentor Peggy gave so I could help her provide the best care for the families we were assigned to. At that moment, unsure what was meant by those two words, and reluctant to question her, I hesitated. Peggy broke her focus from the moaning woman on the bed and the pale man next to her to flick a glance over her left shoulder in my direction and then point with her chin towards the glass.
'Open it.'
'Oh, right.' I hastened to do as asked. A quick glance through the pane offered back the

unappealing though panoramic view of leaden skies and rows of buildings far below, lining the streets surrounding the hospital.

A deep groan of pain from the woman jolted my attention from the bleak view.

'I can't. I can't do this. Help me, please. I'm too scared,' she wailed. Finding reserves of strength, she sat upright and hit her husband on the arm with her fist.

'You do it, I'm done.' With those words she got off the bed and stood wobbling with exhaustion as the midwife steadied her.

I can't do this, help me, I'm too scared. I mentally echoed the weary woman. Mrs Strout, first name Joanie, husband named Paul, I reminded myself. It was my first shift on the labour ward and for what must have been the hundredth time that day, I was wondering if I had made a horrible mistake.

Joanie gave a long drawn out moan, holding onto Peggy and bending her knees as she pushed with the contraction.

'Well done, that's good,' Peggy gently encouraged as Joanie's waters broke and splashed onto the floor. Carefully she moved her towards the bed and helped her on. Kneeling forward, resting her arms on the plump pillow which covered the top of the headboard, Joanie wriggled her hips in pain and her quiet husband began to rub her back, in syncopation to her movements.

'Get off me!' she grunted at him. His hand dropped, as did the corners of his mouth. He looked helplessly at Peggy who flashed him a reassuring smile.

'Could you wet a flannel with cold tap water, please? You can pop it in here so it doesn't drip.' She handed him a kidney-shaped bowl.

Paul hastened to do as suggested, happy to be occupied. The mention of water made me move swiftly towards the wardrobe in the corner of the room, my confidence returning somewhat now that I too had found a way to make myself useful. Grabbing a large handful of absorbent, open broadsheet- sized thin pads, I mopped up the amniotic fluid from where Joanie had been standing. I could hear Peggy murmuring a soothing litany to Joanie as her husband held a cool damp flannel against the back of her neck. Lulled by the midwife's tone, weary from the stress of this day's work, my movements slowed until I was startled to attention when Peggy asked me to get the delivery pack.

I moved quickly and as I left the room my hip glanced off the baby monitoring machine – no, the Continuous TocoGraph, the CTG machine, I reminded myself – that had been placed just outside the door. I tutted, partly in annoyance and partly at the stinging in my hip, but paused as I looked again at the silent machine. It was in the corridor where we had hurriedly shoved it when we first entered the labour room – a hasty removal of this painful reminder to the already grieving parents that their baby had no heart beat to monitor. No precious heart beat for them to cling onto throughout the labour of love.

I rubbed my hip and made my way along the corridor towards the store room where the supplies were kept and wondered why a stock of essentials like delivery packs were not kept in the labour rooms. I grabbed hold of a two-level, square steel trolley from the assortment that lined the walls, pulling it inside the store room. Reading the list on the wall I began gathering items the midwife would need for the birth.

Peggy and Joanie turned expectantly as I re-entered the room, pushing the trolley in front of me. Paul, already facing the door from the opposite side of the bed, went paler still, as he took in the trolley and it's contents. Joanie's body gave her no time to react to the implication of the delivery pack on the trolley as she swiftly moved into another, stronger contraction. She was moments away now. The room seemed to become smaller as we focused on the frantic last moments of the delivery until the tiny baby slipped into Peggy's hands. She barked instructions at me and I operated automatically, not forgetting to soothe Joanie, squeezing her hand as she wept.

Leaving Joanie and Paul together we took their tiny 20-week-old baby into the clean sluice area. Its skin was so thin that we had to take care not to tear it as we peeled the towel away so we could place it on the scales naked. The tiny genitals hinted at the gender that the amniocentesis had detected. Paul and Joanie's baby was a boy and perfect to look at in every respect, except that the top of his skull was missing, his brain covered by a reddish looking membrane instead of smooth bone and skin.

'The most important thing we can do now is encourage Joanie and Paul to see how beautiful their son is. We need to find all of his best features and make sure they have photographs and other keepsakes of these in their memory box. Let's get it done before the chaplain comes up for the blessing,' Peggy said, handling the baby as you might a butterfly, so as not to disturb the fragile dust on its wings.

I helped Peggy take ink prints of his hands and feet, gently placing each precious stamp onto a card, which then went into the memory box along with photos of him dressed in a baby gown, his head covered in a tiny knitted cap. We took him back into the room and passed him gently to Joanie, who bent forward and kissed him softly.

I moved to close the window as we left the room to give the grieving couple time with their son but before I could do so, Peggy reached for my arm and guided me from the room.

Once outside I turned to her, confused.

'It's probably just an old midwives' tale,' she said, 'but I was told when I was a student that the soul of a dead baby turns into a butterfly and that a window should be open so they can fly away.'

I looked back into the room. Outside there were patches of blue breaking through the cloud and, old midwives' tale or not, I was glad I had left that window open.

Chapter 8 - To Downs or not to Downs

A few years after I learned what the term butterfly baby meant I was working night shifts on a busy unit where the neonatal unit was part of the ward rotation. We were expected to work alternately on the antenatal, labour and postnatal wards as well as on the neonatal unit and on a rotation of early, late and night shifts. My preferred bedtime is 9.30pm and I get up at 5am each day to write, so I hated working the night shifts, despite the fact that I quite liked working on each of the wards. Every hospital I have worked in has had a different ward to which they send babies who are to be placed for adoption or who have been removed from their parents and will be placed in a foster home. Some hospitals used a locked nursery on the antenatal ward, some used a peripheral community unit nursery and this particular hospital felt that the neonatal unit's low-dependency nursery was the best place to keep these babies.

I arrived on duty at the neonatal unit after three days off to find that I was working in the low-dependency ward, and amongst other babies I was also assigned to the care of one baby boy who had Down's syndrome and had been placed for adoption because his parents felt they would be unable to care for him. The other babies had their parents visiting most of the shift and would only require minimal care from me throughout the day. My focus was this little boy named Toby who was all alone in his cot in the corner of the room. I have found that babies who are taken from their parents whether for adoption or fostering purposes are often extraordinarily silent. They don't seem particularly distressed, just silent and alert as if they are aware that things are not quite how they should be. Perhaps some primal instinct ensures they stay quiet so as not to draw attention to themselves, and thereby keep themselves safe until their parents return to collect them, much in the way that a lone baby animal will do.

This little boy was no different, and it was no hardship to give him long cuddles and chatter aimlessly away at him telling him what a good loveable boy he was in an attempt to fill the empty space he might sense had been left by the absence of his parents. I knew that he wouldn't recognise my smell or voice but believe there is a lot of good that a soft voice and the warmth from a comforting cuddle from another human can do for a newborn regardless of that fact. Once he had succumbed to a deep sleep weighted down by a tummy full of warm milk I had a chance to catch up on his notes. I had received a handover at the start of the shift but it only covered the basics about the physical care he needed and did not include any other details about his background. I took the notes from the midwives' station back into the ward with me, wanting to remain near him so that when he woke he wouldn't be alone. As he slept I chatted with the other babies' parents for a while, attended to their babies' clinical needs and made a fuss of how well their babies were getting on under the loving care of their parents. After a while I removed myself to sit in the rocking chair near Toby's cot and began working my way through his notes.

To my surprise I found that Toby was not his parents' only child. He was a twin and his parents had chosen to keep his sister but to have Toby removed from them immediately at birth, and to be put up for adoption once they were informed that Toby had tested positive for Down's syndrome. Down's syndrome is one of the conditions from a group called Trisomy and a strawberry shaped skull which had been noted on scan often indicates a condition known as Edward's syndrome. It was this condition, usually incompatible with life, that his parents had grown to believe that Toby had until the blood test taken after birth came back as positive for Down's syndrome. One of the biggest challenges as a midwife is to remain professional by not making judgements about people's choices. This was a struggle at times like this but no one can truly put themselves in another person's situation as we are all affected differently by the same or similar situations. Toby's mum had conceived her babies back when the antenatal screening for Down's syndrome blood screening was still done in the second trimester of pregnancy, when it was a relatively new screening, and had a high false negative rate. It was also no good if a woman was pregnant with twins as there would be no indication as to which twin was showing the high risk for Down's. This meant that the only option available for diagnostic test was the invasive amniocentesis which carried a risk of miscarriage. Toby's parents did not wish to have this test and instead decided that the scan results would have to do until they had the post-birth blood test results. Nowadays with the availability of first trimester combined screening – blood screening and the nuchal fold scan – the incidences of false negatives is much lower. In this case Toby's parents knew they were having twins but had no more than an unconfirmed possibility that one of them would actually be born with the suspected chromosomal abnormality. I can only assume the shock was too much for them once the chromosomal results came back, and that even though they had been carefully counselled by the paediatrician no one could predict the level of disability Toby would exhibit or guarantee whether he would be a happy or angry person so they must have felt that this was their only viable option. Or perhaps it was because they had already said goodbye to this baby during the pregnancy, thinking he had a condition which was incompatible with life.

Some small part of me still believes that if they genuinely did not want Toby then they had actually done him a favour by giving him the chance to be adopted by a family who would love him for the person he was instead of having a constant reminder that he hadn't been born without a disability, like his sister. A bigger part of me wonders how they will ever explain their decision to his sister when she is old enough to understand and if she will ever understand. This case affected me quite significantly as it made me question whether I was strong enough to continue being a midwife as I would be expected to support parents making decisions such as these and to do so empathetically while hiding the fact that my views didn't mirror theirs, and that I feared they were making a terrible mistake that they would come to regret later in life. I decided that to do my job well meant that I had to make sure parents had the information they needed to make informed choices about their own and their baby's care, and that as long as I could assure myself that they were not at risk of harming themselves or their baby then I had to stand by and support them. It hasn't always been easy, and this case is an excellent example, but I can't live people's lives for them and the rewards of being a midwife have, so far, outweighed the distressing situations that I have experienced during the course of my career.

Chapter 9 - Life can be cruel

In direct contrast to most of the other stories in this book which are about people who willingly and lovingly created a child together, some people can have parenthood thrust upon them without their consent and still find they are able to come to terms with it, and to welcome it.

Lisa Polmer was my first client of the shift. I was working as part of the labour ward core team and this meant that many of the women I cared for were strangers to me, as was I to them. When she came in, she was clearly labouring but was very serene and controlled.

'Well, that's your first set of observations done on you and your baby. You are in very early labour and would be absolutely fine to be at home for a while longer but I know you had to take a taxi here on your own. Is there someone coming later on to act as your birth partner? Someone you could rely on to drive you back here later?'

She shook her head. I cursed myself for having asked her two questions as I now didn't know which one she had shaken her head in response to – birth partner or transport availability – or both?

'Would you like some tea and toast?' I offered only to have Lisa shake her head again in response. 'How about a jug of ice water?'

'Yes, please that would be lovely...erm, would it be ok for me to go have a bath? It won't hurt my baby, will it?'

'There is no reason to think it would hurt your baby and besides which your membranes are still intact, completely protecting your baby inside it's little bubble,' I explained in an attempt to reassure her even more.

'Oh, and some women even have their babies born in water, don't they?'

'Yes, usually by labouring and delivering in the birthing pool, doing it by accident in a normal sized bathtub at home isn't nearly as nice. Is the birthing pool something you are interested in?' I asked as I hadn't noticed that specified on her notes but had only had the time to read her medical, pregnancy and other pertinent details so far.

'No...I don't think so...the idea of my newborn floating in a pool of water scares me a bit but I always get in a bath when I've got bad period cramps so I thought that might help now. Plus I'd like to freshen up,' she added, rolling all her words together in a rushed tone, face flushing slightly.

I didn't try to clear up her misconceptions about water birthing; it wasn't the right time as she clearly just wanted to get herself into a bath and sorted out. I escorted her to the bathroom, showed her how to use the buzzer if she needed help or had a question and told her that if I didn't hear from her then I or another member of the team would call through the door periodically to check that she was feeling okay.

I went back to the midwives' station and phoned the community midwives' unit. The community coordinator answered the phone.

'Hi, Tina. I've got one of Mary's women who has just come in. She is in early labour but booked to deliver with us and I'd just like to have a word with Mary about her.'

'Mary's on annual leave but I think Sarah's in the unit, let me just put you through to the office.'

Hi, Sarah, did Mary leave her client files somewhere handy? Only I've got one of her women here, a Lisa Polmer of 19a Worthing Road, and I'd like to know a bit more about her.' Community midwives keep personal files on all of their women, which comes in handy on the rare occasions women lose their hand-held notes but also in instances like this, where a health care professional needs to know if there is anything that couldn't be left unsaid but isn't suitable for the client's hand-held records.

'Ok, I've found her section in Mary's files, there are quite a few pages, what do you want to know?'

'Well she has come in by taxi and has no one with her. I couldn't see the father's details and wondered if there is anyone listed as her expected birth partner or anything else that I need to know?'

'Mary has written that the conception was a result of non-consensual sex and put ? rape next to it. The next of kin has her mother's details but also a note that she lives in Gibralter. Beside birth partner Mary has put to be confirmed. Poor woman!' Sarah exclaimed.

I agreed and rang off. What the hell could I do to help Lisa? Everyone should be able to have support from someone they trust during labour and childbirth. I explained the situation to the lead midwife for the labour ward and we agreed that if Lisa had absolutely no one to come in and support her then I would give exclusive care to Lisa for as long as I was on duty while she was in labour. This meant that I wouldn't be given anyone else to care for while attending to Lisa, a drain on staffing levels but occasionally a manageable necessity. We could only hope that she would deliver while I was on duty as it would be a wrench to leave her still in labour and having to get used to a new midwife but leave her I would have to eventually as I would become unfit for safe practice after too many hours on duty.

When Lisa had finished her bath I discussed the situation with her and confirmed that there was not one person who she felt would be willing to come and support her. She was fairly new to the area and had worked long hours throughout her pregnancy. She had to endure an hour-long commute to and from work each day leaving her too exhausted to pursue friendships outside the usual lunchtime and early evening socialising with her colleagues at work. The best thing was that she was very well paid and had managed to save enough to take a full year off work to enjoy being a full-time mum. She didn't mention the father of her baby and neither did I.

She laboured beautifully. Her serene demeanour remained throughout the labour and eventual birth just before the end of my shift. I stayed on long enough to get her transferred to the postnatal ward and she barely looked up when I said my goodbyes because she was so enraptured with her daughter, and had been from the moment she had first held her in her arms. I was on three days off and Lisa had been discharged by the time I was next on duty.

I phoned Mary, her community midwife, to see how Lisa was getting on. Wonderfully apparently. Delighted that everything was going so well for such a lovely woman I said goodbye to Mary and asked her to pass on my best wishes to Lisa.

Six weeks later Mary phoned me to say that Lisa's baby daughter had died of cot death and Lisa wondered if Mary and I would like to come to the funeral. No, I very much did not want to go to the funeral! I wanted to stomp and swear and rage at a life that could be so cruel to such a wonderful woman. If I felt like this, one removed from the whole situation, then I couldn't even begin to imagine what Lisa was feeling. Mary and I went to the funeral, of course. The sight of that tiny coffin was entirely wrong; no parent should ever have to bury their own child, and most especially not on her own with only two midwives there to grieve with her over the loss of a child who had been her whole world.

Chapter 10 - Time-warp baby

Labour is always hard work, hence the name I suppose, but in almost all cases the parents will come out of the labour and birthing process with a healthy baby feeling it was worth all the effort and be in a celebratory mood. There are only rare occasions when parents endure this process with their joyful expectation laced with grief. The Rogers were one of these couples who were unable give themselves over completely to the happy occasion. Their first son had died due to damage to his kidneys, which had meant he was unable to recover from an infection in his bladder. He had died a year ago to the day that Karen went into labour.

'I do not want to be here. Doing this. Today,' were the first words she said in response to my greeting as they arrived on the labour ward.

Once she had finished the contraction that had overcome her as she was speaking I showed them to the room we had set aside for them. I knew that it was the anniversary of the day their first son had died, thanks to a warning from her community midwife.

'Can't you stop it?' Karen asked me once she was settled in her room.

'Stop what? Your labour?' Karen nodded.

'No, you are just a few days away from being full term and your baby wants to come out and have a stretch. I expect he's feeling quite cramped in there now.'

'I just want him to be born on any day other than today. I want everything to slow down, let me get through today without any distractions and then have this one tomorrow, maybe?' Her eyes filled with tears. 'I do love you,' she said, looking at her belly then patting it. 'He just gave me a kick,' she explained to me.

'But why does he have to be born on the day Joshie's died?' asked Kevin.

'Life doesn't always make sense, does it?' Avoiding giving them a response because I knew the only ones I would come up with, clinical ones related to pregnancy, would all be unsatisfactory answers to that impossible question.

'Maybe I won't have Eddie until tomorrow,' Karen said hopefully.

I looked at the clock on the wall above her head and then at Kevin. It was 5.30 a.m. and Karen was in established labour. I would expect her to deliver some time after her community midwife came on duty at 8 a.m. but likely before lunch. I couldn't imagine her labour lasting until the following day no matter how much she wanted it to happen.

'Maybe, love, maybe,' Kevin said giving her hand as squeeze, his eyes glistening with unshed tears. This would be a long, hard day for them both and I could only hope that they could put their grief aside when it came time for them to welcome their new son into the world.

'I didn't think about the time frames when they put the eggs in last time,' she said guiltily.

'It's not your fault, it's no one's fault,' Kevin said firmly. Clearly they had had this conversation before.

'Babies are a bit unpredictable that way,' I said.

'But I didn't expect him to come early. I thought I'd be overdue like I was with Joshie; they had to force him out in the end.' Karen had been induced with her first son and had ended up with a forceps delivery.

'Each baby is different. Edward, you seem to have skipped over the bit about due dates when you were reading up on how to make your way out of your mum's tummy,' I chided, waggling my finger at her abdomen and managing to coax a giggle out of Karen.

Her lighter mood was soon replaced by a return to sadness. 'I feel like I'm having a time-warp baby!' she cried.

'A what?'

'Edward was conceived at the same time as Joshie but then the rest of the fertilised eggs, including Edward's, were frozen until we wanted to use them again. Then Edward was put inside me and now he is going to be born on the day Joshie died. It makes me feel like we're in some kind of time warp.'

'That makes perfect sense, Karen but we've just got to deal with it. Edward isn't the same baby as Joshie. We've gotta believe that!' Kevin tried and failed to find the right words to make it all better.

'I know that!' she wailed angrily.

As her labour continued Karen began to fight against each contraction, sobbing in the interval between the pains. It was obvious she did not want to be going through this and I suggested she might like some pain relief to temporarily help ease her burden. I was concerned that if she continued to grieve at this intense level it might adversely affect Edward and reduce his ability to cope with the labour and birth process, and it was certainly affecting her ability to cope. Karen had made a note in her birth plan that although she hadn't used pethidine with her previous labour this was one of the types of pain relief that she was considering using this time around. Women are expected to make an informed choice about what types of pain relief they want in labour and this is something that should be discussed at length during the antenatal period. During labour when she is in pain, anxious and tired, the best we can expect a woman to be capable of is giving informed consent. Making an informed choice about what type of pain relief she would prefer will be nigh on impossible at this point. Pethidine is a controlled drug which can be administered as a form of pain relief to labouring women, often after other forms such as gas and air or using a TENS machine have proved ineffective. Although women can chose varying doses of pethidine it is rarely suggested as the first choice for pain relief. To make an informed choice the women needs to understand how pethidine works: that it is given by injection, that it won't take her pain away completely, that it stimulates the vomit centres in the brain so she may become nauseous or even begin vomiting, that there is another drug that can be given to help ease or relieve the nausea. The woman also needs to know the effects pethidine may have on her baby – that it crosses the placenta so her baby also gets a dose of the drug which affects its respiratory centre. Now all the while her baby is inside her this shouldn't be too much of a problem as the placenta will continue to act as an effective gas exchange organ, giving the baby the oxygen it needs and taking away the by products of its metabolism to be dealt with in the mother's circulation.

Pethidine is never given to the mother without first doing an internal examination to ensure that she isn't expected to deliver within the next few hours. However, some women will rapidly become unexpectedly fully dilated within an hour or so of being given the pethidine which means she will be delivering a baby whose system is loaded with a dose of pethidine. For this reason a drug called naloxon is kept handy once pethidine has been given as it will help to reverse the effects of pethidine. The key issue with naloxon is that its effects do not linger as long as the pethidine does. This requires watchful monitoring of the baby by the mum and staff for 24 hours after birth, in case the baby reacts strongly to the leftover pethidine once the effects of the naloxon wear off.

After having chatted about pethidine for a bit in order to go over what Karen's community midwife had already discussed with her, and after I did an internal examination to check how far dilated she was, Karen decided that she felt the possible benefits of pethidine outweighed the risks. About 30 minutes after her injection she was more tranquil and coped with the contractions much more calmly, and then drifted off to sleep in between. Kevin did the same and by the time I handed over their care to their community midwife they were both much more relaxed. I've never been convinced that the benefits of pethidine outweigh the risk but other midwives swear by it because they say it has helped so many of their women cope with labour. However, in cases like Karen's I do feel that this drug did her a world of good and helped her to cope with a most difficult situation.

She delivered in the early afternoon and was discharged home by the time I came back to work the following week. According to her community midwife the labour had progressed slowly but problem free and Edward was a settled thriving baby. After discussion she had referred them on for counselling but was certain that they had already taken big steps towards moving on from Joshie's death and believed that this was in a large part due to Edward's arrival.

'I'm hoping the counselling and extra attention from their health visitor will help them prepare themselves for getting through the run up to

Edward's first birthday without excess anxiety,'
she said.

I agreed completely. I could see how they
would feel frantic that they might lose Edward
too and was glad that they were now getting the
right support and the help they had probably
needed for the past year.

Interlude

Standing Tall

Most movies and TV dramas show women delivering whilst lying on their backs. The fly-on-the-wall documentaries about maternity units are not much better and I have no idea why they choose to show so many women delivering in such an unnatural position – perhaps it is to make the scene more camera- and viewer-friendly. A person only has to think about how the human body is designed and how we tend to be in an upright position most of the time to realise that it makes much more sense to labour and deliver a baby in any position other than reclining – why not let gravity do some of the hard work, too? Having said that I now need to contradict myself because a few women do chose semi-recumbent positions as their preferred way to spend parts of their labour or delivery, and if it works for them then it definitely is the best position for them to be in. However, the only way women can find the best labour and delivery position(s) is through trial and error and they often discover that what worked in previous labour and deliveries doesn't suit them with their next baby. So, it is up to their midwife to encourage them to try new positions and to suggest ones which she thinks may suit the woman best from the way she is behaving in labour and the position the baby is in inside her.

When scared and in pain, some women will head for a nice warm bath, but a large proportion of labouring women will head straight for the bed in the labour room and want to crawl under the covers for comfort. I think it is a leftover instinct built up from being snuggled down when unwell during childhood. One of the ways to pre-empt this instinctive behaviour is to pump the bed up to a level high enough for it to be comfortably leant on but too high to allow the woman to automatically sink down on it straight away. If she wants to get on the bed it has to be an active, cognisant choice, and when faced with this most women will opt to try other positions first. If the labour room is large enough to offer the woman space to roam she will alternate between pacing the room and leaning on different objects of the right height – the sink, the bed, the wall, her birth partner. If she senses that her baby's head is not quite in the most optimal position or the midwife is aware of this then she may want to sit on a chair facing backwards or try to stand with one foot propped up on a higher level than the other, alternating her feet intermittently. Walking up stairs in a sideways crab-like walk is an excellent way for the woman to achieve the same result, though she is unlikely to take herself off the ward and over to a staircase without encouragement from the midwife assigned to her.

I have seen women labour and deliver in so many different positions, and these varied according to the unit I was working in at the time too, most likely because of the wide variety in design of labour rooms and the equipment available in them. Kneeling on bean bags while leaning over the bed or birth partner's legs was a particular favourite in one unit where every room had bean bags and they were used during parent craft classes. Sitting on the toilet has always been a good way to get a woman into a good labour position at the same time as having a little rest from having to be up on her feet. The worry with this position is always that it is a very favourable one for pushing and once a woman starts pushing she is completely into the pushing zone and very reluctant to move to a more suitable place to deliver her baby. The best we can do it to put the toilet seat down and pad the area around the toilet with pillows and sheets in order to make it a bit more comfortable.

Birthing stools made a comeback for a while in some of the units I worked in but because it appeared that women might be more likely to tear or bleed a bit more when birthing on a stool they soon stopped being offered for use. I still wonder if this was a justifiable knee-jerk reaction and wish there was a way to do a more thorough bit of research into the use of birthing stools, but it is almost impossible to do this without possibly making more women suffer the complications of which the birth stool is suspected of causing.

Many years later the abdominal exercise ball came into fashion as a labour support with labouring women sitting on it in order to adopt the most favourable position of their spine and pelvis. It worked well for all women but particularly for those women who had babies in an occipito posterior position, meaning the baby's back was pressing on the mother's back instead of being in the much more favourable position of having its back pressed into the mother's abdomen. Women who chose to labour in the warm shoulder-deep hydrotherapy pools available on some labour wards find it much easier to manoeuvre themselves around and change position as frequently as they wish to, although they lose the option of pacing the room unless they get themselves out of the pool. Some of the favoured positions in pools have been kneeling and leaning over the edge or kneeling with their head and arms resting on a float, side lying with head resting on the edge of the pool or almost floating while their birth partner supports them from the other side.

The position that never fails to make me groan inwardly and frantically try to think of ways to talk the woman out of, is when she is standing completely upright while pushing. This position would make me less nervous if I had hands the size of a catcher's mitt and wasn't wearing gloves that get very slippery when wet. Understandably, babies don't tend to be very happy if they get dropped from a height, even if the midwife has covered the surrounding floor with pillows. I think being born is enough of a shock for them without also experiencing the added indignity of falling. The most challenging delivery I can remember involved a first-time mum who decided that it would be a good idea to get up onto the already raised bed and then stand upright on it. I have no idea how she even managed to perform that move at that point in her labour as I could already see an orange-sized amount of her baby's head distending her perineum. I couldn't get close enough to the baby to be sure I could catch it and so I climbed onto the bed with her, instructed her husband to steady her, and for her to hold onto the headboard so she didn't fall off. In hindsight I suppose it must have been the shock of the feeling of her baby's head beginning to make its way out that made her leap on the bed, perhaps in an attempt to escape the unexpectedly unpleasant sensation. I did ask her afterwards but she couldn't remember why she had thought she should deliver in a standing position on the bed. The baby came quickly and I managed to support it for the few seconds I need to while I talked the mum into sitting down on the bed so she could hold her baby safely. I am happy to say that this was the only time I had to deliver a baby this high off the ground, but working as a midwife never fails to throw unexpected scenarios into most shifts.

Expect the unexpected

Chapter 11 - Modern midwifery is more than just a delivery service

Even at a small maternity unit setting up an antenatal clinic for the day requires a surprising amount of time each morning. There are notes to be pulled from the main note storeroom and checked off against the clinic appointment list. Blood test results to be matched with the notes. Reports to be filed or attached to individual consultant's folders along with referral letters that need reviewing. Equipment to be removed from the locked store cupboard and placed in consulting rooms. Databases that need updating, and most importantly, kettles that need boiling for that all important pre-clinic drink which is often the only one drunk until the clinic ends a few hours later. The clinic I was working in was staffed on rotation between the core unit team and the community midwives and on this particular month I was the core unit team member on clinic duty. Only one person was required to set the clinic up, and as I quite enjoyed this solitary task, I always volunteered to go down and set it up ahead of the rest of the team arriving in from their community areas. The clinic was set off a reception area on the ground floor which staff could access through a connecting staircase leading from the maternity unit above. The reception area wasn't staffed this early because there was no need to have anyone there until shortly before the women and their partners began arriving, which meant that midwives had to pull the notes, a job that fell to the receptionists during the rest of the day.

The notes were stored just off the reception area and after doing most of the setting up duties in the clinic, I busied myself with pulling the notes for the women we expected to see in clinic on this day. I carried an armful of notes into the clinic area and placed them in the appropriate consultant's room with any associated reports. On my way back for more notes, I stopped to unlock the reception area doors so the admin staff could come in that way instead of going through the main hospital. I struggled to find one set of notes that I needed and left a note for the clerk asking for help to locate them before clinic began and then took the final sets of notes back to clinic. With everything set up except for that one set of notes which would have to wait until the admin staff arrived, I decided to catch up on some leftover filing from the previous day. I hadn't had time to finish it because the labour ward had become unexpectedly busy after clinic and I had been asked to return to the wards to fill the gap in staffing as soon as clinic had finished. Sitting at the table in the staff room I got on with that task, laughing intermittently at the DJ's banter on the radio programme while I waited for the rest of the team to arrive.

When I heard a knock at the semi-closed door I said, 'Hello?' expecting one of the midwives to pop her head round the barrier and wondering why she didn't just come in without knocking.

Instead of the expected blue uniform the door slowly opened to reveal a frail-looking old man. 'Sorry to be a bother, Sister,' he said, then stood there looking at me.

'Can I help you, sir? Are you lost?'

'No, not lost, I know I am on the maternity unit but I didn't know where else to go.'

I stood up and walked over to the man, indicating he could sit on a chair just inside the staff room door; he was shaky and I worried he might fall over. 'Where else to go for what, sir?'

He sat silently for a few long seconds then took a deep breath and said, 'For help, Sister.' His eyes filled with tears and he looked away, swallowing noisily then braced himself with a hand on the chair arm next to him before propelling himself into a standing position.

'I'm sorry to trouble you, I feel such a fool.' His voice betrayed his inner shame.

'There is nothing foolish about seeking help,' I tried to reassure him.

He stood there silently looking at the floor, clearly distressed. He was a clean-shaven man who was now a shadow of his younger self. His sagging facial skin and three-piece suit broadcasting that he had once been a much bigger, taller person before the weight of age had taken its toll on him, shrinking and bending him towards the ground under which he would come to lie all too soon.

'I am pleased you came actually. I have never liked drinking my morning cuppa on my own. Join me?' I offered in an attempt to prevent him leaving in such a state.

'Thank you. I could do with a cuppa.'

'Do you take milk or sugar?'

'Both if I may. Haven't had one yet today. On account of having to leave home in a hurry. It's...' He stopped abruptly and took off his hat placing it in his lap, fretting with the rim as he said, 'I do apologise for not removing my hat. Where are my manners today?'

'No offence taken, sir,' I said momentarily reflecting on the generation gap. I had not noticed that his hat was still on whereas he was embarrassed that he had not removed it while indoors.

'You mentioned having to leave home in a hurry this morning?' I busied myself with making our cups of tea in an attempt to make him believe I wasn't desperate to find out what this was all about. I had the feeling that if I put him under pressure he would leave without divulging the reason he was here. Perhaps he had a young grandchild at home and had left in a rush to escape the insufferable noise?

'Yes. I did.' He paused; I waited hoping he would continue.

'My wife...'

I turned and handed him his cup of tea. He wrapped his hands around the mug then raised it shakily for a few sips of the soothing liquid.

'My wife...she isn't...she hits me.' He hiccupped out a sob, sighed, and then regained his composure through a series of slow sips of tea.

'Has this gone on for long?' I asked trying to think of how I would deal with this if it was a pregnant woman sitting before me. A victim of domestic abuse is a victim no matter what the gender but I had never had a man disclose such a thing to me before.

He placed his mug carefully on the chair beside his then rolled up his sleeves to expose an array of bruises in varying shades of painful damage. 'It's gone on so long now that I think it's more habit than the fact that she hates me, though I know I am a disappointment to her. I was raised to never hit a woman. I used to try reasoning with her but she thought I was arguing and that just made her angrier. I know she needs me to take care of her but I get it wrong. I have done such a bad job of looking after her for so long now that I guess someone else should do it for me. Pick up the pieces of the mess I made of my marriage. Solve my problems for me. I can't go back now I have left. I have been walking outside since daybreak with nowhere to go. I came here because I needed some warmth while I decided what to do next. I feel such a failure.'

He went back to concentrating on his tea while my heart broke for him. It wasn't his fault, he should have left long ago and yet here he sat, blaming himself and doing his best to convince himself that he was the bad guy, coming here today only because he had failed in his duties as a husband.

I could hear the chatter of the rest of the team walking toward the office so I got up and stuck my head around the door. 'Morning, ladies. I've got a gentleman in here with me.' They stopped talking and stared at me, eyebrows raised. 'We're just having a chat and I wonder if you would be so kind as to let the EIT know that he'll probably need their support?' By telling them this the team knew that they couldn't come in the office because I had a man in with me who was suffering some kind of abuse.

I closed the office door. 'Would you like another cup?'

'I am sorry, I should go, I can see that I am keeping you from your duties, I don't want to be a bother.'

'No, please don't worry about that. There is a large team here today and our first patient isn't expected for ages yet,' I lied, worried he would leave before I could get him the help he needed.

'There are special work forces who deal with this kind of thing every day. The one at this hospital is called the Early Intervention Team and they would be happy to come and give you any support you want.'

'My wife won't get in trouble, will she? Only I don't want her to be upset. She can't help the way she is, she doesn't deal with stress very well...' He trailed off, perhaps realising that he was making excuses for her.

'It isn't the team's job to get people into trouble; their job is to help people who are in trouble. Like you,' I said softly.

'Thank you,' he said and looked down at his knees.

I let the team in when they arrived and left him alone with them when he said he was happy for me to go. I promised I wouldn't be far and the EIT staff promised him they would get me if he changed his mind and wanted me back in. He left with the team an hour later; they had promised to move him into a secure shelter until his son could come and take him to Spain to live with him until he could decide what steps to take next. He had asked the team to keep me up to date with his progress and I assured him I would wait expectantly for each update of his progress towards a happier life.

I was delighted to hear eventually that he had moved to Spain on a permanent basis and was still there enjoying the sun and lifestyle. The EIT team had gone to his house with the police to collect some belongings for him only to find that his wife had smashed the house to bits in his absence. The neighbours had met the police outside and told them that they were just about to phone them as the noise had been going on for hours. She ended up being admitted for some much-needed treatment but was soon released into the community with a community psychiatric nurse supervising her needs. I still think that old man made a lucky escape and hope sunny Spain made up for all the years of torment he had endured.

As this story has shown, antenatal clinic can be a varied department to work in. However, it isn't just the older men keeping the shifts interesting, the younger ones can behave in unexpected ways, too! In the next story I explain why there is a phone in every scan room and a crash trolley within 'shouting' distance.

Chapter 12 - Scan man

People are so used to scans being used during pregnancies now that they have become fairly blasé about the procedures. However, it wasn't that long ago, less than 40 years, that scans were introduced for the first time and only recently that scans began to be used routinely during pregnancy. They used to be used as a confirmation of a suspected problem rather than a screening and observational tool. This was because the potential for harm to a fetus from scanning wasn't known and so the investigations were kept to a minimum until the safety of more pregnancy routine scanning was confirmed to outweigh the risks of bombarding delicate fetal tissues with ultrasound waves. That isn't to say that ultrasound scans don't disturb a fetus, most of them will start moving around once the scan starts, and I suspect that being subjected to a scan may feel similar to how a fish feels when you tap on the tank it is swimming around in. Some women too, for example those with fibromyalgia, can find the scanning process uncomfortable. Nowadays, most women tend to treat their pregnancy scan appointments as a viewing of their baby and invite relatives and friends to come with them, often bringing along the siblings of the new baby-to-be. As health-care professionals we know this is rarely a good idea because a scan of the fetus is as much of a medical assessment as any other pregnancy investigation and what they may not be aware of, but should be, is that it isn't uncommon for a problem to be noted during the scan appointment.

There have been many occasions when the assembled eager assortment of scan observers have had to be sent out of the room so that the parents can be counselled in privacy about the findings of the scan. It is difficult to properly focus on what the clinician is telling you about the problem that your baby has been noted to have when you are surrounded by distraught relatives or anxious children. Also, scan rooms are small and get hot very fast from the scan machines so extra people in the room just makes it even more difficult for the air-conditioning system to function properly. If a problem with the fetus is noted at an early scan, and thought to be linked to a chromosomal issue, then these women are offered an opportunity to have an invasive diagnostic procedure which will often give them a yes or no result. A chorionic villus sampling of the early placental tissue can be done before 13 weeks either through the abdomen or through the cervix, using a scan to guide the consultant to the right spot. An amniocentesis sampling of the amniotic fluid that surrounds the fetus can be done around 16 weeks, though some consultants will do them as early as 15 weeks if the pool of fluid is deep enough.

These women are advised to bring someone with them for support and also to take them home after the procedure as it isn't advisable for them to drive. When Nicola Tipner arrived for her amniocentesis appointment accompanied by her boyfriend and father, I asked them to take a seat while Nicola and I went into the sluice under the guise of checking her urine and other routine checks. What I really wanted to do was get her alone so I could check who she really wanted to bring into her amniocentesis appointment with her. Both of them, as it turned out.

'Have you brought your urine sample with you, Nicola? Thanks!' I busied myself with gloves and urine sticks at the sink, which flushed the contents away to the same drains as the toilets. 'That's fine, no problems with your urine.'

'Ok, good I guess. Erm, what do you test it for?' Nicola fidgeted, reminding me of a teenager, which she was, just 18 last month according to the date of birth on her notes.

'Each time we see you we test your urine to see if your kidneys are coping with your pregnancy. If your body is feeling the strain a bit then it sometimes pushes out things we wouldn't normally see in urine like protein or sugar. If you have an infection then there might be blood, and if you aren't eating well then we can see something called keytones in your urine.'

'Wow. Sort of like spying on my body then?'

'More like looking for clues because we don't just pay attention to what we do or don't find in your urine, we also look at what your blood pressure is, whether you have noticed any swelling anywhere on your body and what your blood test results are, plus lots of other things.'

'Awesome...I want to be a midwife someday.'

'Well I can definitely recommend it, it is a wonderful job.' I smiled at Nicola then said, 'So which of those two will you be bringing in with you today?' I pointed my head in the direction of the waiting room.

'I thought both?'

'The room where the amniocentesis is done is very small, Nicola; there really isn't room for the ultrasonographer, the doctor, me, you and two other people,' I explained.

'Oh.' Nicola's eyes welled with tears.

'What's the matter?' I said softly.

'I'm scared and want my dad there but Barry, well he's the father of my baby, ain't he?'

'Yes?' I guessed hoping it was the correct response. If Nicola didn't know the answer to that question then no one did.

'So Barry wants to be in there too natch but I want my dad.'

'I can understand your problem, well let me double check with the consultant but I'm sure he'll agree to them both being in the room because of the situation that you're in.' Once Nicola had wiped off the mascara her tears had smeared under her eyes, I took her back to the waiting room and went to talk to the consultant.

'Fine, just make sure they stay on her left,' he said to me, meaning that he understandably didn't want either of them on the side of the couch where he would stand and the sonographer would sit during the procedure. This would put the two men very close together as well as between us and the door but as I was mobile in the room during the amniocentesis assisting the doctor, this shouldn't pose a significant issue. I would remain alert for any signs of aggressiveness from the men which sometimes happened if the woman became distressed during the amniocentesis.

Once the consultant was ready I brought Nicola, Barry and her father into the room. By the time I had Nicola comfortable on the couch with her dad beside her, his hand already clutched in hers and Barry standing awkwardly beside the chair and chewing gum nervously, the room was already uncomfortably warm. The procedure went smoothly and I had my back half turned to everyone as I labelled the pots of precious amniotic fluid on the desk while the consultant removed the long catheter from Nicola's abdomen. As I affixed the final label, I heard a choking sound and a distinctive thump.

I turned to see Barry twitching on the floor. The consultant began to attend to him as I pressed the emergency buzzer then helped Nicola and her dad from the room and the sonographer went to find the junior doctor in clinic to act as back up for the consultant.

'What's happened to Barry?' Nicola asked anxiously.

'Fainted most likely, I'll let you know as soon as possible.' I ran back to the room with a blood-pressure machine. Barry's blood pressure was dangerously low even though the consultant had already propped Barry's feet up. Barry was breathing normally but was completely unresponsive. The consultant asked the sonographer to call for a resuscitation team. The resuscitation team would arrive with any equipment that might be necessary to get Barry ready to be transferred to an observation ward until it could be figured out what had caused him to become unconscious, as this seemed to be more than just a fainting episode. If it had been just a faint then Barry would have been much more responsive to the consultant pressing his knuckles into Barry's sternum. The resus team arrived and decided that Barry was stable enough to be transferred to another ward where they could investigate him in more detail, so we helped them to transfer Barry onto the stretcher and I got a wheelchair for Nicola. We followed the resuscitation team at a distance and I explained to Nicola why they were transferring Barry. I left her and her father in the waiting room of the ward Barry had been transferred to, warned her not to overdo it, to make sure she took the time to rest over the next couple of days.

'I'll see you in two weeks time when you return to get your results. Here is your letter with your appointment details on it and a leaflet explaining what problems to look out for after your amniocentesis. Call the number on the leaflet if you get any of the symptoms listed and call the number on the appointment letter if you have any other questions.'

I made my way back to the clinic, making a mental note to phone the ward that Barry was on at lunch time to see how he was getting on. I didn't get the time to phone the ward until the end of the day but by that time Barry had made a full recovery. Cause of the collapse was put down to Barry choking on his gum, which had triggered a vagal nerve reflex causing his blood pressure to drop and keep him unconscious for an extended period of time. Barry was sent home with the advice to avoid chewing gum during times of stress in the future.

Chapter 13 - Prolapsed cord

Although antenatal clinic has its share of unexpected incidents, most of the time it does tick along in a fairly standard manner. Not so the labour ward, where shifts can be as unpredictable and contrary as a toddler.

The worst thing any midwife can do on duty is be lulled into a false sense of security about how well the shift is going. It is always wise to keep a certain watchfulness and area of alert expectancy going inside your brain. Anything can go wrong and you don't want it to be when you least expect it because your reactions needs to be as speedy as possible in order to rectify the situation before it goes beyond the point of no return. This is especially true of labour ward shifts because you can go from a lazy hour spent cleaning, checking stock and/or catching up on online training to having to deal with an emergency situation in the blink of an eye.

It was on just such a shift that Keema Standmere was admitted in early labour. Her husband had been transferred to the area as part of his job in the past week and they were both still a little disorientated by the change of city, which was why they had come in earlier in labour than they might have in a city they were familiar with. The first thing I noticed about them was that they were a remarkably good-looking couple. Both were tall and slender, and Keema moved towards me with what could only be described as 'presence'; she moved as gracefully and silently as if her feet didn't quite touch the floor. I escorted them to the assessment room where we took women when they didn't obviously appear to be in established labour.

'Please make yourselves as comfortable as you can while I have a look through the notes you've brought with you. Have you seen a midwife here yet?'

'No, we only finished moving here at the beginning of last week; we're booked in to meet the community midwife on Monday when I'll be 38 weeks,' Keema explained.

Because Keema hadn't had a chance to be seen by one of our midwives, it meant that she hadn't been booked into our system or been given a set of our notes. I busied myself with finding my way around the unfamiliar notes that Keema had brought with her from the city they used to live in.

'I'm not really in a lot of pain yet,' Keema began with an apologetic note to her voice.

'I did a few trial runs to the hospital last week, just in case, but couldn't help worrying that I'd get lost on the way here now that it is really happening. So I panicked a bit and told Keema it would be sensible to come in earlier rather than leaving it too late!' John explained.

'We found the hospital ok though. Straight away.' Keema laughed.

'I can understand why John would feel nervous though, new roads can be confusing especially when you're a bit distracted. I'll assess you and see how you're coping, Keema, and we'll make a decision about where the best place is for you to be at this stage of your labour based on that, okay?'

I found the obstetric history page – nothing to note. The antenatal care page gave details of Keema's pregnancy up to 36 weeks. Her pregnancy seemed to have gone smoothly, though she had been seen by a few different midwives and never by the same midwife twice in a row during her pregnancy. I noticed that the midwives had never felt that the baby's head had engaged fully into her pelvic outlet. I found the scan page and checked where her placenta was situated because a low-lying placenta can be one of the causes of this problem. The placenta was in a good position according to her scan.

'Keema, I'd like to have a feel how your baby is lying inside you after I've done your basic checks. Have you brought a sample of urine with you?'

'No, I forgot in all the excitement, I could do one though.'

Once Keema had returned, I tested her urine and took note of her blood pressure, temperature and pulse, which were all normal. When I palpated her baby it was in a long lying position, head down but not firmly lodged in her pelvic outlet. It moved easily when I gave it a gentle nudge. The baby's heart beat was fine but the fact that its head wasn't tightly in the pelvis was a worry. Although Keema was only contracting once every 10 minutes they were lasting 40 seconds and she wasn't able to talk through them, which was a sign she might be going into established labour. Her membranes hadn't broken yet and it could be that the baby's head would lodge itself firmly in her pelvis once that happened but it could also mean the umbilical cord would slip down into the pelvis just before the head did. This would reduce the amount of oxygen the baby would get through the cord to dangerous levels. I explained this as best I could to Keema and John, trying to balance between terrifying them and making them understand that there were additional risks to be navigated for this labour and that their method of delivery might be decided by what happened once her waters had broken.

'I need to let the duty doctor know what I've found and they will want to come and say hello and assess you themselves.' I was nearing the end of the explanation now and not too soon by the look of weariness on both their faces. They needed time to adjust to what they had just learned.

'How soon will we have to decide what to do?'

'Well you need to be thinking about what I've just explained straight away, though I expect you're already doing that. I'm going to go out now to let the doctor know and to grab the things I need so I can take some blood from you.'

'Oh no! What for?' Keema sounded terrified. 'I hate having my bloods taken,' she explained unnecessarily.

I discussed the need for routine admission blood tests, got her permission to go ahead with the blood tests, then took them around to a proper labour room to get settled. They would definitely be staying until this baby was born so there was no need for them to remain in the assessment room.

I bleeped the doctor, who was busy finishing up in theatre and said he would be around to assess Keema straight after. I gathered the blood-taking equipment and made my way back to Keema and John, only stopping to explain to the ward coordinator what the situation was, so she could update the board to reflect that I was with a woman who would likely need my full attention.

'Right,' I said as I washed my hands before taking Keema's blood. 'Do you want to lie down while I do this or sit up?'

Keema settled herself against pillows on the bed while I put my gloves on and the tourniquet on her arm, reluctantly resting her arm on top of the pillow so I could take her blood. John held her other hand, rubbing his thumb over her thumb.

'There, all done!' I said less than two minutes later.

'I hardly felt that but I still hated it. I feel all tense now.' Keema gave a little shudder.

'Some things you never get used to no matter how many times you experience them. It would be a good idea to get changed into the clothes you want to labour in now because it shouldn't be long before the doctor comes to see you, or you can change after he's been, whichever you prefer.'

'I'll do it now; I might not feel like it later.'

I smiled and pulled the curtains around the bed before going to the counter on the other side of the room to finish labelling the blood bottles.

'Ugh...I think my waters have broken,' I heard Keema say

'Can I come round the curtains?' I asked hoping the urgency didn't show in my tone of voice.

'Yes,' Keema said, then, 'What's that?' She sat back down on the bed and pointed between her legs.

My stomach sank as I noticed a short length of grey matter hanging from her vagina. For a split second I dared to hope it was only a string of thick mucosy loss but knew it was probably a bit of umbilical cord.

I gently touched it and felt the firm jelly texture of umbilical cord.

'Keema, could you turn over onto you knees and put your forehead on the bed please and John could you press the buzzer three times?'

Keema assumed the position I had asked, knowing this meant that some cord had come out because it was one of the things I had told her I would ask her to do if this happened.

'Keema, I'm going to put my fingers inside you and lift your baby's head off the cord if necessary.'

'Ok.' Her voice was muffled but the fear was still audible. I gently tucked the cord back inside Keema's vagina to keep it warm and felt the baby's head, still high. I pressed against it with the tips of my fingers to keep it that way, trying not to put any pressure on the cord because I didn't want it to go into spasm.

The door opened and I said, 'We've got a cord prolapsed, can I have some help, please?' without turning to look at whoever had entered as I was already feeling uncomfortable from the position I needed to be in, in order to keep the baby's head off the cord. The midwife left the buzzer going so that others knew they were needed while she listened in to Keema and John's baby's heart beat and reassured us all that it sounded within normal limits. She asked John to stand back against the wall because things would get a bit hectic while we got ready to transfer to the operating theatre. I kneeled on the bed behind Keema and tried to ignore the pulsing ache radiating from my fingers through my wrist. The human body does not like being kept in any position for too long and my body clearly felt that this had been quite long enough. We arrived in the operating theatre very quickly and within a few minutes Keema was unconscious from the general anaesthesia and the caesarean was underway.

Her baby boy was born in a few minutes and after a quick check from the paediatrician and after being labelled by the support worker he was taken downstairs to be reunited with John. John had had to stay in Keema's room during the operation because birth partners are not allowed in the operating theatre if we have to use a general anaesthetic. He was kept busy comforting his new son with the help of the health care support worker until Keema had recovered from the effects of the general anaesthetic and I brought her back to her room. After helping John to settle Michael against his mum for a cuddle I sat in the corner of the room and enjoyed the best part of any delivery from my perspective, catching up on my note writing while this new family enjoyed some quiet time together.

Chapter 14 - Mecconium at home

In fact, it isn't just the labour ward that likes to be contrary and keeps the staff on high alert…labour in the community is equally unpredictable.

I was in the midwifery-led unit doing some postnatal checks when the community coordinator asked me to go out to assess Mrs Moreton who was booked for a homebirth and had phoned in to say she thought she was in labour. She wasn't one of the women in my caseload but was assigned to one of the midwives in my team. I got her card out of the midwife's files and refreshed my memory of Mrs Moreton's history. Because she was booked for a homebirth I was able to jump to some conclusions about her without reading the card: likely to have had a 100% normal pregnancy and not giving rise to any concerns about how her labour might progress. Mrs and Mrs Moreton lived at number 20 The High Street, very nice indeed, I thought to myself. I could remember the inside of their house more clearly than I could remember how the couple themselves looked. They lived in one of the more affluent areas of town with off-road parking and generous-sized houses set well back from the road. The inside of their house was bright and airy, decorated in mostly biscuit and cream which could prove a challenge to maintain in its pristine state in the throes of a homebirth. I made a mental note to send Mr Moreton out to buy a job lot of plastic sheeting once I arrived, if he hadn't already been advised to do so.

I double checked the homebirth equipment, loaded it into the boot, wheeled the trolley back to the door of the midwifery-led unit, pressed the bell, gave the health care support worker who approached the door a thumbs up and left. She would put the trolley back in its place for me and log the time I had left to attend Mrs Moreton at home. I would ring in once I had arrived and had done a physical and visual assessment of Mrs Moreton's condition. This feedback to the unit was important for two reasons: 1 – they had to know I had arrived safely to attend to Mrs Moreton and 2 – they had to know how soon I might need a second midwife to stand by for delivery so that the day's work could be divided up in a do-able fashion amongst those on duty. It was 10 a.m. so I made the relatively short journey in good time and parked in the road outside their drive placing the **Midwife on Call – no drugs on board** sign prominently on the dashboard. I avoided parking in their drive out of habit – as someone who was classed as a lone worker, we had it drummed into our heads to try and make sure our exit was clear at all times. Often easier said than done but some self-help measures like parking on the road instead of in a drive were simple. I grabbed my standard home-visit pack, which contained all I would need to assess Mrs Moreton, and made my way to their house breathing in the scent of the blossoms in their flower beds as I made my way up their drive, an uplifting and most welcoming experience indeed. If only every approach to someone's house could offer this instead of the scent of the urine, dog mess and/or vomit-dodging quick step that accompanied the approach to many inner-city living areas.

Mr Moreton opened the door with a smile before I could knock. I introduced myself as we hadn't met when I had called to visit Mrs Moreton at home previously. He gestured me inside and pointed to the stairs saying, 'She's in the nursery, can I get you a cup of tea?' I declined, preferring to wait until my assessment of Mrs Moreton confirmed that I would be saying for longer than a quick hello. Mr Moreton said he was just going to make a cup of tea for himself and Mrs Moreton and then he would join us upstairs. I called out 'Hello' up the stairs in the hope that Mrs Moreton would respond so that I knew she was really upstairs (paranoid, perhaps, but very sensible when in a house with people who were strangers to me), and to give me some idea of which direction I was headed in once I got up there. A woman's voice responded and I climbed the stairs, making a sharp left once I had reached the top though not before I had taken note of the cleanliness of the bathroom directly at the top of the stairs. Mrs Moreton was sitting in a rocking chair in a colourful, brightly lit room. I sank down onto the bean bag nearby and ran through the gamut of questions which would allow me to begin to assess her progress in labour before I even touched her. After discussing when her pains had started, where did she feel them, how long she thought they were lasting, had her waters broken, was her baby moving normally, was she experiencing any blood loss and what had she been doing when the pains began, during which she had two contractions in 10 minutes, she stood up and began pacing around the room while I made detailed notes on the information she had given me as well as familiarising myself with the information in her notes about how her pregnancy had progressed, where the placenta was situated and all the other information contained within the green folder. I asked if I could do some basic physical observations on her – temperature, pulse, blood pressure and her baby – palpate her tummy so that I could get an idea of which position her baby was lying in and also have a long listen in to her baby's heart beat. Mr Moreton joined us and sat companionably on the bed near Mrs Moreton sipping his tea and filling in responses as and when he could while I went about my job.

Eventually I came to the conclusion that Mrs Moreton, her body and baby were all in the best possible condition for labour and said so, not realising that I was soon to find out just how wrong I was. From what I had observed so far I could tell that Mrs Moreton was labouring with regular contractions though without doing an internal examination of her cervix I was unable to define just how far along in labour she was. Having said that, it is nigh on impossible to tell any mum with any accuracy how long she will be in labour for even after having established how dilated she is. What is possible, however, is to make a reasonable guesstimate based on the average, relatively relaxed mum, labouring for the first time at home. Mrs and Mr Moreton wanted this guestimate, as did I, because it would help me to decide if I could slip away for a while to get some other nearby visits done until Mrs Moreton's labour had progressed to the point where she needed a midwife's constant presence. Mrs Moreton went to empty her bladder before I began the internal examination as a full bladder can make this procedure more uncomfortable than needed and can prevent the baby's head from making its way into the pelvis as efficiently as it needs to. She came back with a towel to lie down on and I was able to establish that she was three centimetres dilated and that the condition of her cervix was favourable to a nice steady progress though her labour as long as she kept contracting as she was at the moment. I could feel her membranes bulging in front of her baby's head and as she was making progress with them as they were, there was no need to discuss breaking them. All things being as they should be, her body would rupture them at the right point in her labour, i.e. before the baby was born.

I left them with the reassurance that I was not going to be more than 10 minutes away, would return in an hour to check on them and for them to call me on my work mobile if there was any change or if they felt they wanted me to come back for any reason before the hour was up. I was just finishing up with a postnatal check on a new mum and baby when my phone rang. It was Mr Moreton informing me that Mrs Moreton's contractions were a lot more painful and she was quite distressed about it. She certainly was, I could hear her calling out with the pain over the phone. I told Mr Moreton I would come straight away, apologised to the woman I was currently with who had been forewarned that I had a lady in labour and made my way back to the Moreton's. Mr Moreton once again greeted me before I could knock but this time all he said was, 'Her waters have broken and they're a funny colour.' I could hear Mrs Moreton upstairs and made my way quickly to her in the bathroom. Her amniotic fluid was coming away on the toilet paper as a greeny yellow instead of the straw colour it should be. I listened to her baby's heart rate which was still fine. When the waters are this colour it indicates that the baby has been stressed enough to void its bowels, though clearly for the Moreton's baby the stress was not something that was occurring at the moment and may have been earlier in the pregnancy judging by the colour of the mecconuim. Regardless of when the stressful event had occurred, the presence of mecconium in amniotic fluid necessitates a hospital-based birth and after explaining to the Moretons why this was necessary I phoned the ambulance control to request a paramedic ambulance and the maternity unit bleep holder to warn her of our impending arrival. I asked Mr Moreton to carry the hospital bags, which we advise every planned homebirth parents to pack, downstairs and to wait for the ambulance. I helped Mrs Moreton get herself ready to make the walk downstairs and once the ambulance had arrived and I had briefed the crew on the situation we made our way to hospital by blue light where the rest of her labour progressed uneventfully and I was eventually able to assist her while she delivered a healthy baby boy. He cried lustily at birth, required absolutely no resuscitation or assistance in any way, shape or form and breast fed as if he had read the textbook, making a mockery of our transfer into hospital, but I am always happy to be proved wrong in cases such as these.

Chapter 15 - Clampers

Luckily the transfer to hospital in the last story went smoothly. Anyone working in clinical or emergency services should be able to go about their jobs without hindrance. Most people would agree, particularly those who have needed a midwife to attend to them in the community urgently. Unfortunately clampers don't always take issues like this into consideration.

I was out on rounds and in transit from one of my client's houses to another one sunny autumn afternoon when my work mobile rang. I pulled over and answered it, expecting to hear the coordinator say, 'Tina Shayner is fully,' and I wasn't disappointed. One of the other midwives in my team had been with her since the start of our shift that morning and I was assigned to be the second midwife – the one who attended as back up – once the woman was expected to be ready to deliver soon. I phoned the family who was expecting me to come and do a postnatal check to explain that I would be delayed and would contact them once I was available to come round if that suited them? It did, so long as I phoned their mobile number so that they weren't housebound waiting for me. I thought was quite a reasonable request; the day was far too gorgeous to be stuck inside. I recommended that they make their way to the seafront for a walk along the promenade in order to make the most of this perfect early autumn weather and said my goodbyes to them. I drove along the seafront from where I had pulled over to answer the phone to the nearby area where Tina Shayner lived in a top-floor flat that overlooked the sparkling water.

I struggled to find a place to park close by Tina's flats and ended up pulling in behind the casino where I had parked many times before while on duty. Placing my **Midwife on Call – no drugs on board** sign on the dashboard, I locked up and walked as quickly as I could manage to Tina's building, cursing myself for not parking on the yellow lines so that I could have parked a bit closer. I was 29 weeks pregnant and climbing the stairs to Tina's flat was no fun at all. I took it slowly enough that I would be able to speak to whoever answered the door once I reached the top. I was already working only as second on call for labours due to the awkwardness of trying to manage to do deliveries in some of the positions women get themselves into with my own pregnancy getting in the way. In three more weeks I would be off the labour call rota altogether. By this point in my pregnancy I had come to the conclusion that as much as it was a privilege to be assisting at births, I wouldn't miss it at all for the duration of my maternity leave. As I climbed the stairs my mind wandered to thinking that one of the worst bits of working while pregnant was when my baby would decide to kick my bladder until the need to go to the toilet was of utmost importance just at the point when I was absolutely unable to leave the person I was attending and go – mid-newborn bloodspot test was a classic example. I had begun to wonder if my unborn baby had launched a personal campaign against me taking blood from other babies; perhaps he could hear them cry and didn't like it.

A rather severe-looking woman who reminded me of my brother's nursery school leader came to the door. She looked at me sternly and I reflexively felt guilty, though for what reason I couldn't define. Was I too late? No, I could hear Tina moaning from somewhere ahead and followed the birth partner as she withdrew to the front room. The curtains were closed which gave the room a soft auburn glow, vigorous green foliage sprouted from pots placed just so on a rickety wooden ladder in the far corner and trailing ferns shadowed the shelves which ran along one wall, bulging with books and ornaments. Tina was kneeling on plastic sheeting which covered the settee and floor. I stood just outside the front room until the attending midwife made eye contact with me and then I gestured back towards the kitchen. I would wait in there unless I was needed to be present at the birth. She nodded then kneeled to help Tina sip from a straw in the glass before her. The severe woman who had greeted me at the door had morphed into an anxious birth partner who was now hovering anxiously near Tina and the midwife. She looked at me and I took the opportunity to mime drinking from a cup and pointed at her, a question on my face. Her face cracked open into a smile as she nodded. I went to the kitchen and made myself useful. Kettle filled and on then rummaging in the cupboards and cutlery drawer. A pot of tea, cup, milk jug, sugar bowl, packet of digestive biscuits and tea spoon went on a tray which I carried into the front room and placed on a side table. I placed a gentle hand on the birth partner's shoulder to let her know that the tea tray was waiting for her though she barely paused to acknowledge me as she was so busy vigorously rubbing Tina's back. I peeked at Tina's now bare bottom half, no head visible yet although I had heard her pushing while I was in the kitchen. Her midwife made a 10p-sized circle with her thumb and forefinger indicating that she could see that much of the baby's head when Tina was pushing. I nodded and made my way back to the kitchen, certain that Tina's birth partner would forget all about her cup of tea in the excitement that was about to follow even though it could be as long as another 15 minutes before the baby was born. I nipped to the toilet to empty my bladder, just in case I couldn't get there for a while after the baby was born, then sat on the chair that was squeezed in between the countertop and kitchen door.

I didn't need to be present in the front room to be able to track Tina's progress now as I could hear the excitement in her birth partner's voice each time she announced how much of the baby's head she could see with every push. The

midwife's voice was a softer but still audible
accompaniment to the sounds Tina made as she
pushed her baby out into that warm, dimly lit
room. Soon the happy words tumbling from
Tina's partner and the cheery congratulations
from the midwife told me that the baby had been
born. I couldn't hear the baby crying but wasn't
concerned as the midwife hadn't called me to
assist. I decided that Tina had one of those
babies who calmly adapted to life outside the
womb, looking around with apparent
wonderment, far too busy taking it all in to bother
with nonsense like crying lustily just because the
text books said they should. Once the midwife
had helped Tina to deliver the placenta and was
satisfied that all was well with Tina physically, I
said my goodbyes to them and left the flat
accompanied by the delicious sound of their
giddy voices buoyant with joy. The attending
midwife would stay for the next couple of hours,
tidying away the delivery debris, finishing up her
notes, helping Tina to latch her baby boy on for
his first feed, making sure Tina was able to pass
urine, eat and have a shower or bath (not
necessarily in that order) and all the other duties
associated with a birth and the immediate
postnatal period before leaving the new family to
enjoy the rest of their first day together. The
midwife had explained in the kitchen that Tina's
birth partner was in fact Tina's life partner. They
had conceived their baby boy through a sperm
donation from a willing donor who they had met
through their own social circle.

I made my way back down the stairs lumbering in a decidedly bear like manner, and walked slowly back to where I had parked my car. There was a gentle breeze now which lifted the wisps of hair which had escaped from the elastic holding my hair off my shoulders. It was refreshing and I approached my car with a smile tugging at my lips only to feel my face drop as I noticed the bright yellow metal clamp on my back tyre. I walked round to my door, tears brimming. I was heavily pregnant, tired at the end of a long day and in uniform which meant I was carrying no money on me and the notice stuck on my windscreen informed me that they would accept cash only. I called the number on the notice and asked if someone could come around and remove the clamp immediately as I was a midwife on duty and allowed to park anywhere in an emergency. Not on private property I was informed and they would send someone round when there was a person free. Not in the immediate future was the implication.

When the clamp release man arrived he actually had the audacity to chatter away to me about his pregnant wife in between explaining that the closest cash point was on the pier. I thanked him then sat in my car and cried and tried to get my tired brain to think of a way out of this mess. I decided to walk to the cash point on the pier if I couldn't talk the wheel clamp remover into taking it off without charge. I alluded to how his heavily pregnant wife might feel if she got clamped while going about her work. He was impervious to my verbal challenge. Realising I couldn't get the clamp removed unless I paid him the cash I gave in and had to make the 20-minute walk to the pier cash point and back. During the walk I thought through all the various scenarios in which I might need to use midwifery related-clamps on his wife if I was assigned her care during her labour and delivery. It wasn't very professional but I have to admit to a smile or two as I imagined myself blatantly refusing to unclamp his wife until he walked, exhausted and overwhelmed by the birth of his first child, to the nearest cash point to withdraw the ransom required.

On my return I gave him my best look of disgust as I handed over the cash, pinched my leg hard and then turned my back on him in order to distract myself from the overwhelming urge to kick him in the arse as he bent over to undo the clamp. I drove off restraining the urge to give him a one-fingered salute in response to his cheeky wink and wave. It wouldn't do for me to behave unprofessionally no matter how severe the provocation as I could never be sure who might be watching.

Chapter 16 - Audience and all

Staff in uniform are always ultra visible and have a tendency to attract attention. Combine this with an actual incident and we have the unenviable ability to draw a sizeable (and unwelcome) crowd in moments, as the next story shows.

It was a warm late spring day, one of those ones which fools you into believing that this summer will be one where the sun shines during the school holidays instead of the cloud and rain which will invariably accompany those six weeks. The hospital grounds were lushly abundant with life from well-covered trees, busy insects crawling around the flowering bushes and tidy borders through to trails of ducklings following their mothers in untidy noisy lines like children on a field trip. I couldn't remember exactly what the weather had been like last summer but it must have been either very perfectly warm encouraging lots of risky frisky evenings or particularly cold and miserable outside encouraging lots of snugly comforting leading to impulsiveness. My colleagues and I had formed this well-researched, completely unscientific theory based on the larger than usual number of women who were pregnant and due to give birth during this month of May.

The postnatal ward was packed full of women, their babies, partners and their visitors. Now I can understand the need for partners to be on the ward much of the day because they are learning how to be a new family and the new mum needs support from the child's other parent and the other parent needs to feel that he/she is also a parent of this new baby. As long as they are not disturbing the rest of the mums and babies on the ward I have no problem with extended visiting for partners. What I am a real curmudgeon about is the fact that the rest of the new parents' families and friends feel the need to turn up on the ward to make a fuss over the new arrival, which only serves to agitate most babies and wear out the new mum, who often has very little in the way of reserve energy. For this reason I think any time spent in hospital should be a visitor-free zone except for the baby's other parent. On this particular day the antenatal wards were also full because it was a place to put women in labour who were in a holding pattern for space on the labour ward. It was mayhem, though well disguised on the surface. Patients were segregated on wards, visitors were at a minimum for some reason so there were very few milling about in the corridors, meaning no one but the ward staff had any idea just how packed out the wards actually were.

There is nothing more likely to make latent labour contractions fizzle out completely than putting the woman in a four-bedded ward where she is unlikely to do anything more than sit on the bed and look out of the window. For this reason we encouraged them to wander the hospital grounds on nice days like this one. It's a good way for them to pass the time, take their mind off the wait for their baby and relax them enough to perhaps tip them over the edge into proper labour. We would never make this suggestion to anyone in established labour, however, as the hospital grounds are quite large and it can be quite a hike from the lower end, where the canteen is, up to where the maternity unit sits at the far side of the hospital. The phone rang as I was heading past the empty midwives' station so I answered it.

'Lower Upton Maternity Unit, can I help you?'

'Security here. Had a report of a woman having a baby by the pond.'

'The hospital pond?'

'Yup.'

'I'm on my way. Can you call for an ambulance and get a screen around her, please?' We would need the ambulance to get her all the way back up to the maternity unit if she really was delivering or incapable of walking for any other reason. I put the phone down and ran to the store room to grab a delivery pack, towels, gloves and plastic apron. I ran so other staff would know there was an emergency in progress. I also said, 'Can I have some help here, please?' loud enough to carry into the adjoining rooms as I wasn't sure where the rest of the team were but had no time to start looking.

A midwife swiftly came out of one of the rooms, closing the door behind here and looking questioningly at me at the same time as one of the labour ward health care support workers came onto the ward. I gestured them to come closer as I moved towards them with the delivery pack tucked under my arm.

'Security rang to say there's a woman pushing by the pond. I've got the kit, he's getting a screen and an ambulance, let's go,' I said to my midwifery colleague and, 'Kim, can you tell Sister where we are?' to the support worker. Our absence would leave the ward too short staffed but this woman was now high priority. The other midwife and I ran along the corridor and out of the back entrance so we could cut down the shortest side of the hospital to the pond. It took us four breath-robbing minutes at full pace to reach the outskirts of the grassy area which had the pond on its far side and one minute of gasping for breath as we moved at a fast walk to where we could see a small crowd clustered and security trying to set up a screen around a woman who was clutching onto the back of a bench.

'Can you give us some room here, please?' I said to the crowd that was doing it's best to look as if they had every right to be there. I put the delivery pack and other supplies down on the bench, tried to slow my breathing, smiled at the woman and the man closest to her as my colleague helped security wrestle the screens around the bench and us. I opened my mouth to ask the woman what she felt was happening to her when she crouched and began grunting in an unmistakable manner. She was pushing and pushing well. I was on the opposite side to her but my colleague heard her too and rushed through the screen on the woman's side of the bench, grabbing and pulling on a pair of gloves as I tore open the delivery pack.

'Ok now?' she asked the woman once she had stopped pushing.

'I can feel the head!' the woman panted, out of breath from her exertions.

My colleague and I looked at the woman, then at each other. Our client was still fully clothed and no ambulance in sight or earshot yet. We had no option but to ask the woman to lower her leggings and then herself to her knees before the next contraction.

'Can you pull your leggings down and kneel so you are in a good position for delivery?' *and not so far away from the ground*, I thought but refrained from saying.

'What? Here? No!'

'We have the screens around you so no one can see,' my colleague coaxed. I moved round the other side of the bench.

'No, I mean, it's coming, nuuurrrgggghhhh!' The woman bent her knees as she pushed and we could see the apex of her leggings bulge as she bore down. There was definitely a baby on its way out but the exit was hampered by what must have felt akin to being shoved against a trampoline. Her husband moved to the side of the bench where I had been and covered her hands on the bench with his in an attempt to comfort.

As soon as that contraction had passed she dropped to her knees and my colleague and I pulled down her leggings as far as we could get them. We could hear the peal of the ambulance as the baby's head dropped onto our waiting hands swiftly followed by its body with the next push. I made a note of the time: 2:04 p.m. The shock of air on its skin instead of the amniotic fluid it had grown used to was enough to make the baby grumble and squawk though it didn't cry. I threw towels down on the ground, leaving two for wrapping around the baby, while my colleague clamped the cord.

'Would you like to cut the cord?' she asked the woman and her husband. The woman shook her head and her husband nodded his.

'Is our baby ok?' the woman asked her husband as he awkwardly leaned over the bench to do the deed.

'He is perfect,' he breathed in response, completely awestruck by the sight of his son's big eyes which solemnly fixed on his face. My colleague wrapped their son up tightly in the towels as I helped the new mum manoeuvre herself onto the towels on the ground. We could hear the ambulance men rattling a stretcher towards us as she held her baby in her arms for the first time.

'Hello, beautiful!' she said and smiled at her son before kissing his forehead. Her son blinked at her, quiet and calm against the warmth of her body. 'Hello, Daddy,' she said as she turned her face to accept the kiss her husband bestowed on her.

'Hello, beautiful Mummy.' The elation in his voice was clearly audible. They both seemed completely relaxed and acted as if they had forgotten that they were outside with a crowd likely gathered within earshot outside the screen. Or perhaps they hadn't, maybe this was their way of sharing their joy with the would-be onlookers.

I took a deep breath to compose myself. Happy parents like this make me feel very emotional every time. It is so lovely when parents are so openly thrilled to be parents and wrapped up in their first few moments after the birth of their baby. I decided that I would wait until we got back to the maternity unit to deliver her placenta because her blood loss was perfectly within normal amounts. With any luck the physical manoeuvring she would have to do getting onto and off the stretcher would encourage her body to do the job itself.

'I think she's had the baby,' we could hear the security man saying to ambulance crew as they stopped outside the screen.

'Someone call an ambulance?' asked a cheery voice and a white blanket appeared over the top of the screen. We swiftly covered the woman's lap with it and called out, 'okay,' so he knew he could open the screen enough to come in and join us.

'Congratulations!' he said to the new parents before asking us anything. Quite rightly too as he could see the woman was conscious, smiling and in possession of a towel-wrapped bundle, so he dealt with the most important thing first.

'Ready for transfer?' he said to us.

'Lochia minimal, placenta in situ, so all set to go,' I responded then turned to our client. 'Do you feel up to walking to the stretcher? It's just outside the screen.'

'I'll give it a go.' She passed her son to my colleague, and the paramedic and the ambulance attendant and I helped her up.

'Ok?' I asked after she had stood steadily for a half minute.

'Fine,' she said firmly and made her way out from behind the screen wearing the blanket like a skirt. A small cheer went up from the people still assembled and she smiled, blushed, ducked her head then lowered herself into a sitting position onto the stretcher. Once the crew had her settled into an upright reclining position with more blankets tucked around her legs they lifted her up into the waiting vehicle. My colleague climbed aboard and passed the baby to his waiting mother and then the husband and I got on for the ride back to the maternity unit.

By the time we had made the two-minute drive there, transferred her into the labour ward and she had shuffled herself from the stretcher to the bed, which we had snuggled up against the stretcher, her placenta had obligingly plopped out with no intervention from us. She was now officially postnatal. A quick check of all her basic observations confirmed her body had coped very well with the experience of giving birth, including not needing any stitches. I made myself useful by making tea and toast for them while my colleague helped her latch on her baby for his first feed.

A short while later my colleague and I sat down with our own cups of tea and began the process of documenting the sequence of events in the woman's notes. The ambulance crew had already filled out their paperwork and we attached it to the notes as part of our documentation process. While we were busy with this the Head of Midwifery came along to get a full briefing from us in preparation for the media attention that was likely to be generated from this event. She then went in to congratulate the parents and to warn them of the possibility of media interest, and to assure herself that they were happy with our care, I suspected. We had done our job and now she was doing hers. The NHS was functioning like a well-oiled machine on that day. Luckily, and sometimes miraculously, it tends to on more days than not. This is always a relief, especially when you need to transfer into hospital with a woman you have been attending to in the community, and have everything ready and waiting for you to do a rapid delivery with, like the woman with an undiagnosed breech baby in this next story.

Chapter 17 - Footling breech

There are many positions that a baby can decide to position itself in for delivery, from the ideal head down and facing mum's back, to the brow presentation, which is impossible to deliver vaginally. In between the former two positions are a whole range of other positions such as head down but engaged sideways in the pelvis, bottom down (breech), arm down (transverse presentation) or foot down. These are all incompatible with homebirths due to the risks associated with them; breech babies can be quite shocked at delivery, sometimes the softer bottom and body will deliver before the cervix is fully dilated but the head can't deliver until the cervix is fully dilated. Feet or arms don't apply themselves very well to the cervix so if the woman's membranes rupture, the cord can slip past them and out of the pelvis, leading to a risk of the cord going into spasm if it reaches the colder air outside the woman's body or being compressed by the baby's body as it is being delivered.

Of course the presentation of the baby is monitored closely throughout the pregnancy; feeling the position of the baby through the mother's abdomen is part of the routine antenatal check where we also gauge how far down the presenting part is in the mother's pelvic outlet. It is also important to know the position of the placenta which is determined at the mid-trimester scan. A mother would be strongly discouraged from booking a homebirth unless the midwife knew the placenta was a good distance away from the cervix, and thought her baby was in a favourable head-down position with the head firmly in her pelvic outlet close to her due date. However some babies, particularly if the mum has had more than one pregnancy, can manoeuvre themselves into unexpected positions even after the midwife has assured herself that the baby is in a good position for delivery. Which was exactly what happened to me one stormy early November evening.

I was called out to attend Georgie who was one of the women in my caseload. She had experienced two previous normal deliveries in hospital after a quick labour both times and she had begun feeling urges to push on the way to hospital with her last one. As she lived some distance from hospital and didn't want to risk delivering en route to hospital she decided that a homebirth would be her preferred place of delivery. Knowing her history I made my way out to her house as fast as I could half-expecting to find her in the final stages of labour when I got there. She wasn't. In fact she was behaving as if she was only in early labour with regular but weak contractions which didn't last more than 30 seconds. A palpation of the position of the baby combined with internal examination confirmed what I had suspected; her baby was no longer lying head down and the part of the baby I could feel occasionally making contact with my finger through the bulging membranes was the heel of one of the baby's feet. I immediately stopped the internal examination as I did not want to risk the added pressure of my finger causing the membranes to break.

Although this baby's heart beat told me the baby was perfectly happy at the moment there was every chance it would change its mind about that if the membranes broke and its cord slipped out in a gush of amniotic fluid. I explained to the mum and her partner what I had found, asked her to shift herself onto her left side and to resist any urges to push that she might get even though this was unlikely as she was only five centimetres dilated. I then called for a paramedic ambulance, informed the labour ward we were going to be arriving shortly and why. They assured me they would have the team on standby. The team in this case would consist of an obstetrician, paediatrician and someone to take notes as the delivery progressed if I was too busy to do so myself. By the time I had packed away my equipment and her partner Simon had brought her cases down (we always advised women booked for a homebirth to pack a hospital case for reasons such as these), the ambulance had arrived. Maternity emergencies are always high on the ambulance services priority list because, in most cases, there are two lives involved. They transferred Georgie onto the ambulance still lying on her left side. Her contractions had disappeared completely and I was quite grateful for this. We could worry about her labour and choice of delivery when we got her and her baby safely to the labour suite. On the way to the hospital I explained to the parents what would happen when we got to the hospital. That they would be examined by an obstetrician who would confirm my findings and discuss their delivery options with them. I warned them that because it was a teaching hospital they were likely to be asked permission for either a medical or midwifery student to be present during Georgie's labour and the birth of their baby.

By the time we had Georgie settled in a delivery room and the consultant had finished examining her she was almost fully dilated and only barely managing to resist the strong urges to push. Simon and Georgie decided that they wanted to try for a vaginal delivery of their baby instead of a caesarean section. They also asked if it was ok if I delivered their baby; it was. The consultant was happy for me to proceed as long as he could be present in the room to jump in and assist me if needed. The birth proceeded smoothly and I didn't need his help but the presence of Mr Honiton, one of my favourite consultant colleagues, was a welcome reassurance anyway. A student midwife was present to observe the delivery and to take notes of what manoeuvres I did and at what time, along with information on Georgie and her baby's well being. Once the shoulders were delivered Mr Honiton pressed the call bell to alert the paediatrician who was standing by outside that the baby was almost born and that she should make her way into the room now. A few pushes later there was a baby with a white body, blue head and loud cry being checked over by the paediatrician. The atmosphere in the room had instantly changed from one of expectation to a jovial almost party-like one. And quite rightly too; there was a new life to celebrate.

One of the more important aspects of being a good midwife is to be able to judge when to step back and observe and when to intervene. Unless of course the baby is in such a rush to get out that it doesn't allow the midwife to do this. The baby in the next story was in such a rush to get out that he came out wearing things he should have discarded on the way.

Chapter 18 - Born in a caul

Routine artificial rupture of membranes during labour has long gone out of fashion. We used to do it once the woman had reached at least four centimetres dilated in the belief that it helped to speed every woman's labour along but now it is only done in certain cases, making its use the exception rather than the norm. We use an instrument called the amnihook which closely resembles a long crochet hook. Before the amnihook is used the midwife assesses the cervix and the position of the baby's head. She runs her fingers over the membranes to ensure that there is nothing pulsing, which would indicate the presence either of cord or blood vessels running through that area of the membranes. Once she has decided that everything is clear then the amnihook is slid into the vagina with the sharp hook side running alongside the midwife's hand already in place inside the vagina until it reaches the cervix. She then uses her fingers to guide it into place against the membranes; one sharp pull back is usually all it takes to pierce a hole in the desired spot. The midwife then looks at the colour of the fluid draining out, as this can give an indication of the baby's well being in addition to the rate and rhythm of its heartbeat.

There are still times when it is necessary to artificially rupture of membranes are still times when it is required, such as when a woman is brought in for induction of labour. Even though artificial rupture of membranes isn't a routine procedure anymore there is always an amnihook on delivery trolleys along with other equipment which may become unexpectedly handy. Many women find that their body will get on with rupturing the membranes at some point in early labour; for some this is the first indication that they are going into labour. For others their membranes rupture and then labour doesn't start, which means they need to be brought in 24 – 72 hours later (depending on local policy) to have their labour induced. The reason for this is that there are indications that the baby is at increased risk of infection without the protection of sealed membranes. Not all babies will become infected but even one poorly baby is too many if the infection could have been prevented by medical intervention. Unfortunately interventions always carry risks of their own, so in cases like these it is often a matter of weighing up the risks and going down the perceived least-risky route.

For pregnancies that have skipped over the bit in the textbook where it says membranes should break before labour and decided to go into labour regardless, then the midwife will know the membranes haven't ruptured yet through talking to the woman on admission and once she does an internal examination. If she has time to do one before the baby arrives, that is. The one and only time so far that I have delivered a baby in a caul, meaning with the membranes still intact at birth, will be forever embedded in my memory as a truly scary event.

I was catching up on discharge paper work for a number of postnatal women who wanted to leave the community unit that day when the phone rang for the elevenmillionth time so far that morning. The ring tone was different for internal and external calls but I had never managed to figure out which was which so I always took the safe route of using the formal greeting.

'Baby Bump Maternity Centre, Midwife Kirkby speaking.'

'Hiya, Dee, it's Clare from reception. I've got a man here who says his wife is in the car in labour and he can't get her out. Can you come help, please?'

'On my way!' I walked quickly to the store room to grab a delivery pack and gloves.

'Sandy, can you let Jean know that reception have phoned to ask me to pop out to bring in a mum who is having trouble walking?' I said to the unit's health care support worker.

'No problem. I'll tell her and then come out to see if you need any help.'

I pressed the door release and allowed myself to run just a little bit on the way to reception. We were advised to keep running only for emergencies but I had no idea whether or not this was one. Running would attract the attention of any patients or relatives in the vicinity but as I was carrying a delivery pack off ward I figured this was going to happen anyway.

'Where is she?' I asked Clare, who indicated the main entrance doors. 'In the car to the left.'

I could see a lot of commotion amongst the patients and visitors loitering outside the maternity entrance with their attention directed to the car in question as I placed the delivery pack and gloves onto a wheelchair and pushed it at a brisk walk to the car, where I could see a man leaning in through the back door on the passenger side. He stood aside as I parked the wheelchair, wincing a little at the cold wind that blew through my uniform.

'Hi, I'm Dee, one of the midwives,' I said to them both.

'Tom and that's Jenny, she says she can't walk,' he said, indicating his wife.

'I can't!' she shrieked, mid-contraction.

'It's okay, I'm not going to ask you to do anything until you have finished that contraction,' I reassured her. I smiled at Sandy who had just joined us and we waited until Jenny's contraction had passed.

'Jenny, can you listen to me now?'

She nodded.

'From what Tom has said you can't get yourself out of the car?'

'I can't, every time I try I get another bloody contraction!'

'Okay well let's get you out in two stages then. First get your legs facing out of the door.'

Tom grabbed Jenny's hand and helped her shuffle herself into position, moving aside as her next contraction hit.

'Ungh, ungh, ungh,' Jenny said, which I assumed could only be translated into 'I want to push'.

'Try very hard not to push yet, Jenny. Just hang on a bit longer and we'll have you inside.'

Jenny ignored me until the contraction had passed then stuck out her hands. 'Tom, you'll have to pull me up.' Tom did.

Sandy wheeled the chair into position and picked up the delivery pack and gloves from the seat so Jenny could sit down on it.

'I can't,' she said pleadingly as she looked at me.

'You want to walk now?'

'No, I can't sit and I can't walk, I feel like the baby will fall out if I do.'

'No problem!' I said trying to sound calmer than I felt. 'Just kneel on the chair and we'll get you in.'

She did and we did, leaving Tom behind to move the car to a parking space and promising to pass Jenny's details onto reception as soon as possible as we went past at a run.

Jenny had one long contraction on the way in and I worried that the baby would be born before we got her into a nice warm delivery room and away from onlookers. Luckily she managed to hold on through that contraction, by which time we had arrived in the delivery room.

'Jenny, as soon as that contraction is gone I want you to stand then lower yourself onto the bed, ok? I'll help you get your dress and pants off if you want.'

'I'm not wearing any pants. I couldn't get them on in between contractions. I just held my arms up and Tom pulled my dress on for me. Then we got in the car and came here.'

'Why didn't you call an ambulance to bring you?' I asked as I washed my hands, while Sandy helped her lower herself onto the bed.

'I didn't feel like pushing. I thought I had lots of time. My last baby took hours to come!' Her last word ended in a groan which grew to a shriek as a fresh contraction ran through her and she turned herself awkwardly to face the head of the bed in a kneeling position. I ripped open the delivery pack and got my gloves on just in time to see the membranes bulge out of her vagina.

'Sandy, open the amnihook for me, please!' I caught the baby as it came out with the next push completely encased in the membranes. As I tipped the baby's head uppermost the amniotic fluid drained out of a hole at the feet end. I sighed with relief. I wouldn't need the amnihook after all. I scrabbled to pull the membranes up and over the baby's head, leaving a surprised-looking baby blinking up at me.

'Hello, little one, you sure were in a hurry. Come on now, say hello to your mummy. Jenny, say hello to your baby!' I prompted as I rubbed the baby with the towel in an attempt to stimulate it into taking the breath I hadn't wanted it to take a few moments before.

Jenny turned herself around with Sandy's help, as she had to manoeuvre herself around the cord which was still attached to her and her baby.

'Oh!' she said and burst into tears, swiftly joined by her baby as it gave a squawk then a lusty cry. I was relieved to hear it because there is a big risk that the baby will take a deep breath in as soon as it is delivered (except during a water birth) because its chest walls are no longer compressed. Being born with the membranes still intact is considered to be good luck, I'm not sure why, but I did know that this baby seemed to be have been lucky enough to have not attempted his first breath while still surrounded by amniotic fluid. I decided to ask the paediatrician to come and look him over just to be on the safe side.

I handed Jenny her new son and placed a dry towel over them both, just as Tom burst in through the door.

'I missed it!'

'Yes, but you are just in time to say hello to your new baby and cut the cord, if you want?'

After Tom had cut his new son's cord I went about the business of finishing up my midwifery duties related to the birth as unobtrusively as possible so as not to intrude any more than necessary while Jenny and Tom were enjoying their time with their new baby.

A few days later I was called out to a planned homebirth for a young first-time mum who still lived with her parents. Her membranes didn't break during her labour and so I made sure I had the amnihook close to hand once she began pushing after an internal examination showed that she was fully dilated. As a first-time mum she was unlikely to deliver fast but just in case she did, and because her membranes were still intact, I opened the amnihook so I could grab it quickly if necessary. She made steady progress once she started pushing and it wasn't long before I saw a bit of her membranes bulging out of her vagina. I could see the vernix swirling around inside the membranes like a mini snow storm and with her permission I used the amnihook to pierce her membranes so that there would be no chance of her baby being born in a caul. One caul birth in my career was more than enough for me.

Interlude

Natural induction methods

Membranes can also cause problems during pregnancy and many methods are used to resolve the problems in late pregnancy. A midwife needs to be able to have some pretty difficult conversations with women and their sexual partners around the time their baby is due if they haven't gone into labour. These conversations involve discussing natural, but also some intimate, methods to induce labour and some midwives find them easier to talk about than others. How I feel always depends on the reactions of the people I am talking to, and this also helps me to decide which natural induction methods to focus on.

Spicy food, fresh pineapple, sex, exercise, castor oil, raspberry leaf tea/tablets, driving along a bumpy road, trauma, hot baths, alcohol, diarrhoea, vomiting, reflexology, getting a fright, bouncing on a trampoline, vigorous walking, bungee jumping, riding a horse, having an infection, excessive coughing, raised blood pressure, stress, food poisoning, allergic reaction, exhaustion. All of these have been alleged to induce labour but some of them are not recommended induction methods, even though many women have mentioned them to me over the years. These old wives tales include driving along a bumpy road, eating spicy food (otherwise women who normally eat spicy food would have to completely change their diet when pregnant), exercise, hot baths, riding a horse (if you can get on a horse at full term never mind without damaging the already softened cartilage in your pubic bone then I would be suitably impressed), getting a fright (I have to hedge my bets here and say that depends on how bad the fright or stress is), vigorous walking (see horse riding response), excessive coughing (may feel like it but no that's just sore abdominal muscles not labour pains) and exhaustion. Some such as bungee jumping, bouncing on a trampoline (seriously people, did you think before you asked that one?), allergic reactions, trauma, food poisoning (including diarrhoea and vomiting), having an infection, raised blood pressure and caster oil will cause more harm than anything else even if they did set off the labour process, and as a result they should never be tried. However, a few have been proven to work for enough women that they get recommended as worth a try.

Fresh pineapple is a good starting point for discussion with the women who need to know about some safe natural induction methods, unless of course they have an allergy to pineapple in which case the topic should be discussed under an entirely different – do not try this ever – category. Many midwives swear that there is an enzyme in fresh pineapple that can trigger labour if eaten in the right quantities though the quantity required has never been defined. I have seen women come in, in labour but with ulcers in their mouth because they have eaten so much pineapple. I have never been convinced that this method actually works and question whether those labours would have started anyway, so I make sure to point this out to the women I discuss this with. People need both sides of the story before they can make an informed choice about what they want to try.

Raspberry leaf tea or tablets go in and out of favour as an alleged induction method. They work by increasing the blood flow to the uterus and I can see how this might push the body that extra step into going into labour but while they don't do any harm if taken when the woman is already full term, I think any resultant labour is pretty much a coincidence and not a method that can be relied on to any extent.

Reflexology is thought to be effective in 50% of women that have it done to them by a qualified practitioner. There are very few midwives with this qualification and I urge the women considering this method to make sure they see and recognise the qualifications of the reflexologist before letting them try this on them. I used to work in a maternity unit that had a midwife qualified to offer this treatment and know that it can be very effective in inducing labour, but she warned me that it could also have detrimental effects if the technique was tried by someone who wasn't properly trained.

Sex at term; under duress most women would agree that this could only possibly be used for medical purposes if at all, at that point in the pregnancy. Which makes this a most challenging topic; the one that many midwives cringe over when preparing to discuss it, and the one that most women are so reluctant to agree to. Men's reactions vary from delightful anticipation to absolute repulsion – usually due to concerns over bumping the baby inside. Women are reluctant for all the reasons that make getting on a horse or vigorous walking nigh on impossible. There is a pregnancy and waddling gait making daily life very uncomfortable so why are we midwives suggesting something as energetic as sexual intercourse? Well, sperm naturally contains the same chemical as the one which we use to induce labour. Having this chemical placed in the right spot by a man you love enough to be having a baby with has got to be preferable to having a clinician place the manufactured equivalent there instead. The sperm is unlikely to irritate you in the same way the medical method can, although both ways of trying to induce labour can be uncomfortable and unpleasant to varying degrees. So the topic is filled with cringe-worthy moments and it just gets worse once you reach the point where you have to explain to the woman or couple before you how to get that sperm in just the right spot. Oh yes, the glamour of being a midwife just goes on and on, let me tell you. The chemical needs to end up behind the cervix at the very top of your vagina and to get it there via the natural method using sperm women need to have sexual intercourse in the doggy- or cowboy-style positions. It is at this point in the conversations that I always hold my breath for just a few seconds, hoping that the couple will admit to knowing what these positions are so that I do not have to go on and describe them further. On one occasion I even had to resort to drawing the position out for a woman whose English wasn't very good and who had refused to have her husband in the room for the conversation. I felt drawings would help ensure that she understood exactly what I was saying but my artistic skills are rudimentary at best and I had to resort to drawing stick figures. She got the message but laughed until tears leaked from her eyes at my artistic rendering, folded the paper and stuck it in her pocket. When her husband was brought back in she began speaking to him in their own language, patting her pocket and laughing again. I didn't dare ask what she was saying to him about the induction methods we had discussed but I suspected that it wasn't anything complimentary about my drawings. However, her laughter was contagious and the room felt light and happy long after they had left.

Wisdom

Chapter 19 - Cabbage leaves – not just for Sunday lunch

Natural methods of health care are also popular at other stages such as labour and in the first few weeks after birth.

During my career I have seen women use many different types of natural remedies. These often make me feel a bit nervous as people don't seem to realise that they aren't just nice-smelling oils and so on. These oils, tinctures, tablets and teas are actually properties with a medicinal nature, which is why a midwife won't suggest or recommend them unless she has had specialist training, as midwives cannot participate or advise in anything for which they have not had specific training.

One woman I cared for, a Mrs Pearson, was extremely fond of herbal treatments and had a veritable cornucopia in her home from which she mixed her own herbal teas, bath products and remedies for various minor ailments. She had several certificates from courses she had attended in order to learn how to use herbs as medicine and had great faith in her ability to treat any ailment she or her husband had. One day I found a note in my pigeon hole from one of the other midwives:

Just to warn you that I need to speak to you about Mrs Pearson's behaviour in parent craft on the weekend! I'm on a late shift Monday and I've

got a free slot at 3pm so can we talk about it
then if you're free. Mandy

How peculiar, I thought. I couldn't imagine Mrs
Pearson causing any trouble or upsetting Mandy
or the other people in the parent craft sessions
but there was no other reason for Mandy to go to
the trouble of warning me that she needed me to
free up some of my time for a chat.

A cancellation from one of my planned visits
meant that I was able to be back in the unit in
plenty of time to meet Mandy at 3 pm.

'That Mrs Pearson is a bit of a trouble maker,
isn't she?' Mandy said, as she unwound her
scarf and shrugged off her coat.

'She's a bit...alternative but I haven't had any
trouble with her at all. What happened?'

'Alternative? Yeah that sums her up nicely but
she's trying to turn everyone else on to her way
of thinking!'

'What? Cuppa?' I said, moving to put the
kettle on.

'Black coffee, ta. It was the pain relief session
last night,' Mandy said, pointing to the parent
craft timetable, 'and your Mrs Pearson was
sitting right up at the front!'

'Well that's good, isn't it? I'd have thought she
wouldn't be interested in pharmacological pain
relief actually...'

'She isn't!' Mandy snapped before composing
herself with several slurps of her coffee, as the
noise level in the room dropped as the other duty
midwives suddenly became more interested in

our conversation than getting ready for their shift.

I sat down and waited.

'So I'm doing my patter about pain relief and every time I mentioned something we have on offer to help with labour pains she had an alternative to it. Massage, mobilisation, hydrotherapy, you name it, she talked about it at length!'

'The session was supposed to be about both, wasn't it?' I asked tentatively. 'She's quite knowledgeable about alternative health care so I guess I should have seen that one coming but I wouldn't have expected her to be so overbearing about it.'

'I never even got a chance to cover the pharmacological pain relief because the whole session ended up being about non-pharmacological pain relief. Every time I broached the topic she would claim that the alternative method would work better and wouldn't harm the baby; she undermined me every step of the way! I'm going to have to hold a separate session on pharmacological pain relief for everyone else so they can get the information they need.'

'I'm really sorry,' I said, then wondered why I felt the need to apologise for one of my client's behaviour.

'You need to go have a word with her and I need to do some damage control at the next parent craft session because she was banging on about massage oils and candles and everything!' Mandy's voice took on a thin reedy sound.

I agreed. This was indeed an issue and one which I would have expected to be covered in the normal parent craft session, except that Mandy seemed to have been bowled over by a side to Mrs Pearson that I had not yet seen. The parent craft session which should have covered both medicinal and alternative pain relief had ended up focusing entirely on the alternative methods, and apparently hadn't covered the risks of applying these.

'Hi Jean, hi Matt, how's everything going?' I greeted Mrs and Mr Pearson as they came in for their antenatal check the next week.

'Oh, the baby's giving me no trouble but I'm mortified about the last parent craft class we went to.'

Here we go, I thought as I braced myself to take a firm line with Jean and get the NHS point of view over to her.

As I opened my mouth to speak she hurriedly said, 'Mortified by my behaviour, that is!'

'Oh?' I said 'What happened?'

'The midwife was talking about alternative pain relief and I started to tell one of my favourite stories about how well they worked and I couldn't seem to shut myself up for the rest of the class. I'm sure everyone thinks I'm a loony now, I know I get too exuberant about herbal medicine...anyway I wanted to apologise to the midwife so, please, would you give her this from me?' Jean handed me a card.

'Of course I will. Now, we do need to have a chat about what pain relief you want to use during labour so that it can be added to your birth plan. I assume you've done some thinking around this already?' I said with a smile to disguise the anxiety I felt about what Jean might expect to use during labour.

'Well...' Jean said with a responding smile and then proceeded to rattle off a list of eclectic treatments and remedies that she planned to engage with in various ways during her labour. I listened in silence until she had finished and looked at me expectantly.

'I'm not trying to be a killjoy here Jean, and most of what you want to use in labour is fine as long as Matt helps you with it, but the midwife who is delivering you may...'

'That'll be you, won't it? You're my midwife!' Jean interrupted, her eyebrows raised.

'I'll deliver you if I am on duty at the time, promise, otherwise it will be one of the others from the team whom you have already met. Don't forget that there will also be a second midwife standing by as you are delivering your baby, though she doesn't have to be in the same room as you unless your delivering midwife needs her help.' Jean nodded and Matt looked around the tiny clinical room as if he was trying to imagine the scene at home.

'So, the midwife who is with you in labour may ask you to ventilate the room if she starts feeling a bit "heady" from the essential oils you choose for your labour massage oil. An open window will be a problem near the time you birth your baby as the room must be nice and warm, so you need to be prepared to stop using the massage oil if the midwife asks you to and understand that there is a good reason for it.'

'I'll switch to TENS then,' Jean said agreeably.

'Great! Only, TENS takes a while to build up to full effect so you might want to put the TENS machine on sooner rather than later. Best not to use massage oil near the TENS pads though,' I said with a rueful expression and Matt nodded while making a zapping motion with his hands.

Jean laughed and said, 'It's all so complicated! It's ok to use the massage oils in early labour though, right?'

'I've never known it to be a problem except when the woman wanted to get in the birthing pool without showering first.'

'Oh well we can't have a birthing pool in the flat anyway because our tenants' insurance won't cover us for it.'

In the end Jean had a relatively fast labour and delivery. I was on a few days leave at the time and didn't get a chance to meet their baby until it was three days old. Jean greeted me at the door with her son held at an awkward position well below her chest.

'Rocks,' she said in response to my quizzical expression. 'Tits made of rock.'

'Ah, your milk has come in, has it?'

'In and not out anywhere near enough to give me any relief! I have to express off a bit just so I can get him latched on but I've got more milk

155

than he wants so I'm not getting any relief after a feed.' Jean looked as if she was about to cry.

I made her a cup of tea and while she drank it I reassured her that her body would soon adjust to meet the demands of her son, which meant that she wouldn't have to endure engorged breasts for too much longer. 'And until then you've always got cabbage,' I said reassuringly.

'Cabbage?' Jean looked at me in astonishment.

'Don't tell me you've never heard of using cabbage to ease the pressure of engorged breasts?' It was my turn to look at her in astonishment as I had assumed she would know about it as part of her herbal medicine training.

'No, never heard of it, though it makes sense now that you mention it. I've got one in the fridge.' She passed me her son and wandered off into the kitchen returning with a white cabbage.

'Those ones don't work as well because it is so hard to separate the individual leaves so pick up one of the ones with looser leaves like a sweet heart type cabbage next time.' I showed Jean how to pack the cooling, soothing leaves around her breasts inside her feeding bra. 'As soon as they get limp and warm, throw them out and replace them with fresh cool ones.'

I finished doing her check and checked her perfect baby boy then watched as she expertly latched her son on for a feed. Some women are natural mothers and unintentionally make the rest of us feel like failures. Jean was one of these. 'Give me a call later on today to let me know how you are getting on with the cabbage leaves,' I said as I departed to go about the rest of my visits.

By the time I got back to the clinic a few hours later Jean had already phoned to leave a message rhapsodising about the wonders of cabbage leaves.

'Cabbage leaves, not just for Sunday lunch,' said the ward clerk as she handed me the message book with a wink.

Chapter 20 - The baby whisperer

Sometimes wisdom comes disguised in the most disagreeable of packaging and it takes the magic of a baby to unwrap the gift.

Employees of the NHS come from all walks of life though some seem to have been dragged along the grumpy path. I don't know if it is their job they hate, the shift pattern/work times, colleagues, or if they were just born curmudgeonly. I am the opposite and have a tendency to come over as all happy and cheerful at work even if I am a seething pit of angst inside. I think we owe it to the women under our care to behave like that; they don't really want to know that we are unhappy or troubled with distractions from our home lives. They want to believe that they, and their problems, are our sole focus. I've been told that my outwardly upbeat mood can be quite annoying to work with and I quite agree, I'd probably piss me off too; if I wasn't me, I mean. However, the women respond well to my seemingly happy exterior and that counts for a lot as far as the midwife in me is concerned. Work is enough like hard work without being miserable about it so for the most part I simply tend to ignore those grumpy co-workers and go about my shift projecting a happy haze. Denial can be a wonderful thing.

There was one co-worker who I always made a point of speaking to despite her constant glower. Dawn Donelly made her way around the wards from early morning to mid-afternoon doing an absolutely meticulous job of cleaning every non-clinical surface and glowering the whole time. The rest of the team called her Dismal Dawn and although I could see why she had been given the nickname I did wonder why she behaved like that. The maternity unit was small and friendly and everyone was considered to be part of the team. Dawn had worked there for many years and so there was no reason for her to feel that she didn't fit in or wasn't welcome. The rest of the team had long since given up on getting a good response out of Dawn but I was relatively new to the team and made it my personal goal to get Dawn to interact more than the rest of the unit staff did.

'Good morning, Dawn!' I smiled brightly at her as she punched in the door code with enough force to make the keys stick momentarily before springing back into their starting position.

'Ugnh,' she replied sounding remarkably like a teenager who had been forced from bed before noon. She shoved the door open, letting it swing back towards me as she made her way rapidly down the corridor.

Niiiice, I thought and steeled myself to keep trying to break through her barrier, surely there was a lonely person inside wanting to join in on coffee breaks with the rest of the team? Several months passed before Dawn began to respond with a mumbled, 'Moaning,' in response to my,

'Good morning, Dawn.' Aha! I thought, there is a sense of humour lurking in there somewhere.

Eventually she began to exchange a few words with me though they never amounted to much more than semi-polite refusals to or disagreement with anything I suggested.

'Not long now 'till Christmas!' I'd say in passing as she swept her dust cloth along the doweling rail that divided the wall the length of the ward.

'Won't miss it when it's gone. Could do without all the fuss and mess.' She rinsed her cloth and moved on to a new section of doweling.

I had expected as much and wondered how I would have reacted if Dawn had expressed delight at the upcoming festivities. The shock probably would have been too much for me so early in the morning, I decided.

'You coming to the canteen with us for Christmas lunch next week? We're going in two or three groups of us staggered during the shift depending on how full the ward is.'

'Nah, got too much to be getting on with what with the decorations collecting dust and all.' Dawn glared at me and then at the Christmas tree perched cheerily on the midwives' station at the end of the corridor. 'The less of you lot around getting underfoot, the better. I'll give the floors a good polish instead. Pick up some of the tinsel and glitter that have come off the decorations already...' she grumbled as she moved off down the corridor.

Bah humbug may just be your middle name, I thought as I left her to her dusting. Still, not everyone likes Christmas as much as I do, I reminded myself. I loved the Christmas season and everything associated with it, but most especially the dust-attracting decorations. I was the one responsible for decorating the ward at Christmas time and this likely had put a black mark against my name in Dawn's book of Things to be Grumpy About.

Night shifts were always a struggle because I am naturally an early to bed and early to rise person and so much more suited to working early shifts, rather than forcing myself to stay awake over night. However, during the festive season it all seemed a bit more exciting and fun to be on the wards. There were always fewer women and babies on the wards as most forced themselves home as early as possible so as not to miss out on anything. This meant that the women who were on the wards were often quite ill and required more of our support with their babies during the night.

One night I had spent a lot of it trying to placate a particularly disgruntled baby without a lot of success. I would get him off to sleep only to have him wake less than an hour later. I had used every technique I knew of including letting him have a supported float in a bucket bath. A dunk up to the chin in a bucket of warm water was usually guaranteed to soothe any baby and did indeed do the trick for this little lad. Until I removed him from the water, that is. Then he would begin raging again, flailing around and generally working himself up into a tizzy. I used the bucket bath on him for as long as I could but it is a hard position to maintain for the person holding the baby in the bucket and my arms tired out far too soon for his liking. So by day break I was in the day room with him, walking back and forth in front of the window, towards and away from the Christmas tree. His mother desperately needed as much sleep as possible and I was determined that she should have it, I was being paid to be there and there was no reason why I couldn't keep trying to placate her son as long as my colleague was happy to carry on with anything else that was required from the women on the ward.

'Oooh, you are a grumpy young man, aren't you?' I said as I switched the position I was carrying him in from up against my shoulder to lying on his tummy over my arm, side of his head nestled in the crook of my elbow and legs straddling my hand. He settled to a disconsolate murmuring and I paused to watch the lights twinkling on the tree. Pausing was clearly not on his list of things to do at that moment and he let me know with a loud wail, propelling me into motion once again.

I smiled at Dawn as she poked her head around the day room door. 'Moaning, Dawn.'

She laughed. 'I knew you had to have a limit on the stock in your good cheer store.'

I smiled. 'I'm a bit tired out because it's been a long night with this young man.'

She walked in and sat down on the settee in front of the Christmas tree. 'G'is here.' She indicated the baby wailing in my arms.

There were strict rules about who could handle babies on the unit and I knew that the cleaners were not amongst those who had this honour. However, I reasoned that as she was sitting down and I was in the room supervising the contact, there was every reason why it would be ok for her to try to placate this baby whose mum was still deeply asleep.

Dawn must have mistaken my thinking for reluctance. 'I just washed my hands and my uniform's clean so you don't need to worry about me contaminating him and I've had five of my own so I won't drop him,' she said gruffly.

I sat beside Dawn, noting that my body felt tired beyond belief and passed her the baby. I rested the remainder of my tired muscles by leaning back into the couch, and watched as she expertly lifted him to her shoulder and spent a few moments smoothing the palm of her hand over his back in an unsuccessful attempt to soothe him. He raged against the stillness of the rest of her body. After a while she raised him higher on her shoulder and turned her mouth to his ear. I watched and listened as she made a strange low-pitched moaning sound. The baby quietened almost immediately and within a minute had relaxed completely, still alert but calm and listening to the noise Dawn was making. Filled with questions I struggled not say anything that might disturb the baby and before too long he had fallen asleep against her chest.

'What on Earth was that noise you made?' I asked in astonishment. Although I had heard a lot of people talking quietly to babies, singing or humming to them, I had never seen or heard anything quite like what Dawn had just done in all the years I had been a midwife.

'I don't know exactly. It's just something my family does. I'm the eldest of eight and can remember seeing my nan and mum doing it. I practised on my youngest brothers and sister and used it on all of my kids. Never fails to work a treat.'

I have spent many years trying and failing to mimic that sound and its effect; I think it must have been something particular to Dawn's family, which is a shame because if we could bottle that sound there would be a lot fewer stressed babies and parents in this world. Some skills, on the other hand, are much easier to pass on. One springs immediately to mind and this midwife was considered quite radical back when I was a student midwife. I'm happy to say the once radical technique in the following story is now standard practice during most births nowadays.

Chapter 21 - Don't clamp and cut the cord before the baby is born

Back when I trained as a student midwife we had to witness a minimum of 10 normal births before we were allowed to help a woman birth her baby with support from a qualified midwife. I learned a lot while witnessing those 10 births and by the eleventh I felt ready to play my part in assisting the birthing process. My usual mentor was not working the day I went on to help a woman birth her baby for the first time and so I was working with someone new. I had learned by this point in my training that each midwife had a distinct way they go about their work and I had become used to my mentor's way of doing things. When the baby's head was delivered my mentor would feel for any loops of cord that might be around the baby's neck, slip them over the head, before clamping and cutting the cord. She would then help the mum deliver the rest of the baby. The other students in my class and I all talked about our mentors and they way they went about doing things so I knew this was fairly standard practice at that time.

The woman laboured relatively quickly and good naturedly, which had gone a long way to making this experience a wonderful one already. I managed to open my delivery pack at the right time without scattering the contents over the floor of the delivery room as I had feared I might. I got my gloves on with my fingers in all the right holes and was poised to help the mum deliver her baby's head with guidance from my new mentor. Much to my surprise this mum needed no help at all and delivered the head calmly while we stood poised for action. Lesson number one for me that day was: women's bodies have been delivering babies forever; midwives are present to watch for and assist with problems not to mess about with perfection in progress. The baby's face was very blue and I explained to the mum that I was just going to feel for any loops of cord around her baby's neck, the mum gave me her permission to do so and my mentor nodded approvingly. As I had expected, I found the cord wrapped around the baby's neck, twice. With help from my mentor I managed to slip one of the loops over the head. I then reached into my delivery pack, which was on a trolley beside me, located the cord clamps and slipped one under the loop of cord which was still around the baby's neck. Lesson number two began when my mentor placed her hand over mine, preventing me from closing the clamp to ligate the cord.

'Why?' she asked me quietly.

'Because the baby is tightly corded and I need to clamp in two places and cut between the clamps before the rest of the baby can be delivered?' I half-answered, half-queried, as I was confused as to why she was asking me this.

Does she want me to explain what I'm doing to the mum or am I doing it wrong? I wondered.

Because Pat always does it this way, I wanted to say.

'The cord will always be long enough to deliver the baby; if it isn't then in most cases it will self-ligate and snap if needed,' she explained. 'We'll discuss this in more detail later,' she concluded.

At that point the mum began to push again and I supported her son as he made his way into the world on the crest of his mother's contraction. The cord stretched long enough to allow all of his body to slip from his mother, though only just. Later, when my mentor and I were in the dirty sluice examining the placenta she explained why she had stopped me when I was about to clamp the cord.

'Suppose you had clamped the cord and then cut it,' she began.

'Yes, Pat always...' She held up a hand so I stopped talking and waited for her to continue.

'What happens when the cord is ligated?'

'The baby's oxygen supply from its mother is cut off completely though it has some residual oxygen held on the fetal haemoglobin which allows for the baby to remain oxygenated while the birthing process is being completed.'

'Almost but not quite right. The residual oxygen on the fetal haemoglobin is used when the blood flow from mum to fetus is restricted during the birthing process however some oxygen is still reaching the fetus from its mum, just a restricted amount.' She paused and looked at me.

I nodded to show I was following so far.

'So if you clamped and cut the cord, thereby cutting off even this restricted oxygen supply what do you supposed would have happened if the shoulders got stuck?'

My scalp crawled and a chill ran all the way down to my toes. I had heard of this happening to some women but being less than a year into my training I had yet to witness an emergency like this.

'Aren't there signs which indicate that the shoulders are stuck?'

'Yes, often there are, but not always. Are you willing to take a chance on a baby's life? If there is shoulder dystocia and the cord is intact then the baby will be getting some oxygen from its mum giving you precious time to go through the emergency manoeuvre to release the stuck shoulder and deliver the baby safely. And alive!'

She was right and her words had a profound impact on me as a midwife in the making. She was the first truly 'Sagefemme' I had ever met, though I would go on to encounter many more over the course of my career – midwives who took all the best of their training, work experience and research and made themselves into expert, confident practitioners of the normal birthing process and able to deal with emergencies until medical help arrived.

As a student midwife you are limited as to what innovative practice you can use, as you have to be guided by your mentor's practice ethos because she is ultimately responsible for the care you give as a student. This meant as a student midwife I had to clamp and cut countless cords before the baby's body was delivered, luckily none of whom ever had shoulder dystocia, the emergency where the baby's shoulder gets stuck under the mum's pubic bone which the midwife had mentioned during her talk in the sluice. Once I qualified I made sure that clamping and cutting the cord was something I did in only the most unusual of circumstances rather than my standard practice. I am happy to say that most midwives now deliver the baby's body before the cord is clamped and cut, but it took modern midwifery practice a very long time to catch up to what that wonderful midwife had already been confidently doing for so many years.

Chapter 22 - Don't hold me to ransom

Some rules are put into practice after extensive research into what is best for mother or baby. However, to a heavily pregnant woman, these rules can often seem unreasonable. Their reactions are varied and often challenging. How skilfully we deal with their reactions is often the key to how well the woman copes long term.

A busy antenatal clinic is often fraught with angst, filled as it is with women desperate for a wee waiting impatiently for their scans, talking in loud tones in order to compete with the rest of the noise in the waiting area. Men long to be back at work or anywhere but where they are and send hopeless looks at each other around the room. Half-feral children circle each other warily as they edge in competition towards the desired toy. Admin staff check people into the clinic, answer the phone, deal with queries, book new appointments, attend to doctors' requests and juggle hospital folders. Midwives chaperone doctors, test urine and blood pressure, take blood for tests, deal with queries, review blood results, support grieving parents who have just found out their baby has a problem or has died, try to cajole the scan department into accepting another woman for an urgent scan during that clinic, try to calm angry patients who have been waiting a long time for their appointment without actually giving away the reason why the doctor is too busy to see them on time, though this is usually because a patient of theirs has been taken ill or come to grief and is requiring more of their time than planned. I always say to women to come to clinic prepared to wait to see the consultant, even if you are booked in for the first appointment as usually a consultant will have been on the ward seeing inpatients before the clinic, which means he could be delayed by an incident there.

Working in clinic always makes me feel as if my brain has to be in two camps because I knew the intimate details of what is happening to each woman who is currently being seen by the consultants. However I can also observe the mood in clinic, see the mothers trying to keep their children entertained and then giving up in preference to staring at the main work station in the clinic as if trying to will their consultant to work faster. I understand their frustration. They have no idea what goes on behind the closed doors of the consulting room for each woman, no appreciation of the fact that the consultants don't rush women because that means they might miss some vital hint or clue in the examination process which very importantly included listening to what the patients are telling (and not telling) them. I know the consultant is already working as fast as he possibly can as are the junior doctors who are there to support him. They know that if the clinic is running late there is every chance they won't get time to sit down and eat their lunch, again. The reason for this is that they often go from being the doctor in clinic for the morning to spending an afternoon as the doctor in the operating theatre. Which means a hastily gobbled sandwich washed down with too hot or too cold coffee or tea on the way to the next set of demands on their time. The same applies to the clinic staff, too, though we at least can step down from clinic duties, one at a time, to go hide in the staff room and hastily eat our sandwich and throw a cup of tea down our necks though it isn't the proper break that any of us should have.

One particular shift I was standing at the desk before clinic began, sorting through blood results in order to make sure the right ones went with the right sets of notes so that there was no delay during clinic because of having to search for missing results.

'Oh, no,' Julie, the admin assistant, said as she was going through the clinic lists for the day.

'What?' I stopped going through the blood results and gave her my full attention.

'Miss Nolam is first on the list.'

'I thought we discharged her back to community midwifery care? How many weeks is she now?'

'She's down as 36 weeks, appointment reason given as: Wishes to discuss induction.'

'I should have seen that one coming,' I muttered. Miss Nolam was familiar to us. She was now on her fourth pregnancy and according to her had not enjoyed any of them. With the past three she had demanded a caesarean in order to get delivered early. Her demands hadn't worked, though she was offered an induction once she was full term and didn't go into labour after a membrane sweep from her community midwife, due to her distress at continuing with her pregnancy.

'Make sure she sees Mr Bryant and not Susie or James,' I advised the clerk. It wouldn't be fair to make the junior doctors see Miss Nolam as they would end up having to check with Mr Bryant, the consultant, as to what they could actually do to appease Miss Nolam, which would delay clinic from the very beginning, which wouldn't bode well for the rest of the morning.

Miss Nolam arrived 10 minutes early, children and harried-looking boyfriend in tow. I couldn't help feeling impressed that she had managed to get three children under five years old up, dressed, presumably fed and out of the house before 9 a.m. I could imagine what a challenge that must be and wasn't sure I would be able to manage the same feat on time. I couldn't, however, imagine where she had found the time or desire to get pregnant again. The clerk checked Miss Nolam into clinic and asked her to take a seat in the far area of the waiting room.

I bleeped Mr Bryant. 'Your first lady is here, it's Miss Nolam.'

'Reason?'

'Wants to discuss induction.'

'Tell her you never heard of me.' He sighed. 'I'll be with you in five mins, make sure she is ready to see me, oh and I'll want a chaperone on this one.'

By this he meant that he wanted me to have checked her urine, blood pressure and blood results before he arrived, so that Miss Nolam was ready to go into his consulting room as soon as he arrived. Many years ago we used to chaperone consultants with every patient but the cuts to the NHS meant that this was no longer an option so we chaperoned only when the doctor anticipated that the situation could become tricky or difficult and wanted a witness to the proceedings or if he was doing an internal investigation and wanted an assistant or a support person for the woman.

Mr Bryant arrived and I squashed into the consulting room along with Miss Nolam, her boyfriend and children. The consultant stood in the corner near the door to allow us all room to get in and seemed reluctant to move from the spot once we had. Wise man, he knew he was going to fight a battle now between trying to meet his professional duties and his client's expectations. His professional duties would win every time of course but it was now a matter of convincing the patient that it was the right thing to do for her. There are very strict guidelines on what stage it is safe to try and induce labour depending on the stage of pregnancy, the state of the pregnancy and how many babies the woman has had previously. He had no choice but to adhere to those but the challenge was to make Miss Nolam understand that her baby was not even due to be born yet, let alone overdue and that to try and induce labour now could be harmful to her and would likely be harmful to her unborn baby. He discussed natural induction methods carefully phrasing his sentences so as not to invoke awkward questions from the children. Miss Nolam looked horrified at the concept of natural induction, leaving me wondering yet again what had made her indulge in the physical intimacy that getting pregnant actually involves. She argued and Mr Bryant firmly repeated the reasons he had just explained at which point she burst into tears.

'I can't be pregnant any longer, I can't stand it, you have to induce me!' she wailed loudly, setting her children off in sympathy or fear. Her boyfriend fidgeted nervously and busied himself trying to shush the children.

Mr Bryant placed the palms of his hands flat on the desk and looked at Miss Nolam until she had dabbed way her tears and composed herself enough to pay attention again.

'The rules are there to protect you and your unborn baby, not to make your life more difficult.'

'I don't care, I'm telling you to get it out of me or I'll be making a formal complaint!' Fresh tears flowed down her cheeks.

Mr Bryant raised his voice slightly to get her attention. 'If I was working in a bank and you came in, demanding I give you all the money in the vault and started crying when I refused, I still wouldn't give you the money. So, don't try to hold me to ransom over inducing you because it is not going to happen.' He lowered his voice to a conversational tone again. 'Now, I think what would do you a world of good would be if you had a chance to get some rest,' he said kindly.

She nodded. 'I'm so tired. That one still doesn't go through the night,' she said indicating the youngest who looked back at her warily, wondering at the sudden attention.

'Is there any way you could take a couple of hours for yourself in the afternoons? Anyone who could help you?'

'My nan might but I didn't like to ask 'cos she's likely to say that I got myself into this mess...' She trailed off.

'Well, how about you tell her your consultant said you need to have a bit of rest in the afternoons from now until the baby comes, do you think she'd help out then?'

She nodded.

'Okay, good. Now, see your community midwife next because it's too much for you to struggle into clinic to see me unnecessarily and I'll see you back here when you're 40 weeks pregnant.'

They left, mollified, and Mr Bryant continued on with the clinic already running 20 minutes late. It was going to be a long day but there was satisfaction to be gained from diffusing an angry patient and having her leave with the feeling that he really cared about her well being, even if he hadn't given in to her demands that she be induced immediately. True skill that can only be learned through years of work and confidence in yourself as a professional. I admired him greatly after that consultation and have spent many years trying to treat women with the same holistic care that he provided.

Chapter 23 - Nine months plus one more for good measure

The Hollywood obsession with the pursuit of bodily perfection has a lot of angst to answer for; particularly for diminishing the pleasure and pride that should be the main driving emotion for women after giving birth and not disappointment that their pre-pregnancy figure doesn't reappear within a few days after having a baby.

'Ready for your shower now, Leonie?' I asked as she handed her newborn daughter to her husband Bruce.

'Oh yes!' She shuffled her legs over to the side of the bed.

'Just sit with your legs hanging over the edge for a couple of minutes until your body has time to adjust before you try standing up,' I warned. I paused to jot down the rest of my observations of her condition.

Leonie had used an epidural for pain relief in labour and it was only now, several hours later, that she felt she could feel enough of her legs again to attempt walking. She had paid to be put in a private room until she had recovered enough to go home.

'A sit on a proper loo and a long shower are going to feel amazing!' Leonie had used a bed pan a couple of times in the past few hours which was challenging with legs still numb from the epidural but better than having a catheter put in, according to Leonie who had refused one when offered the option. I thought both had their disadvantages and couldn't imagine which I would choose if I was in her position.

'What clothes do you want to change into?' Her mum, Holly, asked, poised over Leonie's suitcase.

'Bring the suitcase here, Mum, I'll dig out what I want. Ta,' she said as her mum heaved the case up onto the bed. Leonie dug around in it while her legs dangled, lying the items she wanted to take with her on the bed.

'What do you have those for?' Holly asked as she spotted the box of tampons. 'You can't use those until after you have had the all clear from Dr Richardson at your six-week check-up.

'But, Mum I don't like these!' Leonie whined holding up a pack of maternity pads.

'Tough, you will be pushing up germs with those others, so be sensible and use the pads.' Holly's voice was stern. I completely agreed with Holly but neither Leonie nor her mum asked my opinion so I carried on writing in Leonie's notes. Bruce fidgeted in his chair, holding his daughter firmly with one hand as he pushed against the arm of the chair with the other, boosting himself into a more upright position.

Betsy gave a squeak in her sleep, cried for a minute and then began hiccupping. With each twitch her eyes widened in surprise and the cause for her distress was soon forgotten in her amazement at what her body was doing.

Leonie laughed and said, 'She got hiccups all the time when she was inside me!'

Bruce said, 'That was the first move I felt her do, a bunch of tiny hiccups.' He brought her up to his shoulder, patting her back as he began trying to wind her.

'Try tucking her bare upper half under your shirt, Bruce; she'll soon stop once she warms up and calms down.'

I nodded in agreement; Leonie's mum was right. Baby hiccups came from an immature diaphragm muscle and the comfort and heat would soon stop the reflexive action of the hiccups once the muscle relaxed from the increased temperature against her chest.

'I used to do that with you a lot,' she said to Leonie. 'Got so you wouldn't go to sleep any other way.'

'Yes, I know and Nanna said you made a rod for your own back doing that.'

'Pish! That's one thing we'll never agree on! How can a happy baby be compared to an uncomfortable rod? Once you were asleep you didn't wake, even when I put you down. You were good as gold, just like Betsy will be as long as she knows how much she is loved.'

Leonie and Bruce smiled at each other.

'Ready to try standing?' I asked as I moved to Leonie's side. Holly stayed where she was next to Leonie, which was the perfect support for Leonie as she propelled herself up and held onto her mum's shoulder for comfort until she felt steady.

'Why not have a little wander round inside your room first, pet?' Holly asked and offered her arm to Leonie who slipped her hand through and took a few tentative steps around the bed to the window where Holly fussed with the hospital dressing gown until it covered Leonie to her satisfaction. Bruce stretched his long legs out and groaned with relief.

I hovered until I was satisfied that Leonie was steady on her feet with no residual effects from the epidural, then moved away a few steps so she had some space. The single room was on the small side without a doubt and even more so with four adults inside it.

Leonie turned her back to the window, leaned back against the warm radiator and tutted as she tried to pat down the front of the hospital gown only to encounter the jelly wobble of her abdomen. 'Why am I still so fat?' she muttered.

'Darling, you only just had Betsy a few hours ago...' Bruce began.

'But my belly is empty now so why do I still look like I'm pregnant?'

Bruce shrugged, and I opened my mouth to explain but before I could Holly came to his rescue. 'It took you nine months for your clever body to stretch enough to allow Betsy to grow. You're made of skin and bone not elastic, so it will take you at least nine months to get back to your pre-pregnancy weight. Your shape may never be exactly the same as before, though. Which is exactly as it should be because you are more than you were before Betsy arrived. Also, my lovely, because you are feeding Betsy yourself, your body will hold onto a little extra nourishment to make good milk with. So I would say give yourself at least one more month on top of the nine to reverse the changes pregnancy made to your shape.'

'Really? Clever? I simply feel like my body is fat not clever.' Leonie's face fell and she looked over at Bruce.

'Your body grew our baby. You don't think that's clever?' Bruce's voice was incredulous then softened as he said, 'I don't see any fat...I think you look more beautiful today than ever. Motherhood suits you.'

'Thank you, darling.' Leonie walked to Bruce's chair to give him a kiss and run her finger along Betsy's cheek.

'I am sorry for jumping in and not giving you a chance to speak,' Holly whispered to me at the window as Bruce and Leonie continued to talk. 'You must think I am such an interfering busybody. I just can't bear it when I hear her say things like that. I want her to understand that pregnancy and birth are amazing, complex, perfect and ever so clever and nothing at all to do with looking fat. I want her to know that fat is very different to being pregnant or having the shape of a new mum.'

'I didn't mind at all,' I whispered back. 'I'm happy as long as things get explained correctly. I happen to think you are very wise. I couldn't have explained that any better than you did. In fact I've made some mental notes to store away for future use with women who aren't so lucky to have the support that Leonie does.'

Holly grinned at me then leaned back against the wall as she watched her daughter mothering her own daughter.

As if she felt the warmth of her mum's fond gaze Leonie looked over at her mum. 'We've decided that Bruce is going to stay with Betsy 'cos she is settled so nicely so will you come with me instead, Mum?'

'Of course, Leonie.' Holly bustled about happily picking up Leonie's shower things and I walked them to the shower room, leaving Bruce holding his daughter in peaceful contentment in the warm baby-scented room.

Interlude

Latent Labour

How long is the average labour? When does it really begin? These questions have been subject to fierce debate and numerous research projects for countless years. The accepted definition in clinical arenas is about 12 hours or more for first-time mums from the onset of regular painful contractions. Of course by regular we mean more than once an hour, preferably once every 10 minutes, and lasting more than 20 seconds at a time at least. Those are the pains that mean your uterus is making itself smaller and at the same time pulling your cervix open so that eventually your baby can make its way through your pelvic outlet down your vagina and out into the world to have its first reassuring cuddle with you.

Try telling that to a woman and her family who think she has been in labour for days because she has been suffering cramping pains and uterine tightenings around about once an hour for the past 24 hours. The woman is exhausted because those pains have kept her from sleeping for more than an hour at a time. She is filled with adrenaline over the excitement of her pregnancy coming to an end, meeting her baby for the first time and anxiety about how she is going to cope if the labour pains get worse. This excitement and anxiety has fed into her family's and they are a wound-up bundle of nerves by the time they make contact with the maternity services, who then spoil it all by telling them that the woman is not in established labour yet. The only words they hear are not in labour.

Such was the case with Ann Witterby who arrived at the maternity unit one day. She had travelled there by bus with the father of her baby, who looked terrified, and her mother, who looked very unimpressed with, well, life in general.

'We've come a long way!' she said in response to my greeting at the door, 'and she's had enough, can't cope with anymore pain.' They had come from an area which was about 40 minutes away and by trying to ensure that we didn't turn her daughter away at the door (clearly she thought there was a chance we would do such a thing), she had just communicated to a total stranger that she thought her daughter was a failure, inadvertently or not. I saw Ann's face pale and her lips press themselves into a thin line as her mother's words made contact with her already crumbling confidence.

'Please, come in.' I smiled, biting back on my reflex to try and reassure them that everything was probably going well. I knew it was best to check Ann out before I made that decision and said anything that I might regret later. Sometimes it is sensible to take the empathy out of the midwife for a short period of time. I escorted them to the room where I would decide whether Ann's condition warranted her being fully admitted to the ward or not. Wisely I chose not to mention this fact to any of them. Ann climbed onto the bed and lay down, coat and shoes still on, on the sheet which I had covered the bed with. Her boyfriend Grant slumped into the armchair when her mother chose to stand between the bed and the chair. Either to block Grant's view or to better direct her death-ray glare at me, I presumed.

You're a professional so think like one, I chided myself. I had been with Ann for 10 minutes so far and no sign of any contraction-like pain, though this wasn't entirely unheard of as sometimes the change in environment can alter the rhythm of the contractions that the woman had been experiencing previous to arriving at the maternity unit. So I helped Ann off with her coat and got her to prop herself up on the pillows so I wouldn't be towering above her while I assessed her. I did her basic observations first, temperature, pulse, blood pressure, sent her for a walk to the toilet down the corridor so she could provide a sample of her urine for me to check for ketones, glucose, blood and other proteins. I noted that they were all within normal limits in her notes, using my very best and slowest handwriting. I wanted her to have time to get used to the new surroundings so her body could get back to doing whatever it was that had made them decide to pitch up unannounced at the maternity unit on this day. I had a feel of her tummy to find out which way her baby was lying, to see if it would give me a kick or try to wriggle away because it had taken umbrage to me prodding it around and if her uterus would respond by tightening into a contraction. Yes to a fidget from the baby, no to the contraction. By the time I had finished listening to the baby's perfectly normal heart rate 30 minutes had passed since I had first met Ann and everything about her was normal – for a woman who wasn't in established labour! I was not looking forward to being the one who had to broach this subject with this family. Knowing that the maternity unit was almost empty (those were the good old days), I took the easy way out instead.

'You look exhausted.' I smiled at Ann watching as she smiled in response and closed her eyes. 'So do you both,' I said to Ann's mum and Grant. 'Why don't you take a little while to yourselves and go to the canteen for a coffee and something to eat? Ann will be fine here, I'll see to it that she is and call the canteen if anything changes.' Reluctantly, they agreed and left. I offered Ann a cup of tea and some toast, and went to make it when she accepted, making sure she had the call bell within easy reach should she want me while I was gone. I was certain she would get frightened and call me straight away. I was wrong.

She opened her eyes when I came back with the tea tray and said, 'Nothing. No pains at all since I got here. I don't understand it. I feel like a fraud.'

I smiled, placed the tea tray on her over the bed table, pulled the easy chair close to the bed and sat next to her. 'Sometimes it takes our bodies a while to get the hang of how to go into full blown labour. Especially for first-time mums like yourself. Your body hasn't done this before so it needs to practice; that's why you have been getting the contraction type pains but also why they haven't been coming that often or lasting for as long as they need to in order to tip you into what we call established labour. Often when you come into a strange place your brain will be distracted by the change in environment and won't concentrate properly on what it was doing before. That's why we tell women to try and stay at home as long as possible.'

'I was so tired at home, the pain was really getting to me and I was worried that if I didn't get on the bus when I did then I wouldn't get to the hospital in time.'

'I can see why that would worry you. What made you decide to take the bus? Don't you have anyone who could drive you?'

'Well Grant has a mate who offered us a lift but my mum doesn't like his driving so...'

I let the matter drop for the time being and we chatted about other things, like why latent labour pains were still doing good work by helping to soften the cervix and get it ready to dilate. I could see Ann's eye's lowering as she relaxed and the conversation ground to a halt as she drifted off into a light doze. I stayed put, the rest of the team knew where I was if they needed me, and I finished writing out my conclusions in Ann's notes. Not in established labour, early arrival at hospital related to transport issues, to remain as a ward attender for observation at this time.

All too soon Ann's mum and boyfriend returned to the ward. I answered the locked ward door so I could explain latent labour to them without disturbing Ann. They had relaxed somewhat while they were away and once they knew I wasn't going to immediately send them back home they accepted the explanation of latent versus established labour. I knew they were hoping that Ann would go into established labour while they were at the hospital and there was every chance that she would. I recommended that they encouraged her to sleep while she was here and that they tried to relax and rest, too. They crept into the room with an extra chair and I heard nothing from them for the next couple of hours. Just as I was steeling my nerve to go in and tell them that it looked as if Ann's body had decided to not go into established labour yet the buzzer rang, beckoning me to Ann's room. Ann's mum and Grant were both standing and Ann was sat on the edge of the bed, breathing hard, one hand on her bedside table for support.

She looked up at me and said, 'I feel sick.' I had heard that tone of voice before and hurriedly passed her a ridiculously shallow kidney-shaped bowl.

Ann shook her head, moved herself to the sink in the room and was copiously sick into it.

'Better out than in!' I said brightly, not meaning a single word of it. Vomit was the body fluid I hated the most. Every clinician I've ever met has one they can't bear, usually mucous though that doesn't faze me at all. Even worse, I was the lucky person who was going to have to clean that sink out, which meant getting my gloved hand in to scoop out the undigested toast. Being able to share in people's birth experiences is for the most part a privilege but moments like these put a certain tarnish on the job. However, the good news was that Ann's vomiting was a sign that her body was finally in established labour and she went on to give birth eight hours later.

Latent labour is something which all midwives are familiar with. Its unpredictability in itself is predictable and there are things which we can do to make it pass without causing so much anxiety for the women having to endure it. Sadly there are also many things which we cannot offer reassurance for, such as fetal alcohol syndrome. Many babies are affected to some degree by a mother who drinks heavily but once in a while there comes along an exception to the rule, like this little baby in my next story.

Conundrums

Chapter 24 - There are exceptions to every rule

Birth defects present in about 4% of newborns. A large number of these are for no discernable reason but there are some things that we know will cause damage to the fetus. Some substances include, but are not limited to, medication or drug exposures, maternal infections and diseases, and some environmental and occupational exposures are known to possess teratogenic qualities, and if ingested during pregnancy they will cause harm to the developing baby. Teratogens act in specific ways on developing cells and tissues to cause a series of abnormal developmental events which means that exposure to teratogens can cause death, structural abnormalities, growth restriction, and/or functional deficiencies, depending on the stage of development that the exposure occurs at. Some, such as certain types of antibiotics, will damage the developing teeth causing dental problems for life, other medications such as thalidomide, which used to be prescribed to help with pregnancy-related nausea and vomiting has been linked to structural birth defects. Even widely used additives, such as caffeine, are known to cross the placenta and affect the fetus, which is why women who are planning a pregnancy are advised to reduce their caffeine intake, quite a challenge when it is one of the ingredients of such a wide range of products from soft drinks to energy bars. Infections such as toxoplasmosis (which can be found in animal faeces), rubella and syphilis to name a few of the more common ones are labelled as teratogenic. Luckily you can avoid these if you take sensible precautions such as protecting your hands when handling animal faeces, making sure your immunisations are up to date and being sure that you are in a monogamous relationship and aware of your partner's sexual health before trying to get pregnant. The same goes for x-rays: don't have them if you know you are pregnant or if there is a chance you might be pregnant. If you have a pre-existing medical condition, such as heart murmurs, diabetes or epilepsy to name just a few, then you need to be sure that you take a higher dose of folic acid and that you get pre-conception advice from your doctor before trying to conceive. Some widely used recreational drugs such as nicotine are also thought to be teratogenic and some such as alcohol are proven to be teratogenic.

There used to be a time when pregnant women were advised to give up drinking any alcohol during their pregnancy to avoid any risk of the expected wide range of structural abnormalities linked to alcohol use. The time during the pregnancy when these anomalies were thought to happen was not known and researchers could only make a guess at best, based on the knowledge of how the fetus develops. Then society began to relax a bit about the use of alcohol and pregnant women were advised that drinking in moderation – say one to two units a week – should be safe for the developing fetus. More recent research supports this but it is very rare for any person to drink exactly one unit of alcohol unless a measure is used. Is the enjoyment from those couple of units of alcohol worth the potential risk to a baby? If you didn't drink at all for your entire pregnancy how much would you miss it? Some women would say that they couldn't do without it. Many of those women would be perfectly safe social drinkers but a few would be problem drinkers, or more rarely be dependent on alcohol, otherwise known as an alcoholic. Women who drink heavily during pregnancy can be almost guaranteed to give birth to a child with varying degrees of fetal alcohol spectrum disorder which is characterised by a number of defects, including growth deficiency, neurological problems such as epilepsy, impaired intellect or behavioural difficulties, distinct facial features such as a very shallow or missing philtrum – the groove running between your nose and top lip – very thin upper lip, and eyes set close together. Now these are just some of the problems associated with fetal alcohol spectrum disorders and of course people can have some of these without being the child of a mother who over indulged during her pregnancy. There are exceptions to every rule.

One of these exceptions was Helen Gray. She was a known alcoholic who had been under the care of the mental health services because she needed in- and outpatient treatment for her addiction. She was also educated, articulate, well groomed, and in full-time and full-on, highly stressful employment. Before I met Helen this would not have been my stereotypical image of an alcoholic. I had always envisaged people who struggled to cope without a certain amount of alcohol in their systems at all times to be no more capable of coping than the shambling vagrants dossing on park benches who seemed made up entirely of hangover and regret. Surely alcohol dependant people were more like those discarded men and women who littered the bus shelters and park benches that dotted the perimeter of the park I passed through on my early morning walks to work?

Helen spent a few months off and on the maternity antenatal wards during her pregnancy. She would turn up at the maternity unit when she was struggling to avoid getting drunk.

'Having a hard time of it right now,' she said, grinning disarmingly late one night as I admitted her.

'Hard time with what, Helen?'

'Oh the usual things...but when I'm struggling to get enough sleep too it just makes it harder to cope with everything. This little one keeps waking me in the night and then I find it impossible to get back to sleep once my mind is switched on...I used to have a drink or two to help ease back into dreamland but I want to do right by my baby so I know I've got to do what I can to keep it under control.' I could smell the alcohol on her breath as she spoke.

'How much have you had to drink today, Helen?'

'Ooooh.' Helen scrunched her face as she decided what to say in response. 'I shared a bottle of wine with Rupert with our supper and then had a couple of hot toddies while we watched TV and then I just wanted to finish the bottle of whiskey so I knew I had better come in before I did.'

'Where is Rupert?' I asked after searching for something non-judgemental to say in response.

'He wasn't feeling too well so he stayed home.'

'Well, let's get you settled and then I'll give the doctor a bleep to let him know you're here.'

'I might just have a wander across the way before you go and do that,' Helen said, meaning she wanted to go to the mental health unit for support.

This wasn't unusual and they were quite happy for patients known to them to turn up unannounced but I wasn't sure if this open access policy applied after 10 p.m.

'It's dark and cold, Helen, would you like me to give them a call and see if they'll come over here to see you instead? It might save you a trip?' She would and so I did. Helen was 35 weeks pregnant at this point and unbeknownst to us both, her baby would be born before she left the maternity unit again. The psychiatric team and Helen decided that she was too emotionally unstable to be discharged, and too pregnant to be admitted to their wards so Helen remained on the antenatal ward. Some days were dark ones for Helen, especially the ones where her stash of alcohol was extricated from whatever hiding place she had managed to find, but on the whole she was a likeable person, she tried her best to take the medicines that the psychiatrist had prescribed to treat symptoms of alcohol withdrawal (though she never seemed to display any) and the whole team grew very fond of her.

One morning I came on duty and encountered Helen loitering by the main entrance to the wards. The unit was square shaped at the end of a long corridor with the newborn unit at the opposite end and the labour ward on the ground floor.

'Morning, Helen.'

'Morning, I've been waiting for you!'

'Have you? I'll be in to see you just as soon as I've had handover.'

'Okay, I'm in room 9 now.' Helen grinned widely. Room 9 was one of the postnatal rooms.

'Oh, Helen, congratulations! What did you have?'

'A girl, I've just been to feed her on the newborn unit. They said she's fine, no problems from the alcohol and can come back to my room today.'

'I am so happy, for both of you. I'll be round to see her as soon as handover is finished.'

'Come and get me on your way.'

'Absolutely, I need you to do the introductions.'

Helen's daughter was one of the most beautiful babies I have ever seen. Great big, wide-set eyes and loads of black hair which stood out around her head in a soft frame. There was no hint of any damage caused by the alcohol Helen had drunk throughout her pregnancy. Helen's daughter Mara was an exception to a rule.

'Isn't she just beautiful?' Helen cradled her daughter and beamed at me. I could only agree.

'She looks a lot like you, Helen.' It was true and Helen acknowledged the compliment graciously.

'I've given up the drink for good this time,' she said with a determined expression. 'I don't ever want to put Mara's well being at risk again.'

'Mara is very lucky to have a mum that loves her as much as you do. A sober mum that won't miss a minute of her daughter's life. I will be rooting for you.' I sincerely hoped Helen would succeed.

Social services kept an eye on Mara's wellbeing along with the regular visits from the community psychiatric nurse who kept an eye on Helen and her growing resolve to remain teetotal. Helen came in periodically over the next two years to show off Mara and the last time I saw her, Mara was a robust happy child and Helen was still teetotal. Sometimes the good guys win and sometimes, like the couple in my

next story, it takes a tragedy to break people of
their harmful habits.

Chapter 25 – Hot-boxed house

There is something very distinctly memorable about the acrid yet sweet smell of cannabis. Once the origin of the smell has been identified for the first time, the memory of it remains forever, much in the same way that the essence of cigarette smoke does. This is why I am always able to smell it in people's houses. In my early adulthood it was inevitable that parties would involve at least a few people who liked to indulge in smoking cannabis. One way that was particularly popular at the time was called 'hot boxing' where at least a few people would crowd into a small space such as a bathroom or car to share a smoke of cannabis. I detested the sensation that came from even passive contact with cannabis smoke and would try to avoid going to the toilet too soon after a bathroom had been hot boxed. Some of the houses I have visited as a community midwife are so pungent with the scent that I wonder why they don't realise that it is blatantly obvious to others. I suppose it is because of sensory adaptation. In much the same way you can adjust to even the worst of smells once exposed to them for a period of time, the same happens with the smell of cannabis or, to use a more familiar smell as a reference, cigarette smoke. As I am exposed to neither of those smells by choice in my personal life, I am always very aware of them when I encounter them by chance. In fact the smell of stale cannabis was the first thing I was aware of when I entered Jody Curtis's house to do her booking notes. Oh dear, I thought and made a mental note to raise it as an issue of concern once I got to the medication section on the booking form.

'C'mon in,' Jody said and led me along the short corridor to her front room. 'Want a cuppa or water or something?'

'That would be lovely, thanks. I'll come with you,' I said, keen to have an opportunity see as much of the house as possible in order to learn things about Jody that she might not think to tell me or might avoid sharing with me. Additionally, seeing the state of the kitchen is a good indicator as to whether I should actually consume any of the beverage I have been offered. We kept up a steady chatter, getting to know each other a little as Jody busied herself in her tidy and clean kitchen. Jody's husband travelled extensively due to the nature of his work and therefore was not present for the booking. Jody was articulate, well groomed and confident; a refreshing change from the previous two clients I had visited who were struggling with complex social needs ranging from domestic violence to homelessness and poverty. Jody offered me a tour of her home which I readily accepted and after admiring the room she had set aside to use as a nursery we made our way into the conservatory to work our way through her booking notes.

Reaching the section about medications I asked, 'Are you taking any prescription drugs at this time?'

'Erm...I was on doxycycline for my acne but my GP switched me to this antibiotic cream instead when I told him I was planning on trying for a baby. Oh! Do vitamins count as drugs?'

'Yes, they do count and you must make sure you are taking a pregnancy appropriate vitamin tablet because they will have the correct amount of folic acid and none of the dangerous vitamin A in them.'

I made a note of the name of the topical treatment she had been prescribed for her acne and the advice I had given her about the vitamins. Taking a deep breath I said, 'How about recreational drugs? Are you taking or using any of those?'

Eyes wide, posture stiff, Jody responded with an uncharacteristically short answer. 'Nope.'

Not willing to drop the subject that easily I continued, 'I have been a midwife for longer than I care to remember and have seen more than the average person. There wouldn't be much a person could say that would shock me. The reason I asked you is not only because it is a standard question on the booking notes but also because I could smell cannabis when I came in here.'

Jody avoided eye contact and fidgeted with the tassels on a cushion. I waited. 'It's Grant,' she said eventually. 'He likes a spliff occasionally, says it helps him chill out. I hate it and never use it myself but he's partial to a bit of it once in a while.'

'I would urge you to ask Grant to stop smoking altogether. At the very least he must stop smoking it in the house or anywhere near you and he needs to brush his teeth before he kisses you. THC, which is the active ingredient in cannabis, can cross the placenta meaning a proportion of the THC you breathe in by being with Grant as he smokes it is getting into your baby's bloodstream and also being stored in the placenta.' I explained to Jody the risks associated with cannabis use and pregnancy; small heads, unsettled babies, the risk of placental problems. 'Now there is no guarantee that these problems are solely down to THC but they have been associated with it and just as I have to give you food safety and nutritional advice I also have to counsel you to restrict your caffeine intake along with avoiding other substances that carry a risk of harming your baby.'

'Okay. I understand.' Jody gave me a weak smile and we carried on with the rest of the booking.

As we were nearing the end of the questions I needed answered to be able to book Jody into the maternity system she suddenly asked, 'Have I hurt my baby, do you think?'

Inwardly I cringed. This was the question I had been dreading for there was no suitably accurate response. 'I can't give you a yes or no answer, Jody. It all depends on how much exposure your body has had and will continue to have to cannabis smoke and it is also impossible to predict the extent to which it would affect your baby. I can only compare it to some passive smokers getting lung cancer while others are exposed to it for a lifetime without any obvious detriment,' I finished, knowing my response was inadequate, unhelpful and nothing at all like the reassurance she was certain to be longing for. Once I was sure that Jody had asked all the questions she had at the time I checked that she had the contact numbers for the maternity unit and urged her to phone whenever she or Grant had any other questions. I left feeling I had failed Jody, even though I knew these issues were difficult to discuss in exactly the right way; it was a fine line to tread between providing what knowledge was available so that she could make an informed choice about her lifestyle and the health of her and her baby and scaremongering.

Several weeks later I had a call from Jody to say her stomach was sore.

'What kind of sore, Jody?'

'Well it's been sort of like a mild period pain only constantly there since about seven this morning.'

'A period-type pain for about the past three hours then, is that right?'

'Yes, periody but annoying me all the time.'

'Are you losing anything down below, like blood or water? Is your baby moving about as normal?'

'Not losing anything down below and this is usually bean's quiet time, but there were movements during the night.'

'Ok, you need to come in and get checked over. Is Grant there to drive you in?'

'Yes, he's here. I wouldn't let him got to work today.' Jody's laugh ended in a shriek.

'Jody? What's wrong?'

I could hear Jody sobbing. 'It feels like someone has punched me in the stomach!'

'Jody lie down wherever you are and put Grant on the phone.' A sudden severe pain like that, enough to make a bubbly laughing person suddenly shriek then cry, was likely to be one of a couple things: appendicitis or placental abruption.

When Grant came on the phone I said, 'Grant, I need you to call 999 and ask for a paramedic ambulance. Say that it is a maternity emergency. Listen to their instructions. Then call me back.'

'999, paramedics, instructions, phone you.' He repeated and hung up.

About 15 minutes later Grant called me back. I could hear the sirens and other voices in the background. 'We are in the ambulance on our way to hospital.' The fear in his voice was almost palpable.

'I'll meet you there.' I phoned the matron to make sure she knew the ambulance was on its way in and why. She did and the doctors were on standby. Next I phoned my team leader to let her know what was happening and I was going to the maternity unit. She would call the women who were expecting me to visit this morning to let them know that I would be delayed. I drove to the hospital from the doctor's surgery a short distance away where I had stopped in to look for details of any new bookings.

It turned out that Jody had suffered a placental abruption at 25 weeks' gestation. The doctor had managed to save Jody's life but not that of her baby. Not only did Jody and Grant have to try and cope with the grief they felt over the loss of their baby but they also felt guilty that Jody had been exposed to cannabis in early pregnancy. They were desperate for answers about whether this had caused the loss of their baby but I could offer none one way or the other. Physically Jody recovered quite well from her ordeal but they ended up with a referral for counselling to help them come to terms with their loss.

I received notification from Jody's GP 18 months later that she was pregnant once again, highly anxious and requesting early booking.

I phoned her to book in an appointment date and time.

'I'm looking forward to seeing you!' she said brightly.

I concurred. Well that's a relief, I thought. I hadn't expected her to think of me positively after her previous experience and it wasn't unusual for women who had lost a baby to request a different midwife due to the bad memories associated with the previous pregnancy.

The first thing Jody said to me after greeting me at the door was, 'We're smoke free this time.' She smiled at Grant and rubbed her flat belly.

'Well that's an excellent start and congratulations on your pregnancy. Was this baby planned? Was that what made you go smoke free?' The air in the house was scented with no more than a light dose of air freshener which in no way disguises odours such as cannabis so I was confident that the house had been smoke free for some time.

'I gave it up when we lost Elliott,' Grant said. 'It held no enjoyment for me anymore when I knew it could have that kind of effect.'

'There is no way of knowing for sure that your use of cannabis was solely responsible for...' I began.

Grant cut me off. 'I know that but it was high time I grew up anyway. I want to be the best parent I can and I think that cutting out the spliffs is all part of it.'

Jody smiled fondly in Grant's direction. 'I have the best husband in the whole world,' she said proudly.

'I think your baby is very lucky to have such responsible and loving parents,' I said with total honesty, praying they would have a more successful outcome to this pregnancy.

Due to Jody's placental abruption with her last pregnancy she was booked for consultant-led care. Her pregnancy progressed well with no physical problems for her or her baby and she delivered her daughter at full term on the labour ward at the maternity unit. Whether this was due to the fact that Grant had stopped smoking cannabis is impossible to say but I was so pleased that two such lovely people were allowed to avoid heartache the second time around.

Chapter 26 - Lazy baby

The length of labour varies greatly from woman to woman because so many factors affect it from the mother's genetic makeup and general health, the size and physical fit of the baby in comparison to its mother, all the way through to the mood of the mother on the day she begins to labour. Also there is the existence of latent labour and established labour discussed in an earlier chapter to further confuse the issue of how long labour really lasts. Some women experience something called precipitate labour which is when she labours and delivers her baby in under an hour. I used to think that these women went from zero centimetres dilated to fully dilated in that time but am now fairly certain that they have probably been unaware that they have been labouring silently for a few days until the big contractions suddenly kick in and they rapidly finish the job in less than an hour. I credit Jessie Randall with being the main reason I now think this way.

Jessie came in to see me in one of my community clinics at her GP surgery for a membrane sweep at 40 weeks as we had agreed the previous week. She had three other children and was struggling to cope with their demands while heavily pregnant. Luckily she had the support of her husband and family and could rest instead of doing the school and after school club runs. This pregnancy was unplanned; the result of a weekend away to celebrate their fifteenth anniversary with an unexpected bonus. Too much champagne meant that Jessie's oral contraceptive pill was lost during the after effects of her hangover the next day, leaving her unexpectedly fertile; sperm can live for five days or more after being ejaculated inside a woman's body and once Jessie ovulated the loitering sperm got right down to the business of turning that egg into the beginnings of a baby. The clinic was busy and I was running late with Jessie booked in as my last appointment. By the time I had finished up with everyone else, Jessie was wandering around the waiting room looking a bit hot and tired. I wondered if she had begun to labour while waiting for me.

'Hi, Jessie, how are you feeling?' I indicated the way we needed to go to reach the room I was working in that day, one of many in this large GP surgery.

'Tired and fed up with this bump now. I'd love to be able to sleep through the night without having to wake up so I could turn over. Seems to take me an age to do it now and I'm sure I remember it being effortless when I wasn't pregnant.' She shook her head then said, 'Etc and so on.'

I had heard it all before, she was right about that but not just her, from countless women at this same stage of their pregnancy. I think the body is very clever to make women so fed up with being pregnant that they become willing to go through just about anything, including the pain of labour, just to have an end to it.

'Well with any luck this membrane sweep today will be all your body needs to remind it that it is time to go into labour. It has been eight years since your last labour so it may just have forgotten what to do at this point of your pregnancy. Have you felt anything resembling contractions yet? You look a bit flushed so I was wondering if you might have started without any help from me.'

Jessie shook her head as she put down her bag and shrugged off her coat. 'I think I just got a bit over heated while waiting for you. I should have taken my coat off earlier but it's all a bit of a faff to have anything to carry with this in the way.' She indicated her belly then sat down smoothing it with her hands and giving the baby a poke, presumably in response to a kick.

I busied myself checking her urine then blood pressure. 'Your wee is fine as usual, any swelling in your ankles, hands, face?'

'Nope, Ryan says I don't even look pregnant from behind, bless him.'

'Speaking of Ryan, have you tried any of the natural induction methods we talked about?'

'Oh yes, Ryan was only too happy to oblige, shame I can't say the same! He's done the deed a couple of times since I saw you last. Not that it's worked or anything but he's a happy man now at least.' She smiled fondly, momentarily lost in thought.

I lowered the examination couch and Jessie worked her hips onto it, lay back against the pillow and lowered the waist band of her skirt to expose her belly so I could palpate the baby inside her.

I felt the baby, taking my time in the hopes that I would feel her uterus tightening in a silent contraction but her body refused to play along. The baby was in a good position for delivery though and its heart beat was within normal limits.

'Clearly this baby has read all the text books and knows exactly what it is supposed to be doing, now you just need your body to cooperate. Do you need to do a wee?'

Jessie shook her head. 'Much to my surprise, no.'

'Ok, I'm going to go wash my hands again while you get your underpants off and yourself settled on the couch again. Let me know when you're ready.' I handed her a blanket with which to cover herself.

I pulled the curtain around the examination couch and gathered up the equipment I would need next, gloves and lubrication jelly; oh yes the life of a working midwife is nothing if not glamorous. Hands washed, I stood ready to begin the internal examination that would precede the membrane sweep as soon as Jessie was ready for me to come back into the curtained-off area.

'Ok, done,' Jessie puffed, a bit out of breath from the exertion of getting the bottom half of her clothing off and herself back into position on the couch.

Jessie was quite relaxed as I did the examination which helped to make the whole process a lot faster. It can be difficult to relax during a membrane sweep because of the technique the midwife has to use. It involves running your finger around the outside of the cervix to gauge the length and then inside the cervix if possible to determine how firmly applied the baby's head is to the cervix. It was definitely possible in Jessie's case as her body had clearly been doing a lot of work without her realising.

'Jessie your cervix is already five centimetres dilated and when I spread my fingers against either side of the opening I can stretch it up to eight centimetres.' I ended the examination, pulled my gloves off then had a listen to the baby's heart rate to make sure it hadn't minded the intrusion. It hadn't.

Jessie half sat up supported by her elbows. 'I'm eight centimetres dilated already? Without feeling a thing? Surely that isn't possible.'

'You're five centimetres dilated, not eight, but because your body has done this a few times before your cervix is quite stretchy and I can make it expand up to eight centimetres. I can feel the fore waters slightly bulging through your cervix and that has probably been helping your cervix get into position, too.'

'So what happens now?'

I raised the back of the couch so Jessie was supported in a sitting position. 'Well now you wait. If you begin contracting, and by that I mean even just gentle but regular tightening or regular period-type pains or if your waters break, then you need to phone the unit straight away to let them know you are on your way in.'

'How long do you think it will take now? I mean I won't be having this baby at home, will I? I don't fancy a homebirth.'

'As long as you are sensible and prepared to come in straight away once you start feeling things happening or if your waters go then you should get to the hospital in time. If you feel like pushing then you need to call for a paramedic ambulance. I don't want to jinx you into nothing happening but I do think it would be sensible of you to have your other three stay overnight with someone else just in case you need to rush off in the middle of the night.'

Jessie agreed this was a good idea and I left her behind the curtain to get dressed while I went to wash my hands yet again. Hand washing is one of the most important ways we can keep infections to a minimum and I had often tried to add up how many times I washed my hands on an average work day but always lost count. In the winter my hands were constantly dry and sore from the constant exposure to wet and cold no matter how frequently I moisturised them. If you want to age your hands prematurely then going into a health care profession is a good way to achieve this.

I arrived on duty the following day fully expecting to find that Jessie had come in overnight and delivered her baby. Much to my surprise she hadn't, so I gave her a call at home to find out what, if anything was happening. No change as it turned out. This went on for four days until I received a call mid-morning to say that Jessie's waters had broken, she was having mild backache and she was on her way into the unit. I met her and her husband at the main entrance.

'I need to push!' she whispered to me then stopped suddenly and concentrated hard on resisting the urge to do exactly that.

As soon as that contraction had ended I began walking Jessie towards the lift. As we passed the reception desk I said brightly, 'Can't stop now,' and passed a sheet of hospital labels to them so they would have the basic info about Jessie. Where we were headed would be obvious to even a blind man as Jessie panted and moaned her way through the next contraction at just outside the lift doors.

'Try as hard as you can not to push, Jessie. Just for a couple more minutes,' I coaxed her as I heard the familiar grunt and tried to force the lift door open with the strength of my stare. Jessie sagged against Ryan with relief as that contraction ended. The security guard wheeled over a chair just as the lift doors pinged open. I thanked him and dragged it into the lift refusing to allow the person behind us to get on the lift with us. 'You'll need to wait for the next one.' He nodded.

'Want to rest your weary bones on this, Jessie?' I moved the wheelchair closer to her.

'I can't sit down. Feels like a bowling ball just inside me.'

'Ok, try kneeling on the chair facing backwards instead,' I suggested, 'and keep up the excellent effort at not pushing, we're almost there now.' Jessie kneeled and when those lift doors opened, I pulled and Ryan pushed the wheelchair out of that lift before moving as quickly as possible into the waiting labour room.

No sooner had another midwife, who had come in with us to offer assistance, got Jessie onto the bed, I had got my gloves on and Ryan had helped Jessie off with her leggings and pants then the next contraction came. Jessie couldn't resist pushing and as the contraction ended a head crowned.

'Oh!' said Jessie startled and pushed a little more even though her contraction was gone. A shocked little baby landed on the bed, arms splayed and eyes wide open. A brisk rub all over with a towel pulled from the cupboard soon encouraged a lustful cry from the baby which set Jessie off. A few minutes later both were settled comfortably on the bed and with the help of the other midwife I had the delivery pack lying open in order to be able to use the equipment I still required.

As I went about the business of delivering her placenta Jessie said, 'I didn't think that was ever going to end.'

'What? You were hardly contracting for any time at all.'

'No, the pregnancy, I thought I was going to be pregnant forever. I'm not doing this again.' She shot a stern look at Ryan.

'Nope, I'm booking into the snip clinic, I promise.' He looked ill at the very thought.

'Good, because I don't fancy sleepless nights for the rest of our lives.'

'No, me neither though I think we've got a few coming up,' he said as their new son began to cry lustily again.

Jessie was quite a relaxed mum and once her labour got going she progressed very quickly. Anxiety and fear can have exactly the opposite effects on the progress of labour. Because of the intense unique nature of contractions, a woman needs the constant support of someone who is outwardly calm and confident. In today's busy wards it isn't always possible for this to be provided by the midwife assigned to your care. Student midwives are worth their weight in gold in these (and many other) instances as Debbie Clark was about to find out in the next story.

Chapter 27 - The debilitation of fear

Before I assisted at my first delivery as a student midwife I had worried that everyone would be watching me fumble my way around and that I would be unable to remember what to do. I have never enjoyed being the centre of attention and felt anxious about the time when I would be. I spent several weeks fretting about this when I would have been better occupied with sleeping or studying. What I hadn't taken the time to reflect on was that there is something mesmerising and almost, dare I say it, soothingly predictable about a woman who is having regular contractions. If you have ever been a partner of a labouring woman or otherwise present in the room you will understand what I mean. Somehow a labouring woman draws all attention from everyone in the room to her. The rhythm or otherwise of her travail, the supportive encouraging murmurs from her partner or midwife, makes focusing on anything but her near impossible. The intense experience of being in the orbit of a labouring woman often left me exhausted, even when I was present simply as an observer.

As my training progressed I learnt that despite my fears to the contrary, I had found my niche in being a facilitator of the mechanics of labour and birth. As a student I was able to completely concentrate on the woman and her birth partner, doing all I could to reassure them that the labour and birth were progressing wonderfully and seeking reassurance and advice from my mentor when needed. Once qualified I tried to ensure that I practised in much the same way as I had when I was a student although this proved more challenging when assigned the care of more than one woman in labour at a time. Physically, providing care for more than one woman in labour at once, provided that they are at opposite ends of the labour continuum, is manageable. Emotionally it is less than ideal for both the woman and midwife providing her care. The midwife must make the choice between providing the intense reassurance that a woman in later labour will require against the opportunity to build a relationship with the woman who is in early labour so that she will trust you when you tell her she is doing well later on in her labour. However, it is possible to do both to some degree and that is the goal that most midwives aim for. It is not the ideal but then we do not work in an ideal world.

Debbie Clark was admitted in suspected early labour and assigned to my care. I was already supporting my third-year student with caring for Babs Chigner who was in advanced labour with her second baby. I knew the student would buzz if she needed me urgently before I came back so I left them and went to do Debbie Clark's admission check. This was Debbie's first baby and she seemed highly anxious about, well, everything. After checking her and her baby over, I explained to Debbie that she seemed to be in very early labour. Because of this I hadn't yet done an internal examination to check and see how far dilated she was. I suggested that she go for a relaxing bath and that if she needed anything then she could buzz for me.

'You mean you're going to leave me?' Debbie clutched at her boyfriend's hand. He squeezed it, looked embarrassed and remained silent. I hadn't heard him utter more than a couple of words in the time I had been with them.

'I will be on the ward supervising my student who is looking after our other lady in labour. If you need me you just need to buzz.' I showed her the buzzer on the bed and reminded her that the one in the bathroom was bright red. As part of her admission I had given Debbie and her boyfriend a quick tour of the ward so they could find their way to the bathroom, midwives' station and back.

'But what if I have the baby before you get to me?'

'The frequency and duration of your contractions tell me that you are still in early labour and I am only a few feet away from you so I think that is unlikely to happen.' I smiled reassuringly thinking, never say never, then carried on, 'Also there are other midwives on the ward so if I was delayed for a few minutes one of them would answer your buzzer.'

'Please can you just check me to see how far dilated I am?' Debbie paused to puff and pant her way through a short contraction.

I agreed to do an internal examination on her for her reassurance and did so after checking to see how my student and Mrs Chigner were getting on. Marvellously, as it turned out. I promised to return soon and went back to Debbie. An internal examination confirmed what I had thought from checking her over earlier; she was four centimetres dilated, meaning she was in early labour and safe to be left in a warm bath with her boyfriend for support and an assistance buzzer to hand.

I explained my findings to the duty sister and went back to my student and Mrs Chigner who was nearing the end of the first stage of her labour. An hour later I stood by and watched proudly as my student skilfully supported Mrs Chigner in birthing her baby and delivering the placenta. After the baby checks were finished, and confirming all was well, I left my student helping Babs to latch her baby on for a feed and went back to see how Debbie was getting on. I stopped at the midwives' station to let the duty sister know the situation.

'Debbie has buzzed a few times since you left her. Seems very anxious,' she said with a resigned expression on her face. 'Good thing you've got Amy with you today,' she continued, referring to my student.

Very anxious women can take up a lot of time and this is where students can come into their own as they can be spared to devote that one-on-one time that highly anxious women need but can't always get on a busy labour ward.

'Amy will be a while finishing up with Mrs Chigner so I'll concentrate on Miss Clarke in between supporting Amy with Mrs Chigner. Try not to give me anyone else until we've transferred Mrs Chigner to a postnatal ward, okay?'

The sister nodded her understanding and I went off to see Debbie who was out of the bath and back in her room.

'Oh, oh! I'm so glad you're back. The pain is awful. If you tell me that I am going to be in labour any longer than another hour or so then you'll have to give me an epidural.'

I murmured words of reassurance without giving a yes or no answer as I checked Debbie and her baby were both coping physically with the labour. As I checked them I watched exactly what was going on, noting how hard her boyfriend squeezed her hand as she contracted transferring his tension to her. Noted how ineffectively Debbie used the gas and air she had been given for pain relief.

I got Debbie to stand up and lean over the bed which I pumped up high enough to make it comfortable for her to lean on and high enough to be a bit of a challenge to simply sit down on in defeat.

'If you need a loo break then now would be a good time because I won't be leaving for a bit,' I said to her boyfriend. He checked that Debbie was happy for him to leave before practically running out of the door. The labour ward is not the best place for all men; some would be much happier waiting for the news at the other end of the phone. I stood next to Debbie with my hand on her abdomen waiting for each contraction to begin and talking her through when to begin using the gas and air and when to stop. By the time her boyfriend came back she was much more relaxed, lying on her side and dozing in between contractions.

He sat down in the chair beside the bed, smiled nervously at me and then grabbed Debbie's hand giving it a squeeze. Her eyes opened wide and she began using her gas and air as another contraction began.

'Here. Like this,' I said as I showed him how to offer Debbie just four of his fingers, leaving the baby finger free of her grip. 'It will keep her from squeezing you too hard,' I explained but actually meant that hand position would make it impossible for him to give Debbie anything more than a gentle squeeze with pressure from his thumb. He would have to transfer his anxiety to something else because Debbie had more than enough of her own to contend with.

My student knocked on the door to tell me that she was ready to transfer Mrs Chigner to the postnatal ward. As Debbie's contraction had finished she came in quickly to introduce herself before I went with her to say goodbye to Mrs Chigner.

By the time I returned, no more than five minutes later, Debbie was in a right state of high angst, calling out with her contractions and sobbing in between them like a helpless child.

'What's happened to you?' I exclaimed in astonishment.

'She got like this right after you left,' her boyfriend said, his voice flat, his eyes bright with unshed tears. He pawed at her shoulder in a clumsy attempt to offer comfort. Debbie shrugged his hand off, buried her face in the pillow and cried.

I crouched down so that my face was near hers, arm resting on the bed for support. 'Debbie? Whatever is the matter?'

'Hurts.' She said petulantly though her fear was obvious from the wide-eyed stare she then gave me. 'Can't do it any longer.'

'You were coping well before I left. Why do you feel you can't cope anymore?'

'Too scared it will last forever. And it's going to hurt more as it goes on!' Her voice rose to a panicked shriek as her next contraction started.

I talked her through the contraction, encouraging her to get into a steady rhythm of breathing. 'Better?' I asked once the contraction had died away.

She nodded. 'It's easier when you're here, somehow. I still want an epidural, though.'

'I can't offer you one of those until we know you are making progress in your labour. You're coming up to two hours since you were admitted which is a bit soon for another internal exam...'

'I don't care! I need to know if I can have one!'

I did another internal examination on Debbie, expecting to find that she had either made a lot of progress or none at all. Sadly, it was the latter.

'Although your cervix is a lot softer and tighter against your baby's head, you are still four centimetres dilated.'

'What's that mean?'

'You have not made enough progress to be considered suitable for an epidural right now. Oh, don't cry, Debbie, there are other options for you, I promise.'

I explained Debbie's options for pain relief: TENS machine and walking, keep using gas and air and/or get into a labour pool and as a last resort, a small amount of pethidine once she had made a little more progress. I had a feeling that if I could help Debbie calm down, stop being so scared and get her to relax a bit then she would make rapid progress in labour. She was as tense as a coiled spring and if she could release that energy to be used by her uterus then she would be moving things in the right direction. I was always happy to explain exactly what was going on at any time, knowledge is to be shared after all, and I think parents find this helpful. Certainly many of my women have required much less pain relief than they had expected. I believe that fear often stems from anxiety about the unknown, so once women know what to expect the pain is often easier to cope with emotionally, freeing them up to cope with the physical discomfort more effectively.

'I won't leave you two on your own again for a while if that helps?' I offered. 'Remember my student, Amy, who you met earlier? She'll be back on the ward soon and hoping that you'll allow her to come in and give you one-to-one care.' Women thrive on continual one-to-one attention from a midwife during labour and midwives and students gain great satisfaction from being able to give this kind of attention to women.

'Great,' Debbie said around the mouthpiece of her gas and air. She wasn't contracting but she wasn't willing to let go of it either. She was going to get a sore jaw at this rate and biting on it was also a focus for her anxieties, which I needed to help her get rid of if at all possible.

'Debbie? Would you like to have a go with the TENS machine now? You can use gas and air with it if you want but I suspect you'll find you don't need as much of it with the TENS.' I went for the option that would give Debbie buttons to fiddle with and a semblance of control over the intensity of the pain she felt.

'Yeth,' Debbie murmured around the plastic between her teeth.

Amy knocked on the door then came in when told to do so.

'Hi, Amy. Debbie is still at four centimetres though she has done a great job of getting her cervix nice and soft. I've had a chat about what steps she can take next as an epidural is not an option. Debbie is going to go for the TENS machine with gas and air as a backup if she needs it to start with.' A firm believer in positive reinforcement, I made sure to say it all in Debbie's earshot while acting as if I was briefing Amy on Debbie's progress.

'Debbie, are you happy for Amy to stay with you and talk you through your contractions while I pop out and find you a TENS machine?' Debbie nodded her consent.

The TENS machine helped Debbie through the next couple of hours of contractions and I didn't need to do an internal examination to tell she was making good progress now; her contractions were closer together and more intense and Debbie was operating the dials on her TENS machine as expertly as if she had been using one for days. The internal examination showed that Debbie was seven centimetres dilated and she was quite rightly thrilled with her progress. Her boyfriend just looked exhausted. The poor man had spent the whole afternoon observing Debbie in pain, unable to make it better for her and without the benefit of all the feel-good endorphins that come with the hard exercise of labour. Right about the time Debbie decided that she might want to try the pethidine injection soon the urge to push came upon her. She was fully dilated and an hour and 20 minutes later Amy had helped Debbie to birth her daughter.

As Debbie nuzzled her lips on the tiny fist which gripped her thumb so tightly, she said, 'I can't believe I did it without an epidural! I said to you I was going to have one straight off when the pains started, didn't I?' She turned to her boyfriend whose eyes still shone with unshed tears though for the right reason this time, I suspected.

'What changed your mind?' I asked.

Debbie thought for a while, gazing at her daughter. 'I'm not entirely sure. I can remember feeling so angry when you told me I hadn't dilated any further but then you started talking to me about it all and reminding me about the different pain relief I could still have and then Amy came in and talked to me in her soft voice through the contractions and, well, everything got easier even though it still hurt like hell, I mean heck! Mummy can't be saying words like that around you now can I, darling?' she said to her daughter then tilted her head to the side to smile at her boyfriend. They talked in soft voices while Amy and I sat in the corner and caught up with writing our notes.

'Ready for your shower now, Debbie?' Amy asked.

'Yes, but before I go can you change her name bands 'cos we've decided on a name?'

'Sure, that will look much better than F.I. for female infant. What name have you chosen for her?'

'Amy after you, Louise after Kevin's sister,' Debbie said and her eyes welled with tears in response to Amy's eyes doing the same.

'Thank you. I am so touched,' Amy said and busied herself with proudly writing out the new hospital bands for her little namesake.

A week later a thank-you card arrived and inside was a photo of Amy with an ear to ear grin holding her teensy namesake which Kevin had taken less than an hour after the birth of his daughter. Some memories stay with you forever and I was certain this would be one of them for Amy and that the time she had devoted to Debbie during her labour would be one that Debbie and Kevin would treasure.

As midwives we can provide care for more than one woman in various stages of labour at the same time safely; we are skilled professionals and have a host of electronic equipment designed to assist us in doing our job. More importantly, many midwives have an instinct for sensing when problems are beginning long before the machines alert them to this fact. However, I feel this is of no emotional benefit to either the woman or the midwife even though I understand that this has become necessary due to the ever-shrinking coffers of the NHS. I fear that it can only end badly if midwives are continued to be pushed to stretch themselves further. Sadly, due to less job satisfaction, more midwives are already considering leaving the profession; skilled midwives who nurture and support the newer qualified practitioners of this ancient profession.

Chapter 28 - 'Flat' baby

As mentioned in the previous story support is vital to help newly qualified midwives gain confidence in using the skills they gained during their training as well as when more obscure incidents occur, such as dealing with a baby who was absolutely fine a moment ago but who suddenly collapses.

There are a lot of one- or two-word expressions that used to be used in midwifery that are vastly descriptive to those of us who use them even though they have absolutely no physical reflection on what we are describing. 'Flat' baby is one of these terms. We don't use it to describe a baby who is actually flat, obviously; instead it is used in reference to a newborn baby who makes minimal or no effort to breathe, is very pale in colour, has a slow or absent heart rate, minimal or absent reflexes and poor muscle tone. As I mentioned in a chapter in the Wisdom section of this book, it can be quite acceptable for a newborn baby to have quite a blue tone to his or her skin immediately after birth, but if a baby comes out looking pale then it is of great concern for the midwife. A pale baby will mean that the midwife begins attempts at rousing the baby immediately instead of giving the baby up to a minute after birth, which is the point at which most newborns sort themselves out and will have figured out how to coordinate all the body functions that they now need to do on their own.

It is unusual (but not unheard of) to have a baby born unexpectedly 'flat', as there are often indications that it is beginning to struggle during the second stage which gives the midwife time to call for a paediatrician to be present at the birth. The paediatrician will stand by ready to whisk the baby over to the resuscitaire and do the necessary techniques required in order to encourage the baby to breathe, develop a more normal hue to its skin and otherwise adapt to being outside its mum's body.

A very fast first and second stage of labour can cause a baby (and the mum) to be very shocked at birth, and sometimes these babies can be momentarily 'flat' but they soon pick up with a bit of brisk rubbing with a towel and some verbal encouragement from mum and dad.

This was the case with Liz and Ben's baby boy, Samuel, who had been born exactly one-and-a-half hours after his mum had her first contraction and no more than 20 minutes after she had arrived on the labour ward. As I hadn't had much time to get details from Liz before the birth, we were chatting as she relaxed, Ben had a cuddle with their new baby and I tidied things up a bit. Liz and Ben already had four children at home and this pregnancy had come as a complete surprise to them both, as Liz had fallen pregnant only a month after the birth of their last baby.

'I hadn't bothered getting back on the pill 'cos I was still breast feeding Maggie. I didn't think you could fall for a baby while still breastfeeding.'

'There has been some research into this and from what I know it seems women have to feed their babies at least every two hours for breastfeeding to be an effective contraceptive. Best stick to using contraception even when you are breastfeeding this one,' I warned.

'Separate beds in separate houses, more like, no need for protection,' Liz said, poking her tongue out at Ben who looked abashed.

'I'll be sure and use protection from now on, learned my lesson this time.' He mumbled the promise in Liz's direction, voice hopeful.

Knowing this was the absolute worst time for them to discuss this issue, I interjected, 'I can imagine it was a bit of a shock when you two found out?'

'I only found out last month! Had no idea, thought my monthlies hadn't come back 'cos of the feeding and hadn't lost the baby weight I put on with Maggie so it wasn't until I fell the hard lump in my tum that I thought I'd best get to the doctor.'

'I thought she was joking when she phoned and said she was having another. I kept waiting for her to tell me what was really wrong with her. Didn't believe it until I saw the face on the scan. The baby was too big to see anything else properly, the scan lady said. Having a son after four girls is the best feeling.'

'He's always wanted a boy,' Liz explained unnecessarily. I could see by her sheer joy when Ben discovered their new baby was a boy and the way he tenderly cuddled his son that he was overjoyed and completely besotted with the new addition to their family.

'You and me, eh, son? Evens the odds up a bit against all those females in our house, don't it?' Ben gave his son a kiss and his wife a wink.

'Yeah, yeah,' Liz said in a mock-weary voice. 'Give him here, I'm ready to feed him and I'm sure he must be ready, big lad that he is.' Perfectly on cue, the baby tired of mouthing his fist and gave a squawk of frustration.

He had been quite 'flat' at birth and because his heart beat had been within normal limits during his rapid delivery, I had put this down to shock caused by the speed of the delivery. It had taken no more than a brisk towelling dry and a bit of oxygen to bring him round and he rewarded us all with several minutes of lusty crying, refusing Liz's offer of her breast and only settling once he was snuggled up to his father's chest. Liz latched her son on expertly and he settled into contented suckling, fist wrapped around her finger.

'I'll go out and start putting your delivery onto the computer. It won't take too long and I'll pop in and check on you as soon as I'm finished. Buzz me if he finishes his feed before that and you're ready for your shower.' I reminded them where the call bell was and left them to some family time.

I updated the sister on the baby's excellent condition as she knew that he had needed minor resuscitation at birth. I had no sooner settled at the computer and logged in than an emergency buzzer sounded. All available staff leap to attention at this sound and I rushed into the corridor to see it was Liz's room at the far end of the ward and broke into a run.

'What's happening?' I asked as I came through the door closely followed by another midwife.

'He let go of my finger so I thought he was just done his feed and gone to sleep. Ben wanted him so I went to pass him over and we noticed that he's gone all white and floppy,' Liz explained in the time it took me to take her son from her and take him to the resuscitaire and begin resuscitating him. I had taken hold of him straight away, as I could see that he was in a state of collapse as soon as I neared the bed.

'I'll get someone to put out a flat baby call. Be right back,' the other midwife said and left to find someone to make an emergency call to the paediatricians.

Collapsing during a feed could mean many things but was likely to be one or two conditions; lots of mucous in his body making it difficult to breathe while feeding which I would have been able to hear before he started his feed, or a hole in his heart which he would be able to cope with until he had the extra burden of having to suck and swallow while coordinating his breathing and heart rate. He came round quite quickly and was busily screaming in an outraged manner when the paediatrician got to the room a few minutes later. Sadly the reason for his collapse was the latter condition and meant that he had to have surgery to correct his condition. He was a lucky baby who was born in the right place for his needs and able to have the surgery he needed to correct it.

In this case the baby doctor was bleeped but when there is a problem with a baby during labour then a doctor specially trained in obstetrics is bleeped. If they aren't on the labour ward when needed then they usually respond by phone or in person very quickly. If they don't do this then it is cause for concern, especially for the doctor's well being if Sister Morgan decides to go looking for the unresponsive doctor as she did in this next story.

Chapter 29 - Where is the doctor?

'Can you bleep Mr Blakeman, please? I need to get back in,' Jan asked me part way through a night shift.

'Sure, what's going on? Jonas still in there?' I frowned. All had been fine in her room when I went for a tea break but something had to be seriously wrong to haul a consultant out of bed and even more so for the registrar to stay in the room while the midwife went out to bleep the consultant.

'There are decelerations on the CTG and I want it reviewed. I bleeped Jonas but he hasn't surfaced. Sister has gone steaming up to the 4th floor to pound on the on-call room door and wake him up. I want to make a point though, by calling Blakie, I mean.' She called out the last sentence over her shoulder as she made her way back into the labour room.

I knew what she meant. Jonas often was slow to respond to his bleep, and although this had been brought to the consultant's attention before, the situation hadn't improved. Therefore the fastest way to drive the message home was to get a consultant to come in during the night to sort a problem that was easily within the capability of a registrar, simply because the registrar wasn't responding to his bleep. No registrar but a problem that still needing resolving gave us the perfect excuse to call the consultant in; we were only doing our jobs after all. Cue innocent looks all round. Decelerations on the CTG meant that the baby's heart rate wasn't behaving normally. The heart rate is not only expected to be within a certain range but also to be variable, meaning that it could drop slightly (decelerate) or accelerate but only within the normal range. A pictorial depiction of what the baby's heart rate is doing can be obtained by using a machine called a CTG which transcribes the heart rate and mother's abdominal activity, picked up through transducers placed on the mother's abdomen, onto a continuous paper print out. This meant that if a doctor was called in then he/she could see what had been happening during the period of time when the midwife had concerns about the heart rate. When the decelerations went out of normal range, whether they went back into normal range or stayed low, it was an occurrence to monitor closely and a doctor was called to review the situation if it didn't resolve spontaneously. Often the problem could be sorted simply by the midwife suggesting that the mum change her position or by the mum suddenly wanting to push. The fact that Jan wanted the doctor to come and review the CTG trace told me that the problem was ongoing despite any manoeuvres and position changes she may have talked the mum into.

Sister Morgan came back onto the ward without Jonas in tow which reminded me that I still had to bleep Mr Blakeman for Jan. I phoned the switchboard and asked them to put me through to his pager because he was offsite. When Mr Blakeman rang the ward in response to my page I explained the situation and he promised to head straight in.

'Shall I page you again if Dr Bolbrin answers his bleep?'

'No need. I need to have a chat with him about this matter and there's no time like the present. See you shortly.'

I made my way around the corner to the room where Jan was keeping a close eye on her woman in labour to let Jan know that Blakie was on his way in and then went off on a search of my own for Jonas.

I knew that he had got very close to a student nurse at the last doctor's mess party and had a sneaking suspicion she might be involved in this disappearance. Jonas couldn't be in the on-call room or Sister Morgan would have sniffed him out. She would have called security to use the master key on the door in order to satisfy herself that Jonas wasn't there before returning to the ward. So, I went to investigate the few places I could think of where Jonas might be. The roof was a favourite place to escape for a break or a smoke on night shift for many years until the no smoking policy on hospital grounds became strictly enforced. I climbed the stairs, enjoying the coolness that was offered by the concrete stairwell. I poked my head out of the door and looked around.

'You seen Jonas recently?' I called to the two figures I could see sitting with their backs against the square structure that housed and kept the computer server cool in the middle of the flat roof.

'He was down in the canteen with Shirley about an hour ago,' one of the Operating Department Assistants answered.

Aha! I thought. Shirley was the nurse who had captured his interest at the party. 'Thanks, if you see him tell him Sister Morgan wants him on the labour ward. Ten minutes ago.'

'He's dead meat,' the ODA said to his companion. I quite agreed.

I went to the staff toilets next, opened the door to the men's and whispered loudly, 'Jonas! You in there?' No response.

The sluice was also empty. I gave up and answered a buzzer from a midwife who needed a couple of extra pillows for her newly delivered woman who was going to have a go at breast feeding for the first time.

I walked along the corridor to the linen room. As I opened the door I heard a scrabbling noise. I flicked the light switch, throwing a glare onto Jonas and Shirley peering out at me from the shelf which ran the length of the room just above the floor. They had made themselves a love nest amongst the clean linen.

'Jonas! You're in the shit with Sister Morgan! Why didn't you answer your bleep? Shirley, what's the matter with you? He's on call, for Christ sake! Sort yourselves out and get onto the labour ward pronto, Jonas. Blakie is on his way in, and more importantly there is a woman in labour with decels who needs you a lot more than you two need each other!' I grabbed the pillows I had come for and shut the door in disgust.

Mr Blakeman was in the labour room when I came back carrying the pillows.

'I found Jonas, he'll be here in a minute,' I said to Sister Morgan as I moved past at a fast pace and through the door of the room where the pillows were awaited. I was eager to avoid her questions about where I had found Jonas and let him sort himself out with Sister Morgan. Mr Blakeman took Jonas off the ward for a chat immediately after the baby of the woman Jan had called him in for had been delivered safely. We all agreed Jonas was lucky to still have a job and whatever Mr Blakeman said to him that night must have made that clear to Jonas, as he was always quick to respond to any bleeps after that. As for Shirley, well that night in the linen room must have been more significant to them than it appeared because they married less than a year after that incident. The last I heard they were living in Zanzibar, still happily married with two children of their own.

Interlude

Perfume Room

Over the years it has been proved time and time again that pregnant women can be quite sensitive to things that wouldn't normally bother them when they are not pregnant. Certain flavours and smells are the worst culprits. A lot of women find they are unable to tolerate the taste of tea or coffee within a few weeks of their pregnancies, sometimes the suddenly metallic flavour of their previously favourite brew is their first hint that they might be pregnant. Caffeine can cross the placenta so I can see why a pregnant body would develop an aversion to the chemical; it is an instinctive way of protecting the new life inside from exposure to too much caffeine. Unfortunately the same thing doesn't happen with alcohol, which seems a shame as it is proved it acts as a toxin, and there has been many a young woman who has gone out to enjoy a heavy weekend of clubbing completely unaware that she is newly pregnant. The smell of dogs can set some women off which can be a real issue if it is her own dogs which are having this affect. Many women begin taking circuitous routes around the supermarkets in order to avoid having to walk past the fish counter; a manoeuvre that I don't have to be pregnant to make a part of my food shopping! Women have told me that they found themselves unable to eat jelly baby sweets anymore, though as this often coincided with their first scan, there may have been a very good reason for this as jelly baby sweets do resemble a fetus in the first trimester of pregnancy if you look at the scan photos with new mum-to-be eyes. Pizza and certain strong-smelling cheeses also come high on the list of reported newly noxious substances.

Alternatively, some women begin to crave sweets where they never had a sweet tooth before. The hormone changes associated with pregnancy mean that some women have to give up using cosmetics or bath products that have served them well for many years. This also means that midwives need to consider carefully which perfume and deodorants they apply when they are getting ready to go in for a day's (or night's) work. However, on this along with many other things, I have had proved time and time again that there are exceptions to every rule.

Hettie Hamway, a much-liked, well-known local poet, was to be one of these exceptions. I had met her and her husband, Steve Tyler, several times during her pregnancy. She wasn't part of my assigned caseload but was part of my community team's caseload. Her named midwife was away a few times a month because she was studying for her degree and so I filled in for her, becoming another midwife who was known to Hettie and Steve. They lived on a house boat and for a while had considered having a homebirth. This concept filled me with fear as even though my father spent his whole life working on boats, I did not inherit his sea legs.

Therefore, I began to feel queasy as soon as I stepped onto their boat each time I had to visit them at home. Looking back I can only remember two occasions during her pregnancy that I had to do a home visit but after their baby was born I ended up making several more trips out there on my postnatal rounds. The house boat was immaculate both inside and out, with lots of highly polished wood on display. I did think it was very clever how everything could be stowed away so neatly and out of sight though it was obviously a necessity due to the limited space. One thing I did really enjoy about my visits to their house boat was the smell. There was always a pleasantly mild aroma of rose reminiscent of the occasional waft a person will encounter while out on a walk through a large garden and I wondered, though never actually asked, if it was a particular brand of room deodoriser or cleaner that they used.

By the time Hettie had reached her due date she was, like most women, thoroughly fed up with being pregnant and ready to do just about anything to get the baby out. Isn't nature clever? Unfortunately for Hettie, her baby was quite comfortable with being inside her and showed no signs of coming out any time soon. At 41 weeks I did a membrane sweep, a process where a gloved finger is used to separate the membranes which are tightly applied to the inside of the cervix. Obviously a mum has to have her cervix dilated enough to allow a finger to be inserted, which Hettie's was and which therefore meant that I could reassure her that her body had begun preparing for labour. A membrane sweep is usually a fast but somewhat uncomfortable procedure, similar to the sensation of having a cervical smear taken. It doesn't always work but for Hettie there was every indication that it would. By the time she left antenatal clinic 20 minutes after the membrane sweep she was already getting some cramping pains. I warned her that these could stop especially if she used a hot water bottle or got in a warm bath. She assured me she had no intention of doing either if there was a chance that it could prevent her from going into labour. We had spent the 20 minutes post membrane sweep going over what to expect from early/latent labour and when she should consider coming into hospital which was where she and Steve had decided to have their baby. They left clinic intending to go for a fish and chip supper and a wander along the seafront. I went home hoping she would get her wish and go into established labour in the night.

My phone rang early the next morning to let me know that Hettie was on her way in. This system was used to ensure that the midwife responsible for the labour care for that woman would come straight into work instead of perhaps stopping off to do a postnatal check or antenatal booking visit on the way in. As lone workers we were supposed to phone in if we were going out on a home visit but in reality that message that we planned to 'just pop in' on someone on the way to work didn't always get to the labour coordinator in a timely fashion by whoever had taken our call. Hence the warning phone call to our homes when we had a labourer on her way in to the unit. When Hettie and Steve arrived I escorted them into their labour room. It overlooked a small courtyard, the walls covered in brightly painted murals courtesy of some of the students of our local art college. Many a woman had spent long hours of her labour standing at the windows and gazing at the scenes depicted on the walls which ranged from the comical viewpoint, the more explicit demonstration of the artist's thought process, to downright abstract displays of pregnancy, childbirth and parenting.

After doing a full set of observations on Hettie and her fetus and orientating Hettie and Steve to the ward, I left them to get settled while I admitted Hettie formally to the ward as she was showing signs of being in established labour. When I returned bearing a tray of tea and toast I immediately recognised the scent in the room.

'I have come to love that smell; it was in the air each time I came to your home. I've got to know, what is it?'

'It's mine and Hettie's favourite fragrance, a simple mix of rose absolute essential oil and water. I've made up a whole bottle of it and topped it up with more water than usual. Hettie wants me to mist her with it during her labour.' Steve held up a large plastic bottle with a spray pump attached.

'I find it soothing and uplifting at the same time, sort of like I am cocooned in the smell,' Hettie said.

'I thought it would be best to dilute a lot more than usual so as not to overpower the room with the smell,' Steve explained.

'Good idea,' I agreed.

'I fear that I am quite addicted.' Hettie laughed.

'I can see why, I've loved the smell since I first encountered it at your house.' I sniffed the softly scented air appreciatively.

I quite agreed with Hettie that the scent made one feel cocooned, in a most pleasant way, I might add. I was delighted when they gifted me with a large bottle of the essential oil as a thank you on the day I discharged them from midwifery care. Once I realised how expensive rose absolute oil is I made sure to use it only sparingly but have continued to love the fragrance ever since they introduced me to it almost 10 years ago.

Mirth

Chapter 30 - A family affair

There are a few common themes that a midwife will encounter on a regular basis during her career and included amongst these are the request to have more than one birth partner or to have children present at the delivery of their sibling. In an earlier chapter I talked about midwives having to manage the room and these are instances where that skill comes in very useful indeed. How many people a midwife feels comfortable with in a delivery room will vary between the individual practitioner as well as the personalities of the people that she is caring for at the time.

I remember well the time when I had a young girl arrive in labour with her boyfriend, father, mother, younger sister and boyfriend's mother in tow. She announced that she wanted them all present at the birth of her baby, and after some discussion with just her and her boyfriend I believed this was a genuine request rather than one she had felt coerced into making. I had met them all during her pregnancy as they had alternately come with her to her clinic appointments and parent craft classes. Elise and Lee were both very close to their families and both families got on well with each other so I wasn't entirely surprised to be faced with this scenario. The labour ward was quite busy on the day Elise came in, in labour, and there was only the smallest room left. The family assembled in the waiting area while I assessed Elise and spoke to her and Lee about their wishes for the labour and birth of their baby. I looked around the small room; Lee was perched on the only chair, Elise cross legged on the bed. I could fit four other people in the room and still have room to work, but only just.

I walked out with Elise and Lee to the waiting room.

'Okay everyone let's have a quick chat before Elise has another contraction.' I only just managed to resist the urge to clap my hands together like a school teacher in a bid to draw their attention away from Elise and to me for a minute. Elise's contractions were still 10 minutes apart but what I had to say might last longer than that and I wanted to be sure we had everything cleared long before Elise went into more frequent contractions.

'So, you all want to be in the room while Elise is in labour and while she is having her baby?'

They nodded and looked at me expectantly.

'There is only a very small room left because the ward is full.' I watched as their faces fell. They looked at each other.

'So,' I continued, 'it will get very hot in there and you will all have to remain pretty much in what ever place you can find in the room.' Their faces brightened.

'No problem, I'm good at holding up walls,' Elise's father said.

'We'll stay out of your way,' promised Elise's sister.

'I'll take one side of the bed and you the other?' Elise's mum asked Lee's mum.

'Oi, don't forget about me,' Lee mock blustered.

'You get the only chair so don't complain,' Elise's sister teased.

'As I should, I'm the daddy!' He flung his skinny chest out and thumped it with his fists as everyone laughed.

'Let's just remember who is going to be doing all the hard work today. I expect you to use that chair to sit in while you peel my grapes and feed me ice slivers. And, as for you lot, get your fans at the ready.' Elise propped her fists on her hips and arched her eyebrows at the assembled family.

'Ooooh, diva alert,' they choroused.

'In all seriousness though everyone, if I ask you to leave I want you to do it without question and in a hurry. I promise I won't ask that of you unless it is very necessary.'

They nodded solemnly. 'Absolutely, we promise,' Elise's father said.

'You're the boss!' Lee said.

Elise whacked him on the shoulder. 'Fail!'

'Eeeep!' Lee said, 'Sorry, my mistake! You're the boss!' He pretended to hide behind the soft drinks machine.

After the laughter died down and everyone settled into a position in the waiting room I said, 'Elise, if you're happy out here then that's the best place for you to be. I'll come out and get you periodically when I need to do observations on you and your baby. If you want me in the meantime then come and find me or send one of your happy helpers.'

It wasn't long from a midwifery perspective before Elise decided that she didn't want to go back out to wandering around the waiting room after I had checked her and her baby's wellbeing by doing a series of observations. They found a comfortable position in the room with Lee sitting on the edge of the bed and Elise standing between his legs, resting her arms on his shoulders and her chin on top of his head.

'I'm going to leave you two alone for a bit. Do you want me to let your family know where you are?'

'Yes, please, can you ask them to come in?' Elise said, after she had finished her contraction.

I escorted the family to the room and left them to settle in while I fetched another jug of water. When I returned I passed the jug to Elise's mother who was on the right-hand side of the bed, next to the bedside table. Lee's mother stood on the left-hand side of the bed behind the chair in which Lee was now sat. Elise's father stood next to the sink in front of the window, his arm around Elise's sister's shoulders. They were silent, watching me.

'What? Elise is supposed to be the centre of attention, not me.'

'We want to know if where we've arranged ourselves is ok with you,' Lee said.

'It is a tight fit, isn't it?' I grinned, trying not to betray the doubt I felt over them all staying in this room until the end.

'Yes, but we're happy if you are,' Elise said

'Well I will need space to work so my trolley needs to go there during the labour.' I indicated the square trolley at the foot of the bed on which I had placed basic equipment such as the spygmanometer, thermometer, fetal heart dopler, a box of gloves and Elise's notes. 'If I need to continuously listen to the baby's heart beat then I will need to bring in a large square machine which will need to go between the bed and bedside locker. When Elise wants something besides her TENS machine for pain relief then the gas and air tube will come out of the wall there and will lie along side the bed. When I get the bigger trolley ready for delivery it will be beside me to my right and no one can touch it, not even to brush past it, so you all need to stay in the positions you are in once Elise begins pushing her baby's head out.'

'Promise,' Lee said. The family looked at Lee and laughed then mimicked his hand, which was positioned in the iconic Scout's Honour gesture.

'I believe you but I still reserve the right to ask everyone except Lee and Elise to leave if the need arises. Can you give me a Scout's Honour on that?' I asked doubtfully.

They could and did. I believed them and did my best to relax into the jovial atmosphere that prevailed. I had never assisted at a labour quite like this one and I did hope that they could maintain this ethos throughout as it really did seem to be keeping Elise calm, relaxed and in control of her labour pains. I busied myself with doing basic observations on Elise and her baby while her family supported her emotionally. We made a good team as it turned out, with Elise needing nothing more than a few puffs of the gas and air near the end of her labour and the family made sure that I had all the room I needed when it came time to assist Elise with the delivery of her baby.

Having good support in labour can do a woman a world of good. Often the focus on the labouring woman is so intense that everyone else in the room is forgotten. Until someone faints, reminding us that sometimes the birth partner needs support, too.

Chapter 31 - Standing room only

Having a supportive birth partner can make a huge difference to how well a woman is able to cope with the pain of her contractions and the length of her labour. Occasionally these supportive partners can suddenly become faint and need to be cared for as well. I have been assigned to the care of far too many women whose birth partners have fainted to now believe that this isn't something that is going to occur more or less on a regular basis. The majority of fainters during the birthing process have been men and the same goes for when blood is being taken as well. More men than women tend to faint then, too. Over the years I have come up with the following non-research based theory: our Western society has placed different behavioural expectations on each gender. Women are stereotypically raised with tenderness, allowed to cry over injuries and losses, and given cuddles and comfort when they do. We try to make it all better for them. Men are raised with firmness, encouraged to be a big boy and not cry too long, if at all, over injuries and losses. We tend to jolly them along when they do cry and try to distract them with jokes and varying litanies of it's over now, let's move along, nothing to see here and similar 'ignore it and it will go away' attitudes.

It is likely that this becomes firmly embedded in their psychological makeup and transferred into their everyday reactions to experiences. They try to be the masters of all during times of crises; the ones who can fix things or make situations better, trying to rescue their damsel in distress who has been raised to believe that it is very ok for her to cry out when scared or in pain. Never mind that the man might also be terrified or struggling to cope with the situation around him, he gets busy trying to be a big boy and trying to make it better for his wife or girlfriend. By doing so he is also working to suppress his fears and anxiety over the situation, usually unsuccessfully, in direct proportion to the amount of failure he feels in relation to not being able to make it better for his wife or girlfriend. He becomes more and more tense, especially if he is present during the labour and birth under duress, until eventually he reaches his point of overload. When this happens his brain forgets to send the blood around his body properly, he stands with his knees locked which means he is doing nothing physically to help his blood flow, which eventually drains away from his brain into the lower parts of his body.

Now the brain is a greedy organ which likes to have the large majority of your blood and when it doesn't get what it wants it tends to throw a hissy fit. This is displayed rather dramatically in the form of a faint. The brain does this so that the blood can flow back to the brain more easily as it doesn't have to climb all the way back up the body; isn't the brain clever? No pun intended. This is why I don't think it is right that men are forced to be at the birth of their child. If they are really not keen on being present during the labour and birth of their child, and brave enough to try and tell their wife or girlfriend so, then this should be taken seriously and an alternative birth partner found.

There is never a good time to faint but a few faints have gone rather spectacularly wrong. Mark fainted shortly after I had cut his baby's cord. He had mentioned that he was a bit squeamish but had been present at the birth of his first three children and although he had felt faint at the time, he had managed to stay conscious. This time, without any warning, he toppled over just as I was about to begin delivering the placenta. I don't know what tipped him over the edge from feeling faint to actually doing it; perhaps I was more explicit than the other midwives.

After the birth I had congratulated them on the successful birth of their baby. Sami, flushed with her recent exertion, proudly held their baby while Mark looked to see what gender it was.

'A girl, Sams! We've got a bubba girl!'

Sami cheered, which made their daughter squawk. This was going to be the last baby for them, even if it was another boy. 'Oh yes, please do, neither of us are keen are we, Mark?' she said, nodding at the cord scissors in my hand.

When I made my first attempt to cut through the cord I found that the scissors were a bit dull.

This wasn't unusual as they were cleaned and sterilised but not sharpened between uses.

'Sometimes we need to have a few goes before we get the cord cut. Your daughter can't feel anything though, so don't worry.' I placed the dull cord scissors back on the delivery trolley and picked up the episiotomy scissors instead. They did the job in one but with an audible snick.

'Ready for this?' I held up the syringe.

'Is that to get my placenta out?'

'Yes. However, you had a lovely normal birth and you are losing very little blood so you can try to do it naturally if you prefer, like we talked about earlier?'

'Like I told you before, no chance, I want it all sorted so I can go for a wash!'

I grinned at Sami. 'Just checking; some mums do change their minds once they are cuddling their baby.'

Shortly after I had given the injection, while checking that Sami's womb had firmly contracted down in response to it, I heard a dull thud. When I looked over to the other side of the bed where Mark had been standing, I noticed he was in a heap on the floor. Luckily he had managed to faint into a clear space on the floor, avoiding any of the assorted furniture and equipment that was scattered about the room. He gave a twitch and moaned.

'What's happened to him? Mark? Mark!' An understandable note of hysteria was audible on the last word.

'I think he's fainted; let's get someone in to take care of him while I deliver this placenta of yours,' I said as I moved Mark into recovery position and Sami pressed the buzzer rapidly three times as asked, a signal that we needed help in the room and fast. Another midwife came in almost immediately and began to attend to Mark. I washed my hands and put new gloves on as I tried to coax Sami into relaxing enough to allow me to deliver her placenta before her womb contracted too tightly and the placenta got stuck inside her.

'Sami, look at me, I need to get your placenta out before you can pay attention to Mark. He's with Tracy and she'll get him sorted out,' I said trying to coax her attention away from her husband and back to the job at hand. I needed her to lie back on the bed instead of trying to hold her daughter safely whilst twisting her head sideways trying to keep an eye on Mark.

'Sami!' I said louder.

She forced herself to tear her eyes away from her husband's body on the floor and looked at me.

'I know you are worried about Mark but I don't have long to get this placenta out before your body won't let me do it anymore so I need you to relax back against the pillows, just for a minute. When you sit up it makes it harder to get it out safely because I can't press on the bottom of your womb as I pull. Why don't you have a little cuddle with your daughter? Count her fingers and toes for me'.

Sami forced herself to relax back against the pillows on her bed and delved into the towels wrapped around her daughter to begin counting.

'Oh!' she said as she felt the placenta fill her then slide out as I worked it out of her body just as Mark said, 'What?! Sams?! What?!' in an outraged tone.

Sami laughed and then choked on a sob as she cradled their daughter and looked at her now conscious husband whose pale face stood out in stark contrast to its frame of jet black hair.

'What do you mean what? We've just had a daughter.'

'Yay team us,' Mark said and laughed where he lay; though he was soon feeling well enough to sit on a chair beside Sami's bed and share some tea and toast with her as they admired the new addition to their family. Their daughter's hair framed her face in much the same way as her father's except she had natural caramel-coloured highlights running through the black. She was a truly beautiful baby.

Another man who fainted didn't have such a lucky escape as he collapsed onto the chest of drawers, hitting his head hard on the way down and landing awkwardly on his wrist. He ended up with a broken wrist, a bruised hip, a sore head and a longer stay in hospital than expected.

Students are also prone to ending up in a faint. This probably has a lot to do with too many late nights and improper nutrition rather than them actually being overcome with squeamishness. I can remember one time when we had two students in theatre. One was a midwife who was observing the consultant performing the surgery and one was a medical student who was spending the day observing midwives and hoping for a normal delivery. It had been a long shift and the woman we had been caring for had come in only a short time before we ended up in the operating theatre so that she could have a category one caesarean section. Unfortunately this also meant she had to have a general anaesthetic so her husband couldn't be present at the birth of her baby and in all senses of the word neither was she, due to the fact that she was unconscious. In the short period of time between when the woman falls unconscious, the anaesthetist gives permission for the surgery to begin and the surgeon hands the baby to the waiting midwife, the medical student who had been standing by the anaesthetist decided to sit down with his back against the wall. Everyone else was occupied with the intense tasks that have to be performed during a caesarean section whereas I was only making notes as the procedure went along so I was the only one to notice the student sitting down.

'Alright?' I crouched down beside him, noting his sweaty forehead and pallor.

'Bit woozy. Thought it might be the sensible thing to do...' and then he went into a faint still sitting upright.

'Can you pass me your spare O2 cylinder please, Jane?'

The anaesthetist looked round, barked out a laugh and passed her small reserve oxygen cylinder and a mask. 'Get that on him, slide him down the wall ' till he's on his side and then leave him because the baby's almost out. I'll keep an eye on him. He'll be fine.'

He was and a good thing too, because an operating room is supposed to be treated as a sealed unit while the surgery is in progress so it would have been an issue if we had had to ask someone to come in to tend to him.

Afterwards the consultant congratulated him for having the good sense to sit down well away from the patient before he went into syncope, while his classmate made fainting motions behind the consultant's back. Good sense or not, I suspected he still would be in for quite a bit of piss-taking for having fainted once word got round the rest of his medical student set.

It isn't unusual for people to twitch slightly just after they faint but it can be quite scary if it is isn't something you have seen before and can make relatives think the person is having a fit rather than the normal reflexive action of someone's body during an episode of syncope. I remember feeling quite horrified the first time I saw a woman do this when I was a student midwife. I was escorting her to have her bloods taken so either I was too junior to have mastered this skill or she was having an obscure test done. As we sat in the waiting room she fainted and began twitching. I asked the other person in the room to go and get help and then it dawned on me: I didn't know how to care for someone having a convulsion, we hadn't been taught that yet. Luckily I wasn't alone with the woman for more than a few seconds and by the time the nurse arrived the twitching had stopped and the woman was beginning to come round from the episode of fainting. After a cool drink, a cool flannel and several minutes with her head resting on a pillow she felt well enough to get up only to promptly faint again. I pointed out the twitching and asked the nurse if the woman was having a convulsion. The nurse uttered a short, quiet laugh and then explained, whilst trying to rouse the woman, that this was reflexive twitching and nothing at all like a convulsion. Since then I have cared for numerous epileptic women and have had several exposures to true convulsions, which made me aware how different a true convulsion is compared to the mild twitching that I had witnessed that day. Anyway, sorry, I seem to have digressed there. What I intended to say was that is why I don't mind more than one birth partner because I think sometimes the birth partner needs a birth partner.

A new baby has a huge impact on the family from the moment of conception. Like the fainting birth partners, the effect isn't always felt until after the birth. In the case of the sibling in the next story the new baby didn't appear to be quite what she was expecting to join the family.

Chapter 32 - Jimmy the piglet

A very timid woman named Marsha Tilley was in room 10 recovering from her emergency caesarean section that she had had the previous day. Caesarean babies are often a bit mucousy for a couple of days after being born as they don't get the benefit of having their chest squeezed during birth by the vaginal walls which helps drain the fluid they have accumulated in their lungs and throat during the pregnancy. During the pregnancy fetuses practice swallowing and breathing and while doing so they draw amniotic fluid into their chest and stomach. A natural birth helps to remove most of this accumulated fluid. Because a caesarean bypasses the vaginal muscles these babies have extra fluid left in their bodies and need to get rid of it by other means, usually sneezing, coughing or bringing it up from their stomach for a couple of days. After handover I went around the ward saying hello to the women I knew from the day before and introducing myself to the ones I did not know. Marsha's son had been a bit grunty that morning and she had asked another midwife about it, who had rightly tried to reassure her that temporary grunting was not unusual for babies born by caesarean and that we would keep an eye on him. This had, in fact, been passed on in handover. This meant that the midwives on duty were aware that up until this point her son had been slightly grunty but otherwise well and that a paediatrician had been asked to check him over during the afternoon rounds. Due to a few unplanned caesareans late that morning, we were still waiting for the paediatrician to be free to come and assess the non-urgent babies on our ward. When I got to Marsha's room she was busy trying to coax her three-year-old daughter to come and have a look at her new little brother.

'Come on, Tillie. Come and say hello. Your brother came specially to meet his big sister.'

Tillie crossed her arms and kicked at the wheel on the opposite side of the bed to where her brother's cot was situated. 'Not a brother,' she muttered.

'What? I thought you did want a brother? Your Suzyanne doll wants to meet Jimmy. Shall I introduce her or are you going to do it?'

'Not a brother. A pig!'

Her dad grasped her under the arms and plonked her firmly in his lap. 'Don't speak to your mother in that tone, missy!' Tears welled in her eyes.

'Come here, poppet.' Marsha beckoned for her husband to shift Tillie around so she could clamber on the bed and snuggle in with her mum. 'You wanted me to get you a pig?'

'No, Mummy. I wanted a brother and you brought a pig.' Tillie made a sound that I presumed was a poor attempt to mimic a pig snorting. The sound was familiar and it took a few seconds for the realisation that she had made a sound like a grunty baby.

'Do you think your brother is a pig because of the sound he is making?' I asked. Tillie nodded. 'I'll check him and make sure he isn't a pig if you help me find out exactly where the sound is coming from.' Tillie was up for the challenge. I explained to Marsha and John that the paediatrician was delayed and why. Marsha was near tears from fretting over what might be wrong with her baby and being told that it could be some time still before the paediatrician arrived was the last thing she wanted to hear.

'But I mentioned that Jimmy was struggling to breathe a couple of hours ago.'

'Why do you think he is struggling to breathe?' I asked, walking over to look at her son in his cot where Tillie was waiting to assist.

'Can't you hear him grunting?' Her voice raised a notch on the last syllable of the final word in the sentence.

I paused, listening to her son breathing. He did sound grunty but not to an alarming degree. What did concern me though, was the fact that I could see his nostrils were flaring, which was an indication that he was struggling more than the grunting would make me suspect. I flicked through the notes to confirm what I knew from handover; Jimmy had not shown any sign of nostril flaring earlier nor had any other abnormal behaviour been noted.

'Can you see his nostrils flaring?' I pointed to the outside of his nostrils in time with his breathing.

'Yes?' Marsha answered hesitantly.

'Yes! Piggy pig, oinky oink,' Tillie declared triumphantly

'What does that mean?' John asked me.

'It can be a sign that he is feeling a bit poorly. Do you mind if I check him over from head to toe?' I asked, washing my hands at the sink in anticipation of her saying I could do so.

'Yes please, I'll feel happier if you do.' Marsha sat on the bed and twisted her hands anxiously. John came to stand at the foot of the bed, boosting Tillie up onto the bed so she could see and would be out of my way.

As I began to undress Jimmy I could feel alarm bells beginning to ring, his skin felt cool to the touch which was unusual for hospital babies as, although newborns do tend to get cold easily, the temperature in the hospital is conducive to keeping the babies warm rather than the adults comfortable. A newborn baby with an infection can suffer a drop in temperature as well as a rise in temperature. I used the room thermometer to check the temperature in Jimmy's armpit – 36.2, lower than usual.

'When was the last time you fed him?'

'Not since just after breakfast this morning. He has been asleep most of the morning and as I was told to be sure I demand fed him, it seemed a shame to wake him.' Marsha looked up at me with a guilty expression on her face.

'Well I am about to strip the rest of his clothes off him to have a look at the colour of his skin and other things so that should wake him up in a hurry.' I smiled reassuringly. We could discuss the importance of regular feeding later, at which point I planned to explain how the term demand feeding didn't really apply to babies who went long periods without food at two days old, when they should be demanding food much more frequently in an attempt to encourage the mother's milk production.

Worryingly Jimmy didn't begin screaming the place down as soon as I had his clothes off his chest exposing his skin to what should have felt like the colder air in the room. In addition his skin was a mottled colour, which is another sign that the baby is cold and likely to be fighting an infection unsuccessfully. I could see his chest sinking in with each inhalation which told me that Jimmy was really struggling to draw in as much air as his body was asking for. I knew he needed to be seen before the paediatrician finished up in the operating theatre.

'Do me a favour and press your buzzer again, Marsha. I'll ask whoever comes to the door to call the newborn unit and ask one of the nurse practitioners to come and have a look at Jimmy for you.'

Marsha pressed the buzzer. 'What do you think is wrong with him?'

'Well he feels a bit cold, which in newborns can mean he has an infection, and that combined with his flaring nostrils tells me he might need to have some blood tests and maybe some antibiotics to help him get better.'

While we waited for the nurse practitioner to arrive I helped Marsha tuck Jimmy inside the front of her pyjamas with blankets covering his back and head. His bare skin in direct contact with his mum's was one of the fastest ways I knew of to help raise his temperature besides getting some breast milk inside him. Although feeding worked best for raising a baby's temperature fast, Jimmy was showing no signs of wanting a feed at the moment.

'Has anyone shown you how to hand express yet?'

'Yes, shall I try that now?'

'Please do, the smell may help him remember how much he enjoys a nice warm feed inside him.'

Marsha squeezed a few drops out of each breast and rubbed this on Jimmy's lips, smiling as she watched his little tongue poke out to lick the liquid off. She repeated this process until the nurse arrived to check Jimmy over.

Lifting the blankets to have a closer look, she managed to see enough of Jimmy's condition to concern her without having to remove him from his warm cuddle.

'Would you mind if I took his internal temperature?' she asked Marsha

'Sure, do anything you need to; is that the one that goes up his bum?' Nowadays we have thermometers which measure the core temperature from the tympanic membrane inside the ear but back then the core temperature could only be taken on a baby via the rectal route.

'Yes, are you ok to keep him cuddled up to you or would you prefer I took him to his cot to do it?'

'I'll keep him with me, he'll be less scared that way, won't he?' Her eyes pleaded for a positive response.

'No one has ever been able to ask a baby but we're pretty sure that is what they think!' She smiled and set to work undoing his nappy then opened it cautiously until she was sure that it was clean.

Tillie edged closer to her mum until she was cuddled up to her other side. Marsha wrapped her free arm around Tillie. 'Don't fidget, remember my sore tummy.' Tillie nodded, sucking her thumb vigorously.

'Your legs feel a bit cold young man.' The nurse mock chided Jimmy as he lay on his mum's chest with a faint pink beginning to shade the side of his face that wasn't against his mum's skin. This could mean he was warming up and I hoped it was so but the thermometer told a different story when the nurse removed it from his body. Jimmy's core temperature was only 36 degrees.

'His temperature is lower than it should be and he is acting as if he has an infection so I'd like to take a blood test from him to check his blood sugar level and also some to be sent off to the lab so we can see what kind of infection he has. The other thing that I think would be best to do would be to take him to the newborn unit so he can warm up in an incubator. Is there anything you would like to ask me before I go get the incubator?'

Marsha shook her head, tears silently slipping down her cheeks and onto her son. He made a fast recovery with the help of a course of antibiotics though he did end up with mouth thrush, the poor boy. Although he will remember none of the trauma of his early days I suspect Marsha will never manage to completely forget the experience, no matter how much she might like to.

I was working on the ward the day that Marsha and Jimmy were discharged home. I went to say goodbye to them all at the ward door. Tillie dropped her dad's hand and ran over to meet me.

'He's not a pig, my brother,' she said, tugging at my hand in excitement.

'Oh, that's a relief!' I exclaimed.

'He a piglet! Baby pigs are called piglets.' She skipped over to her mum and dad.

Marsha laughed. 'She knows her own mind and won't be told otherwise. At least she has come round to the concept of having a pig for a brother.'

'Piglet!' Tillie said, clearly fed up with having to remind them. She peered into the car seat in which her father was carrying her brother and made soft sounds at him. Jimmy slept on oblivious.

John rolled his eyes. 'She's going to be a nightmare when she's a teenager,' he muttered, then smoothed Tillie's hair before saying, 'Come on, let's get your brother home so you can show him around his room and show him around your big-girl room.'

Chapter 33 - The funny side of sleep deprivation

Out of the many families that I have visited at home over the years there are a few that are at the forefront of my memory for various reasons; not all of them good. There was one family in particular that I looked forward to visiting because, although beset by mishaps during those first few sleep-deprived weeks, they managed to keep their sense of humour about it all.

With their first child their sleep deprivation had been compounded by the fact that they were having to fit in time travelling back and forth to the newborn intensive care unit which was where their son spent the first few weeks of his life as he was premature, along with spending much of the night awake and fretting because they couldn't spend the night with their son. I would meet the mother on the newborn unit and do her postnatal check in a spare room that was used for parents when they were getting ready to take their baby home with them. The room allowed parents to sleep in the unit with their baby beside them when they approached time for their baby to be discharged home so that they could adjust to providing all the care their child needed 24 hours a day – and would need at home – which included oxygen therapy or tube feeding for some of these children. One day I went over to the newborn unit to do Clare's check and found that Clare had only just arrived on the unit herself. This was unusual because she normally got there just after staff changeover which had taken place a couple of hours ago.

'Hi, Clare, you look stressed, everything ok?' Clare's cheeks were flushed and she was blowing a wisp of hair out of her eyes repeatedly instead of adjusting her hair grip while she rushed about gathering the items she would need to change her son's nappy in his incubator.

Clare laughed and shook her head then clucked her tongue in annoyance at herself for forgetting to wash her hands. 'I'd forget my head if it wasn't screwed on,' she said over her shoulder to me.

'Lack of sleep is a terrible thing for new parents. Unscrewed on heads left forgotten all over the place...very untidy...' I said gravely.

Clare threw her head back as she laughed. 'I'll say, just wait 'till you hear what I did this morning!' She paused as she concentrated on changing Ethan's nappy. Once she had finished and settled in a rocking chair with Ethan nestled under her shirt for some therapeutic skin to skin contact Clare looked at me and said, 'So anyway, wanna know why I got here so late this morning?'

'Yes, that's not at all like you. Did you indulge yourself in a bit of a lie-in?'

'No chance. I don't do lie-ins. I got up with Mick as usual even though he says I'm a nutter for doing so. I like to see him off though and then express off some fresh milk to bring in with me.'

I nodded. Although Ethan was only eight days old Clare had already got herself into a habit of coming with the milk she had expressed off before bed and first thing in the morning.

'So this morning I had the bags of milk ready, my lunch, some clean clothes for Ethan in my day bag...not that he wears them for long at the moment what with the incubator and all but he'll be in a cot soon and anyway it makes me feel like a proper mum to sort his clothes for the day. I tie-dyed this when I was pregnant, bit big for him still but at the rate he's putting on weight it won't be long before he's outgrown it.' She paused to catch her breath and leaned sideways just far enough to pull her day bag onto her lap without unsettling Ethan. Rummaging around she pulled out a parcel wrapped in tissue paper. Inside was a miniature, rainbow-coloured sleep suit. I made appreciative noises about the sleep suit as I made a mental note to discuss the 'proper mum' comment with Clare later and to make sure she didn't have any concerns about her ability to care for Ethan.

'I also had the glass recycling with me to drop off when I do the food shop during quiet time this afternoon.' Quiet time was when the unit closed to everyone except the staff. It was a good way of encouraging parents to get some rest but, as in Clare's case, didn't always work like that as she used the time to do outstanding chores. Mick had decided to defer his planned time off until Ethan came home, which left Clare with empty time to fill during the early afternoon of each weekday.

'You really should use that time to rest in, at least once in a while. You want to make sure that you've got plenty of energy for when Ethan comes home,' I advised.

'Sure, maybe tomorrow,' Clare said, unashamedly dismissing my advice. 'So, I carry the recycling out to the car, bung it in the boot and drive off. It wasn't until I got to the hospital that I realised that I had forgotten everything else!' Clare laughed. 'Back home I went, grabbed everything else, popped the milk on top of the car while I got the other stuff propped up in the foot well so it wouldn't fall over and drove off with the milk still on the car roof!'

'I assume it wasn't still on the roof when you got here?'

'Nope, I should be wearing a "Caution New Mum" badge. Or have a minder. Honestly, where was my head at? Good thing there is plenty more where that came from but life will be a whole lot simpler once you're home, sweetie,' she said to Ethan as he yawned in contentment from his snug position against her chest.

When Clare and Mick had their second child it was a completely different experience for them which ended with a healthy, full-term delivery and prompt discharge home the next day. I went to do a postnatal check on Clare and Abigail the afternoon of the following day. Clare greeted me at the door with an armful of baby and a wailing Ethan clinging to her leg. She managed a smirk and a roll of her eyes in my direction as she crab walked away from the door to let me in, Ethan still clinging to her leg, traces of white visible on his cheek around the edges of his ears and on his forehead near the hairline.

'Ethan, there's no point crying. The talc is not a toy and that's the end of it.'

'Talc baby Bobby!' Ethan wailed louder.

'Not that there is any left. I'll show you why in a sec,' she said to me as I passed her on my way into the family sitting room to the left of her front door. She popped a sleeping Abigail in her Moses basket. 'Cuppa or show and tell first?'

'Oh show and tell definitely,' I said intrigued. 'Who is baby Bobby?' I asked.

'His doll baby. Right, Ethan? Your talcy baby Bobby.'

'Yeth, Bobby nappy!' Ethan said agreeably, earlier angst forgotten.

'Uh oh...' I said getting an inkling of what might have happened. I followed them up to Ethan's bed room.

'Tah dah!' Clare said throwing open the door and holding Ethan back. The room was white, every surface covered in a coating of talcum powder. 'I asked Ethan to play in his room while I went to the loo and when I got back I found this! He had decided to put a nappy on Bobby, hence the talc. Thank goodness Abigail was in the bathroom with me. I thought it would be easier to lie her on the bathmat instead of her starting to cry while I was on the loo and feeling frantic 'cos

I couldn't get to her. It never occurred to me that something like this could happen!'

'I think baby Bobby might like it better if you only put a tiny bit of talc on him next time,' I said to Ethan. He nodded solemnly. 'From an empty talc bottle perhaps,' I said *sotto voice* to Clare, who winked in response.

Clare shut the door to Ethan's room again. 'No,' she said firmly to Ethan who squirmed to go in. 'You can go in there once Daddy has cleaned it up.'

'Where is Mick?'

'He had to go into work for a couple of hours to hand over to the duty manager before he starts his paternity leave. Luckily he should be home shortly. As you can see, I definitely need him home for a while.' She laughed and tousled Ethan's still damp hair. 'You're a handful, aren't you? Come on then, help Mummy down the stairs, there's a good boy.'

Ethan held onto the banister with one hand and went down one step ahead of Clare, holding onto her hand as he coached her down the stairs. 'Next step, Mummy, caaaarefull, well done, next step, Mummy, gooood job, go slow, that's it.' Clare sniggered quietly as she followed Ethan's lead.

'Hello!' Mick bellowed as he came in the front door.

'Daddy!' shrieked Ethan instantly forgetting all about Clare as soon as he heard his dad's voice.

We watched as he ran down the long corridor to the front door where Mick swept him up for a hug. 'How's my big boy? Look what your silly daddy's gone and done!' he said, pointing at his shoes. On each foot was an entirely different shoe to the one on the other foot. On his left he wore a white-and-blue trainer and on his right he wore a black lace-up brogue. We all laughed but Clare ended up with tears of mirth rolling down her cheeks.

'I don't know why I'm laughing; I can't imagine what kind of state I'd be in if I had to get myself together enough to leave the house first thing this morning since madam Abigail kept us up most of the night. I expect I'd have gone out in my slippers but, oh Mick, you must have been so embarrassed when you noticed!'

'I didn't notice until I tripped on the front path just now. I'll never be able to show my face in public again.'

'If no one said anything to you then I would guess it's probably safe to assume that no one noticed.'

'Ah, good thing too as I'll need to keep working to keep that one in all the pretty clothes Clare has her eye on.'

'You'll also need a special fund for talcum powder,' Clare said enigmatically.

Mick looked puzzled then said, 'I don't think I want to know why.'

'Too late!' Clare laughed as Ethan began to drag his dad towards his room shouting, 'Baby Bobby nappy!'

'I'm scared, save meeeeeee,' Mick pleaded to no one in particular as he disappeared up the stairs.

Clare's good-natured attitude seemed to be the standard for both her and Mick; laughing at life rather than letting the occasional foible get them down. An excellent way to live and if their positive outlook could have been bottled for sale then I would have been first in the queue to purchase some.

Chapter 34 - Down the pan

Rebecca Garret bounced gently a couple of times on the edge of the bed and smiled at her husband, shoulders raised in glee.

He smiled back. 'You won't get our kiddo out that easy.' He looked around the room. 'There sports channels on that?' he said to me, indicating the hospital TV mounted on its wall bracket.

'I very much doubt it comes as standard, but you may be able to order it special.'

'Oi!' Rebecca thumped Jim on the knee. 'There'll be none of that; you'll be too busy taking care of me.'

'Pish, you'll be days yet and Wimbledon's on.' His eyes crinkled as he teased her. '

'Shhhhh! You'll bore the kiddo into staying in here.'

'Kiddo! Sweeties, toys, your own room! Come and get them!'

'Hospital radio for you it is then!' I said, pretending to reach over and to turn it on.

'No, miss, please, anything but that!' he said to me.

Rebecca pretended to write a note. 'Watch Eastenders omnibus,' she murmured loudly enough to be clearly audible.

'Soooooo, rapidly changing the subject, how long until Rebecca gets induced?' Jim asked me in a successful attempt to draw Rebecca's attention away from soap operas and back to the reason why they were on the ward in the first place.

'Well almost straight away once I've admitted you to the ward, which won't take me long at all. While I'm off doing that, Rebecca can you get yourself settled in, go for a wee and a freshen up if you want.' I showed her where the bathroom was and left them to get on with things while I got her admitted on the electronic patient system and gathered up the equipment I would need to induce her.

Maternity units have differing policies on most procedures and induction of labour is no different. Some units induce women on the labour ward, some in the day assessment unit and some on the antenatal wards. The form that the prostaglandin used to induce labour is administered in also differs with some units preferring the gel over the pessary. The effects the prostaglandin can have on women are varied from little or no effect to dramatic results. This particular unit favoured the gel and inductions were started off on the labour ward for women who had already delivered one child or more and on the antenatal ward if they were first timers. Rebecca was a first-time mum, 12 days overdue despite eagerly trying out every natural induction method her community midwife had recommended and more besides if Jim was to be believed.

'That curry last night might have been a mistake; she's been several times already today,' he confided in me when I came back in to find that Rebecca was in still in the bath.

'Been to have a bath?' I asked.

'No, you know, been to the loo for a number two.' His cheeks flushed like a school boy who had been caught out by the headmistress after uttering a forbidden word.

'Oh, well that can be a good sign as long as she isn't feeling ill with it or having pains from it,' I tried to reassure.

'She says she feels fine and I'm sure if she had anything even remotely resembling a twinge in her belly she'd let me know. She's desperate for our little pickle to come out.'

'I'm not surprised she's fed up with being pregnant. Nature is very clever that way, most women are willing to put up with labour if it means the end of their pregnancy. A baby is just like a trophy at the end of all that hard work.'

Before I inserted the gel behind Rebecca's cervix I did routine observations on her and her baby to make sure they were both fine and ready to carry on. I spent several minutes with the palm of my hand resting on her belly to check whether she was having any contractions that she might somehow have missed. She wasn't and hadn't.

'Oooh your hand is lovely and cool,' Rebecca said happily. 'Think I might have had the bath water a bit too hot.'

'Your temperature was normal when I took it. Want Jim to open the window?'

'Yes, please!'

Jim rushed to comply and the room filled with the freshness of the air awash with the sound of gentle rain pattering against the ground. 'Anything else I can do for either of you? No? Shame. I thought you might need me to look for the sports station.' He sidestepped Rebecca's attempted hand swat.

Once I had inserted the gel and satisfied myself that nothing unusual was happening on the print out from the machine that continuously monitored Rebecca's abdomen for signs of contractions and their baby's heart rate I left to fetch them tea and toast.

'Oh, lovely, thanks,' Rebecca said, boosting herself higher up against the pillows stacked on the head of the bed. 'Ooooh!' she said and pressed against her abdomen just above her pubic bone.

'Pain?' I asked as I checked the print out. There were a couple of small bumps showing that had happened during the time when I had been out of the room with another being recorded right now.

'Sort of...not really pain, more like periody type niggles.' Rebecca sipped her tea appreciatively.

'This may be the prostin pains that I told you about earlier. The monitor has to stay on for the full hour and you've got a good 40 minutes to go still so we'll have a better picture of how your body and your baby are reacting to the prostin once that hour is up.'

I stayed and chatted with them, laughing at Jim and Rebecca's banter as they told each other jokes, trying to outdo each other until they ended up laughing hysterically, only needing to look at each other to go off into gales of laughter once again. Rebecca's pains were still there, showing as regular bumps on the monitor and able to be felt by hand. Jim's eyes widened with amazement when he felt the first one.

'I can't believe you're so calm! It feels like a sheet of metal.' Jim gazed at his wife in awe.

'Years of practise coping with periods, I guess. Hardly hurts more than that really.' Rebecca shrugged. 'Fed up with this thing though,' she said, indicating the straps around her belly which held the transducers against her skin.

'I could do with a walk about,' Jim said.

'Me, too.'

'Won't be long before you can come off the monitor for a bit. Your baby is quite happy.'

'Not too happy, I hope. I want you out, kiddo!' she said sternly to her belly. 'So, am I in labour now then?'

'If those pains carry on, then yes you are. They may still die off, but going for a wander around is a good way to help things progress.'

Once I had separated Rebecca from the monitor she breathed a sigh of relief and rubbed her belly through her dress. 'Glad that's off. I've got the fidgets, you ready to go for a wander?' she asked Jim.

He was. I reminded them of where to find the day room and they set off, agreeing to return in time for the next set of observations. I was at the far end of the ward answering the door when I heard a shriek and the emergency buzzer sounded, the flashing light over Rebecca's room door indicating where it was coming from.

'Excuse me,' I said to the person at the door and left them standing outside the locked ward. The person could wait, an emergency buzzer could not.

I ran into Rebecca's room which was empty but the toilet door was part way open and I could hear voices coming from inside.

'Careful, don't drop him!' I distinctly heard Rebecca say followed by the unmistakable sound of a newborn baby's cry.

'Goodness! What happened?' I said as I looked around the door where I caught sight of Rebecca standing over the toilet holding her dress out of the way and Jim standing with his hands grasping a crying infant under the arms and around the chest.

'I thought I needed another poo and out he came!'

I grabbed the hand towel Rebecca had placed on the sink and wrapped it around their baby so that I could get a firm grip on it. He squawked as I took him from his dad, blinking in the bright light.

'Hello, kiddo. In a rush were you?' I said as Jim helped Rebecca walk on shaky legs while I carried their baby who was still attached to his mum, making the manoeuvre out the bathroom door slightly tricky.

'Could you get me a delivery pack please and ask a paed to stand by?' I said to the other midwife who had come to see why I hadn't turned the emergency buzzer off.

Jim and I got Rebecca settled onto the bed, baby cradled against her bare skin, towel and blankets covering them both.

'Did he fall into the toilet when he came out?'

'I stood up when I felt him coming out and Jim caught him by the chest and arm.'

'His feet slipped into the water, that's when he started crying,' Jim said guiltily.

'You did wonderfully well to catch him, Jim. A bit of cold water on his feet won't have done him any harm but the baby doctor will be on his way so you'll be able to have him confirm that.'

'I can't believe I had him so fast,' Rebecca gasped as she lifted the towel as if to check that she really was holding a baby.

'Neither can I,' I admitted. I had heard of women who reacted this way to prostaglandins but never without warning after the initial post-induction monitoring had been completed.

'I think we should call him Peter,' Jim said, seemingly at random.

'Peter? Why?'

'Pan. Peter Pan!' Jim said with a smirk.

'Oh, you!' Rebecca rolled her eyes at Jim. 'He's going to take the micky out of your forever about this you know...' she cooed at Peter.

'Too right,' Jim said. 'And so will you once you recover from the shock enough to see the humour in it.'

Neither Rebecca nor her son suffered any ill effects from their ordeal, but I insisted that many women use bed pans during the time it took me to stop expecting every woman I induced from then on to do exactly the same thing as Rebecca had done.

Snippets from my soapbox

Hydrotherapy and other natural methods of pain relief

Everyone has a different pain threshold but many women labour with relatively little pain relief in England. Partly because labour is a 'natural' pain, meaning the body hasn't been broken in an accident but instead is doing what it is built to do. However, natural or not, labour is still hard work and still painful. So, most women use some form of pain relief to support them through the labour and birthing process although this can take a surprising variety of forms, some of which I wouldn't have thought of as pain relief and some which I would never have believed could be so effective before I saw women put them to use.

I'm sure most of you will have heard the term water birth or even know of someone who has used this during their labour or delivery. When I first qualified as a midwife the concept of a woman labouring underwater, never mind delivering a baby underwater, was still quite a radical option and not one that many midwives were qualified to perform. And although I am a big fan of assisting at water births I think that the person who first supported a woman in her wish to actually deliver her baby underwater was a very brave midwife indeed. Nowadays many midwives are trained and confident to support women in having a water labour and or birth, and more maternity units are offering the option of hydrotherapy in labour to suitable women. Most women will have been advised to try warm/hot water for pain relief of period cramps at some point in their life and therefore will know whether this has been of any help to them in the past. The labour/birthing pools used in maternity care are much deeper than a normal household bath, about the depth of a Jacuzzi tub. This adds an anti-gravitational effect to the soothing qualities of the warm water. For any woman who is considering this as an option I always recommend it because it is completely reversible, so if she does not like it she can get out and try something else. The added buoyancy of the water makes it much easier for her to change positions as well. Additionally, she can use alternative pain relief methods in conjunction with immersion in the birthing pool such as gas and air, massage and breathing.

Okay, okay, I know we all have to breathe. I am talking about structured, controlled breathing in this instance. Let me explain… As the contraction begins to build the woman should try to inhale slowly and deeply through her nose, concentrating on how the breath feels as it passes down through her throat. Then I advise her to gently plug her ears with the respective index fingers and close her eyes before exhaling slowly to produce a long and continuous humming sound. She should repeat this as often as required. I can't take credit for thinking up this method because I first saw it used by a labouring woman many years ago and realised that her breathing technique was quite effective because it served to distract her from the pain of her contractions but also had the added benefit of getting a good flow of oxygen to those hard-working muscles. Other alternative pain relief techniques that I have seen women successfully use over the years include: visualisation (you are ambling along a sandy beach, in a meadow, etc), affirmation (your body is strong, is working well for you, knows what it is doing, etc), conscious relaxation of tense muscles, non-focused awareness (notice what you see, hear, feel, smell and then forget about it, move onto the next sensation), vocalising (moaning, making single sounds like 'oh, oh', groaning), singing or prayer.

I mentioned that hydrotherapy in labour was useful because it made it easier for the woman to change position during labour. Moving around during labour is often a great help to women. Changing position and the ability to wander around to some extent during labour, even if only to change your position from sitting to standing to kneeling on all fours, can help to ease the fetus deeper into the pelvic outlet, the start of the birth canal. Walking up and down stairs or stepping on and off a step in a sideways movement is thought to also help shift the fetus deeper into the pelvic outlet, but also goes a long way towards giving the woman something to do during the pain of the contraction; she is up and able to move if she wishes to instead of feeling trapped in one position.

Over the years I have seen several women use self-hypnosis during labour and delivery. It worked very well for a lot of them and for a few it had absolutely no effect that I could discern. I have come to the conclusion that hypnosis is just a fancy term for being really relaxed, and for really focusing in on just one thing, while everything else fades into the background. As far as I have been able to figure out, hypnosis is all about the mind's ability to affect the body's reactions. So self-hypnosis is nothing more than a state of deep relaxation, where the mum remains fully alert and fully in control of what she is doing throughout her labour and delivery. Hypnotherapists may disagree with me on this point though as I'm only guessing, having only seen hypnotherapy used during the labour and birthing process. Regardless of what hypnosis actually is, it is proving increasingly popular, and some small pieces of research have demonstrated that it can make a difference to birth outcome and to maternal satisfaction. Now if we could package that and sell it for the masses then there would be very little need for manmade chemical forms of pain relief with all the nasty side effects. Though obviously there are times when hypnotherapy is not advisable, such as when driving a car, so the option of different forms of pain relief is here to stay.

Massage is a good technique to use during labour as long as the woman is open to the idea of being touched, and it is one which others can do to help which is always a good thing for the birthing partner who otherwise sits beside the labouring woman fretting that they can't do anything to help. It can be especially beneficial for women who are unable to change positions easily, say for example if they have opted to have an epidural. In these cases massage may help prevent muscles stiffening up and the discomfort associated with this. However, massage does not work for every woman and I always advise women to experiment with massage during their pregnancy to find what pressure she can tolerate and which parts of her body she prefers to have massaged. Some women find even gentle massage too uncomfortable and labour is not the right time to discover this, though it has happened countless times and I have always felt sorry for the birth partner who has to endure the backlash when it does happen. Some women really abhor massage and in these cases there are some similar techniques which work in much the same way as massage but without the rubbing sensation that winds some women up: hot compresses such as a flannel or hot water bottle placed on the back or wherever else she feels the pain is particularly intense, or ice packs used in the same way, a warm blanket over the woman's entire body or a lengthy warm shower where she takes the shower head off the wall and directs the spray to precisely the area she needs it most.

I used to work in one unit where the consultants would refer women to one of the antenatal clinic midwives who was trained in using reflexology whenever they had a woman who needed to be induced. This midwife focused her technique on a certain part of the woman's feet and averaged a 50% success rate, which is pretty good going and well worth a try before admitting a woman to the labour ward and putting chemicals into her body, which is the medicalised version of induction. The one pain relief technique that I have seen used by a few women, and the one which completely baffles me, is acupressure, which seems a shortened form of reflexology. It seems to work by the woman or her birth partner pressing firmly on certain parts of the woman's body to provide pain relief. I can only assume it works by somehow interrupting the pain signals as they travel along the body but I do wonder if these women would have laboured equally well without any technique at all. However, if they believe it works for them and that belief provides them with pain relief then it's a good job done well, regardless, isn't it? The mind is connected to the body after all...

Is breast really best?

This is a topic of great controversy and ongoing debate. I would have to say that unless you are a severely immunocompromised woman with a blood-borne virus such as HIV or on medication that passes into breast milk then, yes breast milk really is the best food for your baby. Additionally, in countries where sanitation and water hygiene isn't as good as ours, and where the risk of gastrointestinal illnesses due to contaminated water outweigh the risk of all else, then breast feeding, even for women with high viral load HIV, is the best food they can offer their baby. The one irrefutable fact is this: the woman's body grew that baby so therefore it must know exactly what that baby needs in the way of food, and certainly it is going to know better what kind of food that individual baby needs than a baby formula manufacturer. However, although breast milk is the *best food* for babies, breastfeeding is not always the *best option* for all women. Some women are not able to breastfeed for medical, physical or psychological reasons. Some women choose not to breastfeed for other reasons.

I think there are a couple of main reasons in relation to these women making that decision. The first is that it is no longer an expectation of modern society and we have generations of women growing up without seeing a baby being breast-fed. This is then passed onto the next generation, who think that offering a bottle full of generic formula to their baby is the norm. Secondly, breasts, unlike the hidden womb, have become highly sexualised objects which are displayed like trophies to varying degrees from almost every form of media that we connect with. If society could come to terms with the fact that breasts are not only sexual objects but also have another purpose, then I think the breast-feeding issue would be largely resolved. Until that time women who chose to breast-feed will struggle to do so openly without coming under criticism from total strangers whether by word or stern look. These women also have to defend their decision to assorted family members who bottle fed their children and look upon the decision to breast feed as a personal rejection of their ideals. It is not, of course; it is simply the decision of a new parent trying to make one of many hard choices about what is best for their child.

Maternity and children's services are doing their best to support women with their feeding choice although there is a strong focus on breast-feeding with many hospitals attempting to gain 'Baby Friendly' status. This accolade directly reflects the number of women who leave hospital breast-feeding their baby, amongst other standards. It even goes so far as to look at what the education provision is in relation to the physiology of the breast, the psychological aspects of breast feeding and how students are taught to teach women how to breast feed and their support of breast-feeding women. This has led to formal breast-feeding support training being given to midwives and being part of the midwifery education curriculum for student midwives.

I think the education of staff and students is vital in helping women to make the right feeding choices for their baby, whichever that may be. However, if we are not trained properly then we run the risk of giving women the wrong information, or giving it in the wrong way and may end up putting women off breast feeding because they feel pressurised to do something they are not at all comfortable with. Women who breast-feed under duress are rarely going to continue on to make a success of it and will often endure a week or two of angst before giving up and feeling a failure. No woman should ever have to feel like this about motherhood and it is important that midwives have the right tools to support women during this period. One of the best tools midwives can offer women is their time, but sadly this is fast becoming one of the rarest commodities in maternity services.

So, will breast-feeding ever become an acceptable norm? Yes, but it will be a slow process because until we have had enough women successfully feeding their babies and confident enough to support their friends and family in doing so for their own babies, it will remain down to midwives to provide this support as and when their work demands slow down enough to afford them the luxury of the time newly breast-feeding babies and women need. Additionally there are also those women who make an informed choice to feed their babies formula as well as the few women who are physically unable to breast feed and therefore have no other option. These people need as much support as women who breast-feed because making up bottles is an additional demand on their time on top of feeding their baby. The midwife needs to assure herself that the parents understand how to safely sterilise the bottle-feeding equipment and how to make and heat up the bottles safely.

Don't touch the placenta!

The one instance where a placenta needs to be delivered almost immediately after the baby is born is if the woman is experiencing heavy sustained blood loss. Then it is important to get the placenta delivered so that the uterus has a chance to clamp down and naturally cut off all those bleeding points under the placenta. When midwives or obstetricians deliver the placenta an injection is given to encourage the uterus to contract and sheer the placenta off the uterine walls. Once the uterus is a nice firm shape, pressure is then placed against the uterus to hold it in place while the placenta is pulled out; if this is not done exactly right then there is a risk the uterus can prolapse – to be pulled out of the pelvis and into the vagina. No traction should ever be applied to the cord if the injection has not been given and if the uterus is not being held in place once the injection has worked. If the woman has an acceptable amount of blood loss after delivery and wishes to be left to deliver her placenta naturally then the cord should not be pulled. If this occurs it will send signals to the uterus which can confuse it causing it to relax at best and at worst can cause the placenta to detach partly. Should this happen then it may leave a big bleeding point open because the placenta is still attached to the rest of the uterus which will keep it from clamping down and closing that bleeding point off. The great difficulty is how to judge blood loss effectively. Women naturally bleed after they have given birth, some more than others but they can still be within normal limits, and when the uterus clamps down and sheers the placenta off there is often a big gush of blood. Newly delivered woman can safely lose more blood than any other type of patient due to their increased plasma volume which can be frightening for students but this is a normal physiological process. Once the baby has been born the extra plasma volume is no longer required and therefore it makes sense for the woman's body to dispose of it immediately in the fastest way possible.

Visiting hours

Is the hospital postnatal ward really the place to have visitors? I think not. If a woman is well and rested enough to focus on her visitors then the hospital isn't the place for her. A hospital is a place for sick people on the whole or, in the case of most women in postnatal wards on maternity units, the place for new families to get to grips with everything they need to know how to do as new parents. If you are in hospital only short term then your visitors should wait until you are settled in at home before descending upon you. If you are in a four-bedded ward then your visitors may arrive while one of the other women is trying to catch up on much-needed sleep, which will be nigh on impossible if there are visitors at another bed making a fuss over the woman and baby. If you are in the hospital postnatally for longer periods of time then you or your baby are ill and your visiting should be restricted to the birth partner only so that you can have the time you need to rest and heal.

The 12-month pregnancy

So you've decided you want to have a baby? Congratulations, you have taken the first step towards becoming a parent. As a midwife I am all too frequently reminded that many people put more effort into planning a holiday than they do into organising one of the most important events of their lives. Your body is going to be your baby's home for the duration of your pregnancy and by making sure you make your pregnancy part of a 12-month process then you have recognised the need to make it the best you can offer to your unborn child. The better prepared you are, the better you will cope with this major life change, both physically and emotionally.

At least 12 months before you begin trying to conceive a baby, you should stop smoking, drink in moderation only and increase your exercise by at least walking or cycling on a daily basis. Try to do this instead of driving to and from work or a friend's house or the shops. Exercise helps your body do everything more efficiently. When you exercise, your body digests food better (helping you on your way to maintaining a more healthy weight), your sleep patterns are more restorative, and your mood is elevated in comparison to when your body receives no exercise.

If you are using oral contraception then you should stop taking this and begin using another form of contraception at least six months before you begin trying to conceive. It is also sensible to consider taking 400 micrograms of folic acid (0.4mg) each day, even though you won't be trying to conceive straight away. It won't do you any harm and starting before you begin trying to conceive will give you time to make it into a habit. Folic acid helps prevent some structural defects in babies, particularly ones of the brain and spinal cord; this is also known as neural tube defects. You should also eat foods which are rich in folic acid, such as green leafy vegetables, nuts (avoid peanuts during this period, pregnancy and until you have stopped breast feeding), cooked dried beans, citrus fruits, avocado, raspberries, raw mushrooms and vegemite. It is also important to make the switch to a vitamin supplement which is suitable for pregnancy as certain vitamins are not. Your pharmacist can advise you on which vitamin supplements are suitable for you.

If you drink herbal teas I advise you to check they are safe to drink during pregnancy and the same goes for any essential perfume oils you may use, such as rose and clary sage, which can be harmful if used during pregnancy. Try to eat foods in a variety of colours with each meal to ensure that your diet is balanced. For example, if you had free-range meat, red, green and yellow roasted peppers (try brushing them with pesto sauce before popping them under the grill), carrots and broccoli and a choice of either some potatoes with the skin left on, wholemeal pasta or brown rice, then your meal will contain many vitamins and minerals which are vital for health. Men can maximise sperm count and motility by eating regular portions of fish, eggs, mushrooms, oysters, pumpkin seeds and other zinc-rich food. Smoking and alcohol have been found to reduce sperm counts and to increase the production of damaged sperm.

Visit your dentist early on in your 12-month pregnancy to complete any dental work you may require and to gain advice about what changes pregnancy may cause to your teeth and gums. If you haven't managed to quit smoking yet, you and your partner should do so at least four months before you begin trying to get pregnant, as well as avoiding alcohol and any unnecessary drugs. Finally, and perhaps most important of all, enjoy and cherish the company of your partner during this exciting time in your lives.

Come fluff my pillows

The ward was busy enough to induce feelings of anxiety about whether we would ever find time to get all our work done, let alone time to stop for a cup of tea and/or lunch and other vital bodily functions that so often got ignored on shifts like these. I was hurtling down the corridor at a pace I had perfected over the years: not quite running because that would signal an emergency but fast enough that I had hope of getting all the work done in time for, well yes, for me to be able to stop long enough for a cuppa after I had been for a wee, which had now become my number one priority. How I managed to turn off the urge to void my bladder when the buzzer went off over the door to room number 15 I'll never understand but luckily it did. One of these days I was certain I was going to embarrass myself by having a not so little 'wet accident' in public on the ward. The woman in number 15 had undergone an emergency caesarean section two days ago and wasn't responding well to post-surgical expectations that she care for herself as much as possible. Unlike other surgery of a similar nature, we expect new mums to be as self-caring as possible in order to ensure that they adapt to the demands from their new baby as seamlessly as possible. Babies thrive on care from their mums, so we encourage even post-caesarean mums to attend to as many of their baby's needs as possible, only stepping in when they are unable to do something. Not all mums agree that this is such a great idea and the woman in number 15 was one of them. I braced myself and opened the door.

'Hello. Everything ok?' I whispered, because I could see her baby sleeping.

'No. My pillows have gone all flat and horrid. I need to have them fluffed.'

This is a wind up right? I thought, feeling slightly hysterical, wondering if there were hidden cameras somewhere in the room. 'Here, let me show you how you can manoeuvre yourself into a position where you sort them out more easily,' I said, still keeping my voice low so as not to disturb her sleeping baby, determined not to do it for her but to help her learn to cope for herself.

I know staff that have ended up in the main hospital wards with renal colic after shifts like that and it is no wonder. Your body can only go so long with no fluids and improper bladder emptying before things begin to go seriously wrong. The problem is that we have a bit of a Pavalovian reaction to room buzzers going off and feel the need to respond to them immediately, because we can never tell what might be going on inside that room that needs our attention. This, on a bad day, will lead us into long periods of time where we forget to attend to our own needs.

Separate beds, please

A woman can ovulate within 21 days of giving birth. This strikes me as a very ridiculous thing for the female body to do. Surely it could take a few more months off? Apparently not, and for this reason, midwives ensure that contraception is a topic that we bring up with women within 24 hours of birth. Now that seemed a mad thing to do when I first began my student midwifery training but it soon became clear that this was a necessary discussion for a small – but prolific – proportion of the childbearing population. There are a surprising number of women who commence penetrative sexual intercourse within a few weeks of giving birth and a number of these women will become pregnant again almost immediately. I can think of several women who have asked to have their 'down below' looked at because they 'got a bit frisky last night' and it is now feeling a bit sore. Of course there are also women at the other end of the spectrum. When we begin discussing ovulation, the risk of pregnancy within three weeks of giving birth, and the need to use a suitable form of contraception should they have sexual intercourse these women look at us as if we are utterly insane. Rebuttal from these women, when asked to suggest suitable contraception to be used as a new mother, have ranged from sleeping in separate beds to divorce. Personally I can't imagine any new parent having the energy for such luxuries as an indulgent bath or more than a few hours sleep in one go, let alone the time to enjoy sex. However, the number of women who deliver their next child 10 months after giving birth to their last is proof that some parents do indeed make the time.

Informed choice

As a student midwife I worked with an eclectic mix of qualified midwives, observing their practice and developing my own from their guidance. By spending my shifts with them on the wards and out in the community I learned many valuable things about human nature that text books could never prepare me for. The nicest people sometimes have the biggest secrets, such as excessive drug habits, abusive partners, psychological problems, child protection issues, or having to share their partner with another person, to name just a few. The very well-educated and affluent people are often the most challenging and time consuming to give maternity care to as they have a tendency to be extremely well read and will question everything. This is actually the maternity care ideal as you can be sure that these people are making fully informed choices. However, due to staffing levels it can mean that those who are more readily accepting and/or less well read are not getting as much of their midwife's time. It is this group who probably need it more as the midwife should be able to discuss each topic in a way that would encourage this group of people to ask any questions they might have.

Hygiene

There seem to be as many different ideas about what constitutes good hygiene as there are pregnancies. Some women go to great lengths to maintain their grooming, to the point of asking their husbands or friends to do their pedicure in the later stages of pregnancy, while others come in with decidedly whiffy feet and we end up trying to think of ways to get them into a bath or shower without offending them. Whilst working in the community I learned that the state some houses are kept in make you want to wipe your feet on the way out and you certainly think twice about washing your hands while there. In fact, you often can't wash your hands because there is no soap and anyway the only available towel looks crusty. The invention of soapy hand wipes was a wonderful thing for situations such as these. The hand rub gels have a purpose, too, but are no good for hands that are visibly soiled. In these situations only soap can lift off the grime and soapy hand wipes allow the midwife to lift the grime up with one and then wipe it off with a second.

Filming the birth – good or bad idea?

Whether or not it is a good idea to film the birth of a baby depends on who you ask. Many women are perfectly happy to have their labour and childbirth experiences filmed, in fact, as I'm sure you will have noticed, some even agree to have them broadcast on documentaries and childbirth channels. Some women think the concept is appalling from a personal perspective, though they may have watched a few of the films available and, indeed, this may be what has put them off the idea as it is an infrequent occurrence for a nice, normal, intervention-free labour and childbirth to be shown on TV, and even that might be enough to put off a woman who is about to go through the same process. Does she really want to know that the head looks that big on its way out of a woman's body? I strongly suspect the average woman really doesn't. However, some pregnant women find the birth shows beneficial because they feel stronger and more in control when they know what to expect. Knowledge is power after all.

Lots of student midwives have told me that they have found the birth shows very useful when they are looking for visual clues as to what their first witnessed birth experiences might be like. I always feel that I have to warn them that most of the birth shows they have watched are not representative of what really happens on the average labour ward. This is particularly true if they have been watching the American ones where the very large majority of women seem to have an epidural and deliver in positions that make them look as if they have simply fallen over and can't get up. There is absolutely nothing natural about trying to give birth while lying on your back. Women's bodies are physiologically designed to deliver babies in a more upright position, but most epidurals often don't allow women to feel and respond to urges to get into these positions. However, it is quite difficult to choose one birth scene which will represent the average one on a modern labour ward, which is why I rarely show birth DVDs in class. Instead we talk about what they think they may see, the myriad of birth scenes that happen in unedited real life and some students share their memories of their own personal birth experiences. I also discuss the types of births that I have been present at while they were being filmed and whether I still think it was a good idea to agree to be part of that.

I have been assigned to the care of several women who wanted to or had agreed to have their labour and childbirth experience filmed. I know of a few who even watched the video afterwards. I admire their bravery in being able to do that. I wish I had asked who they planned to show the films to: was it just for them or did they offer to show it to visitors who came to welcome the new baby into the family? I do wonder how many of these films will be wheeled out on the child's 18th birthday and whether they will be scarred for life through sheer embarrassment.

Many midwives are reluctant to have the births that they are assisting at on film and either refuse to allow it or okay the filming but insist that they are not captured on film. I am not one of those midwives and therefore can be found making an appearance on a few birth films, though mostly it is my hands that are a part of the movie and even then they are not the main focus of the film because the real star of the show is, of course, the baby who is slowly making its way out into this brighter, nosier world. That is the one thing I really dislike about births being filmed, the fact that the camera needs a lot of light to capture a good recording of the sequence of the baby's birth, because of course this means that the lights can't be dimmed in an attempt to soften the shock a newborn baby might experience during its first few moments after birth. I do wonder how the babies would vote if anyone could ask their opinion on whether it is a good idea to film their births or not.

Epilogue

Postpartum Oppression

Whether this is your first baby or your sixth, the thrill of seeing your own baby for the first time is still there – a wonderful fresh chance to bring about positive change in this world. All those months of expectation have come to life in one tiny infant; your own miracle. Your baby's journey to get here is complete but a new parent can expect more physical and mental changes otherwise known as the postnatal rollercoaster, during the weeks following the birth. Mostly to blame for this somewhat bewildering sensation is the fact that the new mum's endocrine glands have slammed on the brakes (hormone production wise) and are now in reverse without having given you time to get settled into the idea of being a parent with overwhelming feelings of responsibility. So yes, you do have an excuse for weeping copiously when your favourite house plant dies.

Added to the jumble of pressures you put upon yourself as new parents is the expectations of others. One of my favourite cartoons of all time is one with the above title Postpartum Oppression, that shows a pregnant woman surrounded by three new mums holding their babies. The new mums are regaling the pregnant woman with tales of their horrific pregnancies and birth experiences all the while cuddling their smiling, sleeping babies. That pretty much sums up what I have overheard women doing to each other for as long as I can remember. We seem to have an urge to amplify the negative aspects of labour and birth and gloss over the good aspects of the postnatal period. So women who have had relatively easy and enjoyable pregnancies and relatively enjoyable birth experiences say nothing for fear of being lynched when these stories are exactly what pregnant women need to hear in order for them to develop a balanced perspective on what they can expect.

As for the smiling, sleeping babies; well nothing worries me more than new parents who tell me how their newborn sleeps all night. A human baby is physiologically designed to breast feed. This means small amounts frequently for the first few weeks of life, meaning the baby should wake throughout the day and night at regular intervals. Now breast feeding might not be the method of choice for all mums but their baby is still designed to wake for frequent small feeds even if they are being given a bottle of milk made up from formula. So if your baby wakes frequently when it seems that everyone else is telling you how well their baby slept take comfort in the fact that your baby is the one who is behaving normally and that others may be exaggerating the amount of sleep their baby actually is having. Try to sleep when your baby does. You'll turn your life upside down for a while but you will be happier and healthier for doing so.

Another thing that people feel the need to gloss over when they have a new baby is when they don't feel the expected surge of love and 'bonding' with their new baby, or experience baby blues and postnatal depression. During your pregnancy you may have formed expectations about the gender, appearance and behaviour of your baby. It may be difficult to adjust these expectations with reality. It may take a while for you and your family to get to know your new baby because every baby is unique and every parent's relationship with their baby is also unique. The first few days and weeks of your baby's life can be a marvellous adventure as long as you remember to accept all help that is offered with shopping, housework and so on. The vacuum cleaner won't mind if someone else uses it and your most important job is to care for your baby and yourself. When you are sleep deprived it can be a struggle to try and do all your tasks of daily living, never mind trying to also form an immediate deep bond with a unexpectedly demanding infant. I know of people – mothers and fathers – who took up to two years to feel that they had 'bonded' with their child. This didn't make them bad parents but it did mean they were filled with guilt and fear that someone might find out how they felt and decide they were a failure as a parent.

Despite efforts to raise awareness about depression it would seem that there is still significant stigma attached to this relatively common side effect to becoming new parents.

Baby blues is relatively common around three days after birth and postnatal depression is not unusual either, though this often becomes apparent after the first week instead of during it. Parents are often quite accomplished at hiding feelings of depression, wrongly assuming they need to prove they are coping, worrying that their midwives, GP or health visitor will think less of them for feelings of depression; fear we will think they can't cope. This couldn't be further from the truth and the sooner we are made aware that they are struggling the faster we can help them get treatment and support so they can get on with enjoying their new baby instead of struggling.

There are ways in which we try to pre-empt and encourage parents to disclose these feelings so that we can offer help early on before the feelings become overwhelming. Certainly one of the most effective ways is to develop a good relationship during the pregnancy, building trust up in layers so that parents feel they can discuss anything with us. This sometimes means we hear about intimacies that we don't need to know but this is worth it if it means that people feel able to trust us enough to discuss fears and feelings of inadequacy in relation to childbirth and parenting. Sometimes we have to do a bit of detective work when we are first getting to know parents during the pregnancy. If a woman tells me that she has a history of depression then I am on the alert for a reoccurrence of this during the pregnancy and in the postnatal period. It also means that I can put work into building a woman's confidence around telling me or her GP if she is beginning to feel low or downright depressed at any point.

Communication is a key midwifery skill but it works best when it goes both ways. So, talk to us, tell us when and what things are worrying you and don't ever worry that you are just being silly or wasting our time. We train for a long time to become midwives and then continue building on our knowledge for the rest of our careers, so we would never expect you to know all the things we do. There have been countless times that a woman has phoned to say her baby is spotty, lethargic or hasn't been behaving normally all day. She is frantic with worry by the time she phones in but when questioned as to why she didn't phone sooner the response is invariably that she didn't want to be a bother. You can rest assured that whatever question you may want to ask will have been asked hundreds of times before by other new parents. No question is a stupid one and rarely is it going to be unique but sometimes people ask the question too late. Don't become one of them. We trained to be midwives because we wanted to be 'with women', it is the classic definition of a midwife after all, and we rather like to be asked for advice. We are on duty in order to be available to care for you; so make good use of us.

Working on the antenatal or postnatal ward can be just as rewarding as carrying a community caseload or working on the labour ward; in fact some midwives prefer it to all other work rotations. The wards are extremely busy more often than not with everything from complexly ill antenatal women to women needing post-caesarean care or routine overnight stays after having had a baby late in the evening. Often the women and babies are not there long enough for the staff to get to know them so we make a point of reassuring them on admission to the ward that it is ok to come and find us or to press their buzzer if they have any questions. Sometimes we regret having advised them to do that because very occasionally a woman will call for us because she is bored or lonely or just wants a chat, but that is preferable to a woman sitting on her own and worrying about something that is happening to her or the way her baby is behaving, but reluctant to call us for fear of bothering us. So, let me set the record straight, once and for all: we are the ones who are trained to decide if there is something wrong with you or your baby and to bring it to the correct clinician's attention if there is. We are paid to be there to answer your questions and would rather you called us unnecessarily than not at all. So, feel free to call upon your midwife for advice so you can enjoy your parenting experience as much as possible. Other maternity/parenting caregivers such as your health visitor will also be happy to answer your questions. Finally, I hope this book has shown you how much maternity healthcare providers appreciate the privilege of being able to offer you

advice, support and care during one of the most significant experiences of your life.
The End

Now that you have finished reading Special Deliveries: Life Changing Moments please consider writing a review, and posting it on your favourite review site. Reviews are the best way for readers to discover great new books. I would truly appreciate the time it will take you to write and post a review.

Also by D.J. Kirkby

My Mini Midwife
The pocket companion for your pregnancy with clear answers to confusing questions. Due for publication February 3rd 2014

My Dream of You
"D.J. Kirkby writes with compassion and energy, creating characters you can really care about." – Sarah Salway - Canterbury Poet Laureate.

Without Alice
"Governed by duty, lost without love. A truly insightful narrative, controlled by a delicate hand" – Caroline Smailes, author of *The Drowning of Arthur Braxton*.

A Collection of Writing
This collection includes *My Dream of You*, *Without Alice,* which has been in Amazon.co.uk's top 100 'Women Writers & Fiction' bestsellers list for over a year (at the time of publication of *Special Deliveries*) and excerpts from other books by D.J. Kirkby.

The Portal Series
Mid grade chapter books written by D.J.
Kirkby using the name Dee Kirkby

"This is great for children to be read to or those who are progressing into reading on their own. It reminded me of childhood books like *The Lion, The Witch and The Wardrobe*, as well as the wonderful lands that could be found at the top of *The Faraway Tree*." - Jo D'Arcy - Vine Voice top 1000 reviewer.

About the Author
D.J. Kirkby lives in the South of England in a home otherwise filled with males – husband, boys and pets – she writes to escape the testosterone. Dee is a registered midwifery lecturer, teaching midwifery two days per week, a registered public health practitioner, working two days per week for her local Public Health Department and the other day per week she uses for author events and other writing related activities.

Find D. J. Kirkby online
Website for adults: djkirkby.co.uk
Website for children: deekirkby.co.uk
Twitter: @djkirkby
Facebook:
https://www.facebook.com/DeeJKirkby

Join Dee's quarterly newsletter mailing list to be kept updated about future releases, giveaways and more.

Feel free to get in touch: djkirkby@gmail.com

Acknowledgements:

Thanks to my new editor Sarette Martin for her work on this book before it was published in paperback. I look forward to working with you on many more books.

Thanks to my cover designer Andrew Brown for your endless patience and for knowing exactly what I want in a cover.

Last but not least - thanks to all of my readers - you are the reason I get up ridiculously early each day to fill blank pages with words.

Printed in Great Britain
by Amazon